BEYOND MADNESS
45°N

JOHN MARKS

BLACK ROSE
writing™

ISBN: 978-1-61296-881-0
PUBLISHED BY BLACK ROSE WRITING
www.blackrosewriting.com

Printed in the United States of America
Suggested retail price $18.95
Beyond Madness 45°N is printed in Adobe Caslon Pro

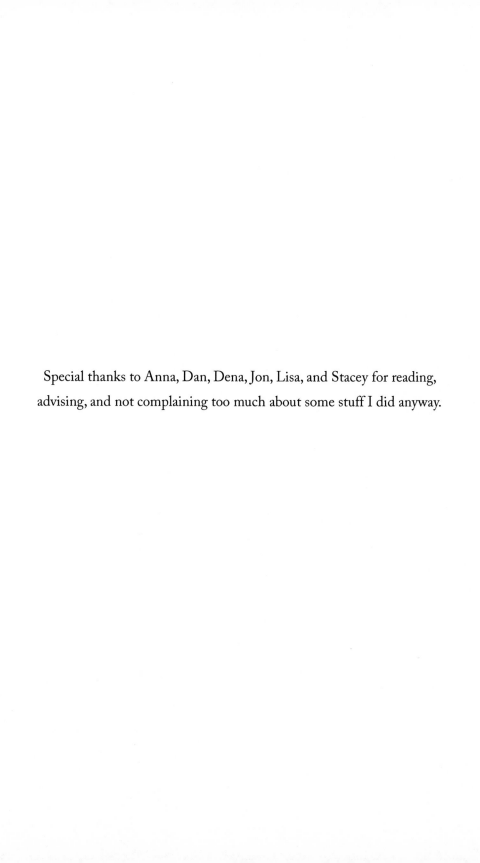
Special thanks to Anna, Dan, Dena, Jon, Lisa, and Stacey for reading, advising, and not complaining too much about some stuff I did anyway.

BEYOND
MADNESS
45°N

C1

3:25 a.m., Tuesday, April 5.

"What's this, a Rolex watch? Stop jerkin' me around, man, and just gimme the damn money!"

The rant erupted from nowhere, as if a dream had gone sideways. It propelled Joe Rylands to the edge of his bed. He woke, poised to spring forward, stomach churning. A pinpoint of light glared from a cell phone on the nightstand beside him.

Jeez, what a nightmare, Joe thought, until—

"Please... I... I only need a little more time to get you the money... a-all of it. And you can just keep the watch... for all the trouble I've caused."

That clearly was Joe's roommate, Leo Surocco. He couldn't have been more than a few feet outside the door.

But who's he talking to?

"Dammit, Leo, the money's owed today."

"But I... I... won't have it until—"

"Listen, you little—"

A crash against the wall was all Joe heard next. He bolted for the door.

C2

4:35 a.m., Tuesday, April 5.

Harlan Holmes woke to a dual attack on his senses: a high-pitched beeping sound blasting from his computer across the hall; and the smelly breath of his German shepherd standing beside the bed, panting. The dog's face was within inches of his and closing in. "Okay, Dozer," Harlan said, turning away to find breathable air. "I'll take care of it."

As Harlan reached for yesterday's pants, his thoughts about the day ahead derailed. It had been nearly two years since he lost his job as a state trooper, yet the sting of it still insinuated itself into most mornings. After twenty years of service, they just let him go. And he couldn't let that go. They said it had nothing to do with job performance. It was simple economics. The department had to be downsized, and that meant cutting a lot of good cops. What they never explained, though, was why a younger officer—a woman he had trained—was retained to do what he used to do.

Harlan's knee popped loudly as he dropped his six-foot frame into a chair in front of the computer. He pushed aside an empty beer bottle and reduced the volume of the speakers. A few mouse clicks later, he learned that the alarm had begun just minutes ago, at 4:32 a.m.

"Does the kid ever rest?" he complained, glancing at Dozer.

The dog cocked his head sideways.

A program running on the computer provided a trace to the location of a GPS tracking device that Harlan had planted on a pickup truck used by Leo Surocco. It appeared on the computer screen as a blinking dot on a map of Michigan. The alarm signaled that the truck was moving and that Harlan, these days a private eye, might have to do the same.

Please, Leo, just let me go back to bed.

Harlan had been retained by Leo's father, Angelo Surocco, to surveil Leo and report any problems that might arise while Leo attended law school away from home. Leo's problem was a gambling addiction. Harlan's had become the boy's determination to feed it.

Aggravating the problem was the monotony of Leo's legal studies at Grand Traverse University. Last fall he coped with it by skipping half his classes and doubling his time in the local casinos, where mounting losses showed up as thousands of dollars of credit card debt. Angelo, a resident of Chicago, bailed out his son and looked for someone in Traverse City to keep an eye on him. The case struck Harlan as an unusual one for a PI, but the size of the fee Angelo offered overcame his reservations.

Harlan scrolled through zoomed-in images of the blinking dot, beginning with a map of Michigan's Lower Peninsula, which looks like a gigantic mitten. Along the mitten's northwestern edge is what appears to be a slightly protruding baby finger—the Leelanau Peninsula—surrounded to the north and west by Lake Michigan and to the east by the Grand Traverse Bay.

The blinking dot was on the baby finger. Harlan zoomed in some more. It was moving slowly along the bayside coast, southbound on M-22.

Replays of earlier transmissions showed that Leo's truck had spent the night at Omena Point, just a few miles north of its current location and about twenty-five miles north of Traverse City, which sits at the base of the baby finger. Leo lived in a townhouse in Traverse City, near the law school. But there was nothing unusual about his truck's presence at Omena Point the prior evening. Leo's family owned a cottage there, and every semester at this time—the week before final exams—he used it as a place to hole up and study.

Harlan returned to the blinking dot's real-time movement as a small clock in the corner of the computer screen advanced to 4:44 a.m. Seconds later, the alarm stopped. Leo's truck still appeared as a blinking dot, but it was no longer moving. It had stopped near the small coastal community of Peshawbestown, where, at this hour, only two things were open: the 24/7 BP gas station and, directly across the street from it, the 24/7 Leelanau Sands Casino.

That damn kid.

Monitoring Leo Surocco had become an unbearable task, nothing like the spy games Harlan was more used to playing with the cheating spouses of other clients. GPS tracking, phone taps, computer hacking—none of it worked on the kid. Not only did Leo quickly figure out that he was under surveillance, he actually seemed to enjoy the new element of risk it added to playing games of chance—for risk, at bottom, was his narcotic. Eventually at wits' end, Harlan had offered his surrender.

And that's when Angelo, an overbearing parent, to say the least, really imposed his will—on both Leo and Harlan.

"Alright, let's talk about money, first," Angelo said. He removed an envelope from his pocket and handed it to Leo, who sat beside him at a kitchen table in Leo's townhouse. Harlan sat across from them.

Leo opened the envelope and removed its contents, two hundred dollars. "What's this for, Dad?"

"It's the first installment of your weekly allowance until you finish law school."

"Just two Benjamins for an entire week?"

"That's right. And don't even think about credit cards or bank accounts. I've closed them all."

"No way, Dad, I can't make it on this. My last semester's coming up. That means tuition and books, and I've got rent and utilities on this place, and—"

"Just pass your major bills along to Mr. Holmes, at the weekly meetings that the two of you will be having this semester."

"What weekly meetings?" Leo said, just as Harlan was about to ask the same question.

"The meetings where you'll be producing purchase receipts to prove how every penny of that weekly allowance was spent. And if you can't, Mr. Holmes is going to assume that you blew it in a casino and withhold the next installment."

"He's gonna control my finances?"

"That, and a hell of a lot more, Leo."

"Wait a minute, Angelo," Harlan said. "This doesn't sound like a very—"

Angelo jerked his head to face Harlan directly. "How many clients you got right now, Holmes?"

"Well, just a couple others."

"Get rid of 'em. I'm your only client until I tell you otherwise."

"But—"

"Here's *your* weekly allowance," Angelo said, as he slid a thick envelope across the table. "Go ahead, open it and count the money. Then tell me if there's a problem."

Leo scooted close to the table and leaned forward when Harlan began counting the stack of hundred-dollar bills. There were fifty.

"What the hell, Dad? He gets five large, and I get two lousy yards?"

As Leo continued to complain, Harlan stared down at the stack of hundreds. It would more than cover a stack of past-due bills sitting on his desk at home. But it didn't feel right. "This isn't going to work," he eventually said.

Angelo's frown at Leo turned to a scowl at Harlan. "What, that's not enough, Holmes?"

"It's not that. Look, the kid obviously knows about my surveillance, and—"

"So what? You're going to continue it anyway, along with some other things I want you to do."

Angelo slid a document across the table.

"Hey! That's my class schedule for next semester," Leo said as it passed by him.

"That's right," Angelo said, "and Mr. Holmes is going to make sure that you attend every single one of those classes for the whole semester."

"What? You can't be serious, Dad. Do you have any idea how lame most of my profs are?"

"The boy's got a point," Harlan said. "You can't really expect me to make him go to school every day."

"Oh yes I can. And you're also going to make sure that he does this after-school thing I read about on the school's website. It's some kind of program where they work on courtroom skills, called Moot Court."

"No way," Leo said. "That's for law geeks who've got nothing better to do than volunteer for extracurricular bullshit."

"Well," Angelo said, "it's either volunteer for that bullshit or start attending a program that your mother found online for dealing with... uh... gambling addiction."

Harlan could see the difficulty Angelo had saying it—addiction. The man's denial ran as deep as his son's. That's what was making this feel so wrong. Angelo wanted Harlan to serve as a babysitter—*in loco parentis*, as Leo would later expound in law school legalese—tasked with suppressing a real illness in dire need of a very different kind of intervention. Some job for a professional investigator. But the truth was, he had no other clients and really needed the money.

Harlan zoomed in further and squinted at the blinking dot, trying to determine its exact location. *The gas station? The casino? Or somewhere else nearby?* Unfortunately, his after-market GPS program was almost as imprecise as his vision had become in recent years at computer distance.

He reached for his reading glasses but stopped short. It was 4:47 a.m. on the computer's clock, and the blinking dot began moving again, but only for a few seconds. According to the program, in those few seconds the dot rapidly accelerated and then suddenly stopped.

Then it vanished.

Suddenly the room was filled with an ear-piercing sound, like an EKG machine when it flatlines. The program had overridden his speaker settings with a shrill alarm signaling complete malfunction.

Dozer ran from the room, howling, as Harlan tried to kill the alarm using the mouse and keyboard. He quickly gave that up and resorted instead to pulling the speaker plugs from the power strip. "What the hell just happened?" he shouted.

Harlan settled back into his chair and ran a recording of the tracking device's final minutes of life, but his thoughts digressed. *It doesn't make sense. If the kid found it, he would have disabled it before going to the casino, not after he got there.*

Confounded, Harlan decided to do something that always led to Leo: he called the boy's cell phone.

C'mon, Leo, pick up.

He didn't.

Harlan then texted, "Don't make me call your father in the middle of the night," and waited a minute. Still no answer.

Recalling that Leo's roommate, Joe Rylands, often joined Leo for trips to the cottage, Harlan looked up Joe's cell number and called him. There was no answer there either.

Suppressing the anxiety was getting difficult, but Harlan tried. He imagined the boys being up late, or early, studying for exams and deciding to take a break, maybe go out for something to eat, and stopping for gas along the way. And maybe the tracking device just happened to quit when they stopped, and they both just happened to forget their cell phones—*which they take everywhere they go!*

Harlan slammed his fist on the desktop. "Dammit, Leo! What are you doing?"

The recording was reaching its final seconds when Harlan slowed it down and then froze it on the last image of the dot, at full zoom. He snatched up his reading glasses and leaned in.

"Hey, wait a minute," Harlan said to himself. "He didn't even reach the gas station or the casino."

The last blink of the dot was in the vicinity of a tiny, densely wooded park located at least a mile north of the casino, on the bayside of M-22. The park itself was bordered to the north and south by reservation land, also densely wooded, that belonged to the Grand Traverse Band of the Ottawa and Chippewa Indians. A lone driveway cutting into the park provided the only point of vehicle access to that side of the road for at least a mile in either direction.

Why did he stop in the middle of the woods, next to the bay, and then...

C3

4:48 a.m., Tuesday, April 5.

Stabs of freezing pain jolted Leo into full consciousness—trapped in complete blackness as frigid water blasted over his body. He blindly fought through the icy deluge, terrified and disoriented, only to slam into walls in every direction.

He couldn't get out of whatever this thing was.

Pressing upward into a shrinking pocket of air, Leo felt panic yielding to despair. And then he felt something else—*someone* else—trapped with him, also thrashing around inside this thing, this coffin-like box, occasionally thrashing up against Leo himself.

Leo instinctively reached for the unfortunate soul trapped in there with him. He got hold of some body part and clung to it like a terrified child to his mother, so tightly that his fingernails burrowed deep into its flesh.

The pocket of air then vanished.

A moment later, Leo lost hold of the body part.

Joe? No! Don't leave me!

C4

5:26 a.m., Tuesday, April 5.

A white SUV screeched around a bend and crossed the center line, forcing Harlan off the road toward a ditch. "What the—" he shouted as he slammed on the brakes. He caught a glimpse of the vehicle, a Ford Explorer, in his rearview mirror just before it disappeared.

The sudden stop had thrown Dozer into the dashboard and then to the floor. Harlan checked on his partner, slowly palpating his ribs, while taking in the desolation that followed the Explorer's disappearance.

Local vineyards and cherry orchards would soon blossom, and the area, lush with fruit, would become paradise for countless tourists and part-time residents. But at this moment, dormant beneath the lights of the night sky, the Leelanau Peninsula looked more like the Arctic coastal tundra.

On one side of M-22, endless rows of lifeless grapevines trembled in a breeze chilled by the northern waters of Lake Michigan. On the other side, the same breeze rippled the dark surface of the Grand Traverse Bay. What captivated Harlan most, however, was the thing in between—a sign off to the side of the road standing just inches in front of his Jeep. It read, "45th Parallel North." He was three-fourths of the way to the top of the world, geographically speaking.

Back on the road, they eventually passed the Leelanau Sands Casino and the remainder of Peshawbestown. About a mile north of town, a small sign barely advertised the entrance to Pontiac Park, which required a hairpin right turn to the bayside of M-22.

The dirt driveway leading in, like the rest of the park, was carved into a dense mass of four- and five-story evergreens that blocked out nearly all of the sky's lights. The Jeep's headlights cut through the blackness into the park's center, revealing a few old picnic tables and rusted cooking grills.

Harlan clicked on a flashlight as he stepped out of the Jeep. He slowly turned full circle, working the light along the perimeter of the tiny park.

As the bayside wall of trees appeared, Harlan's thoughts raced through various scenarios, eventually turning to the possibility that the GPS device went dead after somehow being immersed in the bay. But there was simply no way that a vehicle like Leo's Avalanche pickup truck could get through that wall of trees—not without leaving a trace.

Harlan then walked the park's perimeter and eventually back up the entrance drive. The crunch of dead pine needles ceased when he emerged from the tree-lined driveway onto the shoulder of M-22. An isolated car drove by, just a few yards in front of him. He shook his head. It made no sense.

When he returned to the Jeep, Harlan spotted his partner in front of a "No Dumping" sign—squatting. He wondered whether Leo might have stopped in the park to take care of the same kind of business when the GPS device just happened to quit.

Am I overthinking this?

Dozer looked back at him. *What the hell are we doing here?* the dog's expression seemed to say as he crapped.

The former K-9 police dog essentially was all that Harlan, at age fifty-two, had in the way of close family. His adult-age children seldom visited since graduating from college, and his ex-wife would never return after leaving him about a year ago. She claimed that he had become impossible to live with after the state police discarded him for some younger blood. Not until the divorce was final, however, would he learn of a developer from Petoskey whom *she* had decided to trade up for.

He didn't know what pissed him off more: being usurped again, or not seeing it coming when he, after all, was supposed to be in the business of busting cheating spouses.

C5

5:49 a.m., Tuesday, April 5.

The patient gasped and writhed despite a nurse's efforts to comfort him. "Leo? No! Let me go!" he shouted.

The emergency room fell silent. Nurse Dailey froze momentarily and stared into the patient's face. "Did he just say something about a guy named Leo?" she asked.

Doctor Forrester nodded. "He said something like that to me too when I first found him."

"The kid actually talked to you?" Nurse Dailey asked.

"Just a little," the doctor said, "and he made no sense then either."

"I still can't get over it, the way you just happened to find this kid and save his life," the nurse said, shaking her head.

It was about a quarter past five when Doctor Forrester returned home from an extended shift at the hospital. As he opened the door to his beachfront home, his dog darted outside and ran straight to the water, barking wildly.

"Rufus! Get back here!"

The doctor's shout to his usually obedient golden retriever went unheeded. Minutes later, Rufus ignored a call for breakfast.

Maybe he got into something down by the water, the doctor thought. He grabbed a windbreaker and headed for the beach.

The windbreaker snapped and rattled in a gust of wind chilled by the frigid water over which it passed on its way to this spot, Stony Point, located about midway along the Leelanau Peninsula's bayside coast. At the very tip of the point was the dog's find.

"What do you have there, boy?"

Rufus hovered over something extending out of the water onto the beach. His barking mellowed to rapid pants that drove bursts of steam into the cold morning air.

When the discovery fell within the beam of the doctor's flashlight, a surge of adrenalin pulsed through his body.

A drowning victim had washed onto his beach.

Doctor Forrester, a heart surgeon at Butterfield Hospital, suddenly found himself providing paramedic services to the unfortunate stranger. He dragged his new patient out of the water and untangled him from a snarled mass of surface weeds interwoven with the straps of a swim buoy that had a near chokehold around his neck—but that had also provided a relatively buoyant wreath beneath his head.

The doctor quickly checked for a pulse and placed his face close to the patient's mouth to check his breathing. Just then a faint groan pushed through the patient's blue lips, which began to quiver.

"Talk to me, son," Doctor Forrester said. "What's your name?"

The patient struggled. "Joe," he said. "What the... where... wh-where's Leo?"

"Who's Leo?" the doctor asked. But the conversation was over.

Doctor Forrester ran back to the house, grabbed some blankets and the keys to his Ford Explorer, and rushed through the kitchen to a door leading into an attached garage. He barely noticed his wife entering from a dark hallway into the bright kitchen, squinting. "Where are you going?" she asked.

"Back to the hospital, honey. I'll explain later."

The Explorer roared out of the garage in reverse and continued through the backyard, down to the beach. Doctor Forrester jumped out and quickly wrapped the patient in blankets and loaded him into the SUV.

The drive to Butterfield Hospital usually took him at least thirty minutes. The unexpected return trip this morning took less than twenty. Weaving southward down the remainder of the Leelanau Peninsula, Doctor Forrester passed without notice a panoramic view of the rippling bay to his left and rolling vineyards to his right. Also unnoticed was the Wrangler Jeep that he ran off the road while screeching around a bend.

"I'm transporting a male drowning victim, approximately twenty to twenty-five years of age," the doctor shouted into a Bluetooth device attached to his head. "The kid's into advanced stages of hypothermia, unconsciousness right now... What? Where'd he come from? Hell if I know. I found him washed up on my beach wearing nothing but pajamas, damn near dead!"

Upon arrival at Butterfield Hospital, Doctor Forrester was met by Nurse Dailey and some other ER personnel, who removed the patient from the Explorer.

"We can take it from here, Doctor," she said.

He ignored the offer and followed along to assist.

Nurse Dailey leaned over the patient and placed her face close to his. She noticed the blue hue to his lips beginning to fade back to a healthier pink. "You're doing great, Joe. What's your last name, son? Who are you?"

The nurse jerked straight up and laughed. "He just said 'Joe Law Student.' Our John Doe patient is Joe Law Student."

"Maybe he goes to GTU Law," suggested Doctor Garratt, the head ER physician.

The patient gasped again, thrashed on the bed, and began to shout.

"Leo! Where's Leo?"

Nurse Dailey leaned back in and placed her hands on Joe's shoulders. "Easy does it, Joe. You're okay. You're safe now."

Joe's movements began to slow.

"There you go," she said. "Do you want to tell me about Leo?"

"Oh my God... B-Bucknell... wha... what happened to Bucknell?"

"What's he talking about now?" Doctor Garratt asked. "Who is Bucknell?"

"Well, obviously," Nurse Dailey said, "you've lost track of March Madness."

Doctor Garratt looked puzzled.

"You know, Doctor, the basketball tournament? Certainly you've heard of it."

The doctor remained perplexed.

Nurse Dailey looked over the top of her glasses, stunned. "You see, Doctor Garratt, there's this college basketball tournament—you know, Doctor, *March Madness*—played every year around this time. Practically everyone in America with a heartbeat knows about it. Of course, basketball is that game where they try to shoot the little ball through that round hole called a—"

"Okay, Dailey, you've established my ignorance of college sports. Now please, just tell me who this Bucknell person is."

"Bucknell's not a person, Doctor. It's a basketball team—the Bucknell Bison. They were an underdog in the tournament, a Cinderella team, that made it all the way to the final game last night. Nobody figured them to go anywhere in the tournament. But there they were last night, in the championship game against Michigan State."

Nurse Dailey shook her head and then turned back to the patient. "Joe, the Bison got blown out by thirty-some points. They were never in the game. Is that bad news?"

There was no response. Nurse Dailey tried again. "Please, Joe, stay with me. Why are you asking about Bucknell? Did they bust your bracket, like they did mine?"

"What'd you just ask him?" Doctor Garratt said.

"Well, he seems so upset. I thought maybe the Bucknell Bison busted his—" Nurse Dailey stopped and shook her head. "Oh, never mind, Doctor."

The patient had slipped back into a deep sleep and seemed likely to stay that way for a while. Nurse Dailey turned from him and looked into Doctor Forrester's bloodshot eyes. "We've got this, Doctor. You should talk to the police and then go home for some rest."

"What police?" Doctor Forrester asked.

"The cops right outside the ER," Nurse Dailey said, "who we blew past when we brought the patient in."

"Oh, okay, I guess I can see why they might want to talk with me."

"You think?" the nurse said as she rolled her eyes and then glanced back at the patient. In addition to impact injuries to his head and torso, he had deep fingernail grooves in a dislocated arm, which was now dressed with gauze and tape.

C6

6:21 a.m., Tuesday, April 5.

Harlan turned north onto M-22 after visiting the Leelanau Sands Casino. Although Leo's reputation among the casino's pit bosses and dealers bordered on legendary, nobody there that morning could recall having seen him for weeks.

A few miles later, Harlan took some back roads toward Angelo Surocco's getaway dwelling on Omena Point. The so-called cottage was set deep in the woods in a secluded area along the bay. Its dirt driveway typically was blocked by an iron gate and monitored by cameras. Today, neither security measure was in place.

Harlan parked his Jeep about halfway up the drive, stepped out, and scanned the area. "You stay here, Dozer," he said.

The sun, though still beneath the horizon, cast a dark red glow on the bay's surface. Glimpses of the blood-like hue rippled between the naked branches of surrounding trees. Against the impressive backdrop stood a monstrous brick structure capped with a black slate roof—nothing like the real cottages of neighbors to the north and south.

On Harlan's way up the dirt drive, multiple tire tracks and, eventually, footprints fell within the glow of his flashlight. He stepped around the remnants, onto the lawn beside the driveway, and made his way to the front door. A security code usually had to be entered on a keypad to disable an alarm before entering. Today that was not necessary. Nor was the key that was usually needed to unlock the deadbolt.

Beyond the entryway was the main floor's great room. "Leo? Joe?" he shouted as he entered the room. "Is anyone here?" The shouts bounced from the room's walls and vaulted ceiling, spilling over an upper-level loft high overhead and into adjacent bedrooms and bathrooms. There was no answer.

Thinking about where to begin his search, Harlan recalled a wall safe located in the first-floor master bedroom. During a tour of the cottage after Harlan was first hired, Angelo had said that the safe was off-limits to Leo. *May as well start there.*

Harlan pushed aside a chest of drawers to get a look at the safe. An intricate, unbroken spider web extended over a corner of it, where the door opened and closed. He tried the handle anyway. It was locked.

He then made a quick pass through every room of the cottage, slowing down the search in two upstairs bedrooms. In one a backpack and a suitcase were sitting on the end of a neatly made bed. Leo's name was on a tag attached to the suitcase. Packed within it were enough clothes for at least a week's stay somewhere. The contents of the backpack—law books and other study aids—also suggested an intent to go somewhere for the week before final exams. Harlan paused over the backpack and wondered, *Why didn't he unpack? Or did he repack his things to go somewhere else?*

After closing the luggage, he crouched down beside the bed for a look underneath. Something was down there. Harlan clicked on his flashlight for a better look. It was a cell phone. He paused again. *What's up with that? Leo doesn't go anywhere without that damn thing.*

He grimaced at his knees' objection when he rose to his feet and then headed to a closet where there was another wall safe. Leo had purchased and installed this one a few years ago when he started law school. He was the only person who knew the combination—that is, until an autodialing machine, once left overnight by Harlan, figured it out after thousands of tries.

Harlan opened the safe and sorted through the contents, mostly miscellaneous items that he'd seen on prior sweeps of the cottage. His main reason for checking the safe in the past was to make sure that Leo didn't hock for gambling cash something of significant value usually stored inside— a Rolex watch his parents had given him as a college graduation gift.

As Harlan looked for the watch, a USB flash drive slid out of an unmarked envelope and fell to the floor. Leo used the flash drive as a backup storage medium for important information, including his passwords for online activities. Harlan had discovered the flash drive the first time he breached the safe and had since used the passwords to access virtually every aspect of Leo's cyber life. He returned the flash drive to the envelope, and the envelope to the safe. *Where's the watch?*

The bed in the other upstairs bedroom was unmade, as though someone had slept in it the night before. Under it was a suitcase. This one was empty. On a nightstand next to the bed were a laptop, cell phone, and pair of eyeglasses. Harlan recognized the glasses as Joe's. In fact, he had never seen Joe without them on, and for good reason. *The kid's practically blind*, Harlan thought as he looked through the lenses.

After returning the glasses to the nightstand, he looked around for any sign of corrective contact lenses—saline solution, cleaning fluid, or a contact case. Nothing of the sort was in the bedroom or its adjoining bathroom. *Where'd he go without his glasses?*

Harlan stepped out of Joe's bedroom, into the loft, and scanned its shag carpet. Something slightly protruded from the carpet's fibers across the loft and beneath a window. A closer look revealed that it was Leo's Rolex watch.

As he stood over the watch and raised his head, Harlan noticed a thin crack, about an inch long, in one of the slats of the wooden blinds covering the window. It looked like a fragment of wood had been chipped away. He looked down from the damaged blind to the floor, crouching as he scanned it.

Sure enough, resting on top of the carpet's shag fibers was a thin splinter of wood. He picked it up and placed it against the crack in the blind. It fit like the last piece to a jigsaw puzzle.

Still standing by the window, Harlan looked back across the loft toward the stairs. *Did someone throw the watch across the loft?*

He dropped the splinter, left it and the watch on the floor, and returned to the stairs. On the way down, slowly, he studied the handrail, each spindle extending from it, and each hardwood step to which each spindle attached.

His pulse elevated when he reached the bottom and saw blood—small splatters of it—at the base of the last two spindles and on the adjoining steps.

Harlan dropped to his hands and knees on the hardwood floor at the base of the stairs and lowered his head toward the largest of the splatters. It was thick and roundish, about three-fourths of an inch in diameter, and had something sticking out of it.

Dammit, I need to start carrying my reading glasses, he thought.

He leaned in close and squinted. There was a single hair plastered onto the step by the blood, a hair that was probably too light and way too long to be either Leo's or Joe's. *Who left this?*

And then something that should have been obvious struck him as he knelt there, at the base of the stairs, right where he had seen something during past visits to the cottage—a rug. *Where is it?* Then he remembered. *It was a white rug. Blood on it would have been a lot more obvious than blood on the wood stairs. Did somebody screw up when they cleaned the place?*

Harlan exited the front door. Stopping briefly on the lawn beside the dirt driveway, he looked again at the tire tracks and footprints. They were fresh. One set of tire tracks was consistent with the big tires on Leo's Avalanche pickup truck. The other was left by tires of a more ordinary size. Among the footprints were some that were far too large to be Leo's or Joe's. They led straight to and from the porch steps, which, in turn, led straight to and from the front door.

Leo or Joe must have let some big bastard walk right in. But if things got violent, why would whoever it was let such obvious tracks remain?

Harlan then realized why the footprints were so obvious even without the use of his flashlight. *The sun's coming up.*

He glanced at the cottage's outdoor lights. They were all off.

C7

6:42 a.m., Tuesday, April 5.

Harlan gazed at the rippling bay waters that flickered between bare tree branches as he thought about the phone call he had to make. Normally, his communications with Angelo Surocco about matters relating to Leo went through Angelo's attorney. But this was no time for that protocol.

It's not even six o'clock yet in Chicago, Harlan thought as he glanced at his watch. *And he's gonna wake up to the news that his overpaid PI lost his son.*

Harlan's thoughts briefly turned to past efforts to learn what he could about his client's background before agreeing to take the case. The check had raised some red flags. By outward appearances, Angelo ran a legitimate import-export business out of a Chicago-based company. But that wasn't true of some of his business associates who also operated in the Great Lakes region, including one currently doing time for smuggling untaxed tobacco grown on Aboriginal reserves in Canada.

Suspicions about Angelo's involvement in trafficking contraband eventually were confirmed by Leo. The boy and Harlan had managed to develop a bond of sorts over the course of their weekly meetings. It grew out of their shared frustration with Leo's controlling father and led to many candid conversations about the man and his business dealings.

Harlan finally made the phone call and matter-of-factly recounted for his client the events of the morning, beginning with the mysterious movements and death of the GPS device and ending with his discoveries at the cottage.

"I... I'm coming up there... immediately," Angelo said, his voice quivering uncharacteristically. Harlan could only imagine the impact of the report. Leo may have been his second son in birth order, but he clearly was

25

Angelo's favorite child and heir apparent to the family business.

After a productive smoker's hack, Angelo seemed to steady himself. "Harlan, I want you on this nonstop until my son is found. Is that clear?"

"Yes."

"And I expect to see you at the airport when I arrive."

"Of course, Angelo, I'll be there. Look, one thing I think we should do, right away, is call the police. They might be able to—"

"We'll talk about that when I see you," Angelo said. "There's something else I need you to do before we involve them."

The bad feeling Harlan had before making the call grew worse.

"I want you to remove some things from the cottage: a briefcase inside the safe in the master bedroom, and anything Leo has that might relate to any work he's done for my business or to any of his personal issues, you know, like the gambling problem."

There was a lengthy pause after Angelo provided the combination to the safe in the master bedroom. Harlan was being instructed to remove things from a potential crime scene. He'd likely be crossing a line.

His thoughts flashed back to the day he lost his job as a state trooper. As upset as that had made him, he never imagined the old job and his new one working at cross-purposes.

"What is it, Holmes?" Angelo said. "You got some fucking problem with this?"

At that moment, Harlan's regrets about taking the case were stronger than ever. He always knew that any trouble Leo might get into would, in his client's mind, be on him—the 24/7 babysitter. And that responsibility in this situation would extend not only to doing everything he could to find the boy but also to anything else that Angelo might deem necessary to mitigate any collateral damage.

"There's no problem here," Harlan finally said.

"Alright then, I'll call you soon with my flight information."

C8

7:45 a.m., Tuesday, April 5.

The John Doe patient at Butterfield Hospital wouldn't be able to give a statement for a while, so the state troopers assigned to the case followed their only other lead.

The front entrance to GTU Law School led them into a four-story, glass-enclosed exhibition hall that provided a stunning view of the Grand Traverse Bay. One of the officers, Detective Riley Summers, headed for a receptionist, who was at his desk even though the school didn't officially open for another fifteen minutes. Riley's partner, Sergeant Frank Tice, lagged behind, taking in the grand exhibition hall.

"So this is the school for the one percent that those Occupy Wall Street hippies always complain about," Frank said when he caught up to Riley. Her gaze drifted up and down one of the hall's ornate columns and settled on the marble floor. "More like one percent of that one percent," she said.

They were directed to a top-floor suite of offices, where they met the associate dean of students, Janice Fletcher. As Dean Fletcher approached, it was hard not to react to her disheveled appearance in this otherwise formal business environment. She wore baggy jeans and an oversized hoodie, and she had her hair pulled back into a ponytail, exposing tired, droopy eyes.

"Is this really necessary?" Dean Fletcher asked immediately after they introduced themselves.

"Excuse me?" Riley said.

"Well, just how many more police officers and university officials must I talk to before I get to go home?"

"Which police officers have you already met?" Riley asked.

"The ones who were here when I got called into the school in the middle of the night."

"I'm sorry," Riley said, "but I don't know what you're talking about."

"The disturbance at the school, Detective—that *is* why you're here, right?"

"Actually, no. We're here about something else, I think. What happened?"

"Seriously, Detective, you don't know about the vandalism that happened in the library around half past two this morning?"

Riley shook her head.

"Oh, for crying out loud," Dean Fletcher said. "Come into my office."

"Okay, look," Fletcher began as the officers seated themselves. "It's dead week around here and—"

"Dead what?" Riley asked.

Fletcher sighed. "This is the week before final exams, Detective. Our students call it 'dead week' because no classes are held and all they do around here is study—at all hours. At night, students get into the building with access cards that unlock some of the doors. Apparently, one of them somehow let in some people off the street who caused a problem. Either that, or some of our own students trashed a study area in the fourth-floor stacks of the library."

"Was anyone hurt?" Riley asked.

"It's not entirely clear. One of the carrels was damaged badly, and there were some blood splatters by it, though not a lot. The campus police took samples of the blood for testing."

"How'd they get involved?"

"A student called them on his cell phone. He was studying on the third floor and heard some yelling and a crash overhead. He also told the librarian on duty. But by the time she checked it out, nobody was up there."

Riley glanced at Frank, who shook his head and shrugged.

"Well," Fletcher said, "if you didn't know about any of this, what brings you here?"

"A semi comatose patient at Butterfield Hospital," Riley said, "who's been able to identify himself only as 'Joe Law Student' and who's been asking about some guy named Leo. We thought that perhaps—"

Dean Fletcher leaned toward her desk and tapped a button on a phone. "Mrs. Palsgraf?" she said.

"Yes, ma'am," a voice called back through the phone's speaker.

"Please compile some contact information on two of our students, Joseph Rylands and Leonardo Surocco—their home and local addresses, phone numbers, that sort of thing—and bring it into my office."

"Yes, ma'am, right away."

"Sorry to cut you off like that, Detective. Please, tell me, what happened to Joseph?"

"Well," Riley said, "the Joseph I'm talking about—Joe Law Student— nearly drowned in the bay this morning under some very suspicious circumstances. But you tell me, with so little information, how can you possibly know that he's this student of yours, this guy, Joe Rylands?"

"Because that's Joseph's nickname around here: Joe Law Student. His friends sometimes tease him with that name because he's one of our more serious law students—a real gunner in the classroom."

"A what?"

"A gunner. You know, one of those students who's always raising his hand in class to answer the professor's questions."

"And you know Leo because—"

"Detective, I know every one of our three hundred and fifty-two students. It's my job to know them. It's also the result of an unusual gift of memory that I happen to have. The truth is, I remember everything I've ever seen or heard regarding every student who's attended GTU Law during my thirty-year tenure here at the school."

Riley glanced at Frank, whose eyes widened. "That's amazing," he remarked. "Is there anything you can tell us about Joe and Leo before your secretary brings us their contact information?"

Fletcher paused for a moment and shrugged. She then leaned over her desk, wrote a note on a piece of paper, and gave it to Frank. "This is something my secretary won't find on file," she said. "It's another phone number for Leo. It popped up on my caller ID last semester when he returned my call to discuss a class-attendance issue. I asked him to come see me at the school immediately, but he said he couldn't because he was calling from a family cottage up north."

Frank looked up from the note, shaking his head. "How can you possibly remember—"

Riley gestured for Frank to stop. Dean Fletcher was staring into space, apparently concentrating on something. Then she wrote another note. "These two people, Professor Andrew Caparo and his secretary, Nikki Ybarra, are pretty close to Joseph," she said, extending the note to Frank.

"What do you mean?" Riley asked.

"Well, Professor Caparo has become something of a mentor for Joseph over the years, and I think Joseph and Ms. Ybarra have some kind of dating relationship."

"She's his girlfriend?" Frank said. "How would you know something like—"

This time Frank stopped himself. The woman was staring into space again.

"You know," Fletcher eventually said, "I can't think of anyone on the faculty or staff that Leo might be close to. I've seen him hanging around with only two students: Joseph and—"

"Excuse me, Dean Fletcher," a woman's voice called from the telephone's speaker. "I have the information you requested." Fletcher leaned over to the phone. "Thank you, Mrs. Palsgraf. Just bring it in."

"Yes, ma'am."

"Oh, before you do that, Mrs. Palsgraf, please call Professor Caparo and Nikki Ybarra up to my office."

Riley looked up from the contact information and asked, "What about the other friend of Leo's you were talking about a minute ago? Can you tell us that person's name?"

"I can tell you a lot more than that," Fletcher said. She leaned over her desk again to work on another note. This one took a little while to write. When she finished, she extended it to Frank, whose eyes widened as he looked it over. He leaned toward Riley so she could see it too.

At the top of the note was the name of Leo's friend, Craig Davies, followed by a detailed list that included his complete mailing address; his home and cell telephone numbers; and even the make, model, and license plate number of his car.

"Okay, Dean Fletcher," Frank said when he looked up from the note. "I don't mean to sound like I doubt you, but don't you think your secretary should check this information to make sure it's—"

"There's no need to," Fletcher said. "It's all correct."

"Alright," Frank said, "if you say so, but why do you know all this stuff about this guy?"

Fletcher didn't respond. Her gaze drifted away from the officers.

"C'mon, Dean Fletcher," Frank said. "What's up with this guy? Does he play a lot of hooky from school?"

"That, and other assorted mischief," Fletcher said, still looking away.

Riley leaned forward and managed to gain eye contact. "Just what kind of mischief does Craig Davies get into around here?" she asked.

"Look, Detective, our students have privacy rights, and I have to respect Craig's when you ask questions like these."

"I get that," Riley said. "But certainly you can appreciate the seriousness of the case we're investigating. Please, tell us what you can."

Fletcher sighed. "I really doubt that any of this matters to you, but if you must know, Mr. Davies is one of those law students who just can't seem to outgrow his undergraduate mindset."

"What do you mean?"

"I don't want to give you the wrong impression about our students, Detective. The vast majority of them take seriously the rigorous Juris Doctor program offered at GTU Law. But year in and year out, I find myself dealing with an unruly handful of students who can be shockingly juvenile despite their postgraduate status."

"And Craig is one of those unruly few?"

"Perhaps the worst I've ever had to deal with in my thirty years here. The boy is single-handedly driving me to an early retirement with his constant nonsense."

"Like—"

"Like his repeated tardiness and unpreparedness for classes, and his insistence on parking that damn car of his in spaces near the building that are reserved for faculty, including the space reserved right up front for me."

Riley glanced at Frank, hoping that he, too, was able to suppress a smile. "That does sound pretty unruly," Riley said. "And that's why you know all of this information about Craig's car—because he sometimes swipes faculty parking spaces?"

Fletcher nodded and then stared into space once again.

"What is it, Dean Fletcher? There's something more, isn't there?" Riley said.

Fletcher nodded but didn't say anything.

"Oh, c'mon," Frank said. "What the hell is it?"

"Easy does it, Sergeant," Riley said.

"But she's the mother hen around here, Riley, and she's got a brain like a steel trap. Obviously, she's not just fretting about the guy's parking violations."

Fletcher winced at the remark.

"I'm telling you, Frank," Riley said, "that's enough."

Riley, a reserved and methodical investigator, had come to appreciate the more reckless style of her subordinate. But this grandmotherly witness hardly seemed like the type who required any bad-cop interrogation.

"I'm sorry if we've offended you," Riley said.

"It's okay," Fletcher said. "The sergeant is right. There is something else bothering me. It's Craig's history of violence, though I don't think it's serious enough to merit any suspicion in the matter you're investigating."

"Well," Frank said, "why don't you tell us about it and let us try to gauge his character?"

Fletcher nodded. "Craig used to play college hockey at Michigan Tech, and he seems to have quite a reputation for fighting, on and off the ice. It hasn't been a big issue here at GTU Law, but there was one occasion about a year ago when he was involved in a bar fight and caused our school some embarrassment."

"No shit," Frank said, "a privileged college kid from GTU Law mixing it up with some dude in a bar."

"Actually, Sergeant, the way I heard it, he mixed it up with *two* dudes in that bar."

"Two guys?" Frank said. "Did he kick both their asses?"

"Yes, I believe he did. But from what I heard, one of them provoked it, and no criminal charges were ever brought against any of them."

"And that's the extent of Craig's violent history?" Frank asked.

"Yes, as far as I know."

"But you said he has a reputation for fighting. So what else—"

"Excuse me, Dean Fletcher," a voice called from the speaker on the telephone. "Professor Caparo is here."

"What about Ms. Ybarra?"

"Nobody knows where she is, ma'am. She's not at her desk, and she hasn't called in to report any illness or other issue."

"Okay, Mrs. Palsgraf, just send in the professor, please."

C9

8:01 a.m., Tuesday, April 5.

Harlan was walking across a parking lot toward Butterfield Hospital when his cell phone rang. The caller ID said, "Leo—Townhouse." It stopped him in his tracks, just short of the hospital's main entrance.

"Leo, where the hell have you been?" Harlan shouted into the phone.

"No, Mr. Holmes," a woman's voice replied. "This is Nikki Ybarra. I'm at Leo and Joe's townhouse, looking for Joe. I saw your business card on their refrigerator and thought I'd call to see if you have any idea where he might be."

"Sorry, Nikki, I don't. To tell you the truth, you were on my list of people to call today about Leo. You haven't seen him either, I take it."

"No. Neither of them is answering my calls," she said, her voice beginning to shake. "This isn't like Joe. He calls me every day before I go to work, and today he didn't. Are you sure you can't help me, Mr. Holmes? I thought you of all people would at least know where Leo is with all that surveillance he says you're doing."

"What surveillance has Leo told you about?"

"Oh, you know, Mr. Holmes. The phone taps, the GPS, and all that other stuff you use to keep track of him."

"He knows about all that?"

"Well, yeah."

That little shit, Harlan thought as he remained standing in front of the hospital and watched an ambulance pass with its siren blasting.

"What was that, Mr. Holmes, a cop car?"

"No, an ambulance. I'm at the hospital."

"What are you doing there?"

"Just checking to see if Leo's been admitted."

Nikki gasped. "Really? Why would you think that's even possible?"

"At this point, I don't know what to think," Harlan said. "It's like the kid vanished."

"Did you check the cottage?"

"Yes, and my next stop is going to be the townhouse. Why don't you stay there and wait for me so we can talk about this."

"Okay, Mr. Holmes, but I can't stay long. There's somewhere else I need to be soon."

Harlan glanced at the hospital entrance. "Alright," he said, turning away from it. "I'm coming right now."

As he returned to his Jeep, Harlan wondered, *Why's she so worried about the guy missing one lousy phone call?*

Nikki sat motionless after the call ended. Her bad feeling was getting worse. She looked down at the engagement ring that Joe had given her last Christmas. She still wore it despite her recent decision to break their engagement. It wasn't an easy decision. She hadn't told anyone yet.

Harlan punched a button on his steering wheel to activate his hands-free calling system. After a prompt, he recited the phone number for Butterfield Hospital, which he had Googled on his smartphone. Eventually his call was transferred to someone at the hospital who could answer his question.

"I'm calling to see if your hospital has admitted a patient named Leo Surocco."

"And what is your relationship to this Leo..."

"Surocco," Harlan said. "I'm a friend of the family, calling on behalf of Leo's father."

After a pause, the person answered, "No, sir. We have no patient in the hospital by that name. Have a good day."

"Wait," Harlan said. "How about any patients whose identity is not—"

The individual had hung up.

35

After Harlan punched the button on his steering wheel again, he was distracted by something Nikki had said earlier. "The phone taps—I forgot all about them," he said, glancing at Dozer. "I'll have to check them after we stop at the townhouse."

"Sorry, I missed that," said an automated voice through the Jeep's speakers. "Please repeat the name of the person or telephone number you are trying to call."

Harlan glanced down at the screen on his smartphone. The number for the hospital was gone. He then reached for the redial button on the Jeep's touch screen but stopped short, recalling the medical alert bracelet that Leo wore for his asthma. *They'd know his name*, Harlan thought.

"Call Leo Surocco, cell," he said instead. *Who knows, maybe he's returned to the cottage.* After several rings, however, Harlan imagined the cell phone still lying under the bed. He ended the call when it bounced into Leo's voicemail.

The cell phone rang several times from across the room. He walked over to it, checked the caller ID, and then let it bounce into voicemail. It was Harlan Holmes, again.

Why does he keep calling?

C10

8:07 a.m., Tuesday, April 5.

Riley had never met a law professor before, but she had some preconceived ideas of what one might look like, and Andrew Caparo, with his greying beard, wire-rim glasses, and tweed jacket, seemed to fit them. The way he moved also suggested a desk-bound life. Upon hearing about Joe's near drowning, he stumbled to his feet and tried to make a run for Fletcher's office door. He wasn't hard to catch.

"Take it easy, Professor," Riley said as she grabbed hold of his arm.

"You don't understand," Caparo said. "I have to find Nikki and tell her what's going on. She's the closest thing Joe has to family."

Riley moved her hand to Caparo's shoulder and guided him back to a chair. "So Joe and Ms. Ybarra have more than a casual dating relationship?"

"Yes, they've been together for almost three years and got engaged just last Christmas."

"And I understand that you also have a close relationship with Joe—that he sees you as something of a mentor."

"That's true."

"Can you tell me a little about it?"

"I guess," he answered, still distracted by the news. But his fondness for Joe quickly engaged and he spoke about him at length. The professor explained how Joe, unlike many students at GTU, came from a disadvantaged background, yet he had managed to put himself through seven years of higher education, aided currently by a scholarship at the law school that he was awarded because of his strong undergraduate performance.

"And Joe's not one of those students who's just looking for a ticket to practice law," Caparo said. "He genuinely embraces legal studies, as I do. Over the years, he and I have spent many hours in my office sharing that interest."

Riley had remained on her feet, pacing the room, since the short race to the door. But at this point she dropped into a chair opposite Caparo and leaned forward. "Professor," she said, "given this close connection you have with Joe, can you think of anyone around here—and I mean *anyone*—who might have some reason to hurt him?"

Frank looked up at Riley. He was across the room, standing by a window, trying unsuccessfully to contact Leo and Craig by phone.

"Absolutely not," Caparo said. "It's not even imaginable."

Riley glanced back at Frank with a look that said *not yet.*

"Nobody at all?" she pressed. "There's not a single friend or acquaintance of Joe's that you, as his mentor, have ever had any concerns about?"

"Look, I've only seen one person give Joe a problem around here, and that's Joe himself."

"What do you mean?"

"Nothing that would concern you, Detective."

"Try me."

Caparo glanced at Fletcher, apparently seeking permission. She shook her head.

"It's just an anxiety issue about taking exams," Caparo said, somewhat vaguely, "a kind of enemy from within that Joe deals with. He certainly doesn't have the kind of enemy around here that you're thinking of. Everyone around here loves Joe."

Riley glanced at Frank again, and then she leaned back into her chair and folded her arms.

"Oh, c'mon, Professor!" Frank shouted from across the room. "What about these guys, Leo Surocco and Craig Davies, who won't answer my calls right now? Can you imagine either of them having something to do with Joe Rylands getting his ass kicked and then thrown into the Grand Traverse Bay?"

Caparo's eyes widened as he turned toward Frank.

"And what the hell's up with the Bucknell Bison?" Frank added.

"The Bucknell Bison?" Caparo said. "What do they have to do with this?"

"Why don't you tell us, Professor. In the ER this morning, Joe was all freaked out about Bucknell getting throttled by Michigan State last night. What's up with that?"

Caparo's mouth fell open and his eyes darted around the room, until they locked onto Dean Fletcher's. "Janice," he said, "do these officers know about the... uh ..."

"About the what?" Dean Fletcher asked.

"About the... uh... March Madness pool."

Fletcher's eyebrows crunched together. "The March Madness pool? What are you talking about?"

"Well, March Madness is a reference to a college basketball tournament that's played mostly in March. A lot of sports fans throughout the country get pretty excited about it because—"

"I'm familiar with the tournament, Andrew. What I want to know is what *pool* you're referring to."

"The one Craig Davies was running here at the school."

"That boy was running a gambling operation out of our school?"

Caparo nodded.

"And you knew about it?"

Caparo nodded again.

"And you didn't tell me about it?"

"But... but... Janice, I didn't think that... uh—"

"Andrew Caparo, did you even *think* at all?" Fletcher snapped. "You are aware of this school's honor code, are you not, Professor?"

"What's the honor code?" Riley asked.

"A code that requires our students—and faculty—to abide by the law, among other things," Fletcher answered, all the while glaring at the professor. She then sharpened her cross-examination of him.

"You must have known, Andrew, that Craig's conduct violated many anti-gambling provisions of the Michigan Penal Code and quite likely some federal statutes too. So why didn't you report it to me?"

Riley and Frank shared a glance as Caparo stammered, "I... I... just didn't think a March Madness pool was a big deal. I mean, half of America does that kind of gambling during the basketball tournament. It just seemed like harmless fun to me."

"Well," Fletcher remarked, "it seems to me, Andrew, that you exercised some monumentally poor judgment in this matter. And there are going to be repercussions for this. To begin with—"

"Excuse me, Dean Fletcher," Riley said, "but could you hold off on the repercussions for the moment? I have some more questions for the professor."

Fletcher nodded but continued her stern stare at Caparo.

"Professor," Riley asked, "this guy who ran the March Madness pool, is he the Craig Davies who used to play hockey at... uh—"

"Yes, at Michigan Tech."

"How big a pool did he manage to create here?"

"I don't know exactly, but I heard rumors that more than half of our students were playing in it, at ten to forty dollars apiece, depending on how they filled out the entry form."

Riley recalled the student enrollment number that Fletcher had mentioned earlier and did a rough calculation in her head. "So, assuming that half the student body was involved, if the average contribution was in the middle—twenty-five dollars—the pool would have been over four thousand dollars," she said.

Caparo nodded and then looked at the floor.

"More than half the student body gambled thousands of dollars right here at our law school?" Fletcher shouted. "My God, Andrew, how could you possibly think this was no big deal?"

"Please, Dean Fletcher, I want to hear more about the operation of this pool," Riley said. "Tell me, Professor, how did it work?"

Caparo lifted his head and looked directly at Riley. "Detective, are you familiar with the NCAA basketball tournament?"

"A little," Frank interjected.

Riley rolled her eyes at her partner. Around this time of year at the stationhouse, Frank was known as the "doctor of bracketology." It was a distinction he had earned by winning the stationhouse's annual March Madness pool in four of the last five years, including the one that had paid him several hundred dollars just that morning.

Frank couldn't resist taking it upon himself to explain the tournament's structure in great detail and how, in the usual March Madness pool, the person who can best predict the winning teams in each round of play wins the most money.

"It sounds like you may have some experience with this sort of thing," Caparo said, as he shot a glance at Fletcher. He then reached into a pocket of his tweed jacket and removed and unfolded a piece of paper. "The pool Craig ran had a much simpler structure. Here's a copy of the form he distributed around the school. It's the one I submitted."

"Andrew Caparo!" Fletcher shouted. "Are you saying that you participated in this pool yourself?"

Caparo nodded sheepishly as he handed his form to Riley. "Actually, Janice, a lot of faculty members played."

"What?" Fletcher gasped. "Why did nobody tell me about this?"

Fletcher continued to scold Caparo while Riley and Frank studied the form.

March Madness—Unbracketed

To win, all you have to do is predict the ultimate winner of the tournament. You may pick up to four teams, at a cost of $10 per pick. A player may submit only one form, and it's every player for him or herself. If you guess right, you'll share equally in the entire pool with anyone else who picks the winner. Good Luck!

Michigan State
North Carolina
Arizona
Gonzaga

"So you paid forty dollars to submit those four picks," Frank said.

Caparo nodded.

"And because Michigan State won last night, you get the money."

"A share of it," Caparo said, "along with a bunch of others who also picked State."

"Well, isn't that special?" Fletcher interjected sarcastically. "Congratulations, Andrew, on being one of the big winners of an illegal gambling operation run out of our school—behind my back!"

"Did anyone pick Bucknell?" Frank asked.

Caparo nodded. "From what I heard, Craig himself did. He submitted only one pick—the Bucknell Bison—and he was the only player to choose them."

"Who'd you hear that from?" Frank asked.

"I don't recall specifically. But I do remember that after the regional rounds ended and Bucknell had advanced to the final four, a lot of us wondered if anyone in our pool had actually picked them to win out. I mean, with them starting out as an obscure twelve-seed in their region, they were such a long shot."

"Well," Frank remarked, "they weren't so obscure to those who really know college hoops. They caught on fire at the end of the regular season, and then got into the region with the weakest one-seed."

Riley rolled her eyes at her partner again. She'd already heard Frank's breakdown of the entire tournament at the stationhouse that morning. "Alright, you guys, enough hoops talk," she said. "Let me just make sure I have this straight, Professor. Am I correct to understand that the whole jackpot would have gone to Craig Davies if this Cinderella team, the Bucknell Bison, had won last night?"

"Yes."

"So this guy is fairly sharp when it comes to college hoops, and he almost took his classmates for thousands of dollars."

"So it would seem," Caparo said.

"What do you mean by that?" Riley asked.

Caparo looked away.

Fletcher spoke up. "Andrew, the detective asked you a question."

Caparo sat silently, staring into space.

Riley persisted. "Professor, what did you mean by that answer? Was there something about Craig Davies or his March Madness pool that wasn't as it appeared to be?"

"You're getting into something that I can't discuss," Caparo finally said.

"What the hell, Professor? Stop jerking us around here," Frank said. "A kid was damn near murdered this morning and you're not gonna—"

"I can't tell you about the problem because I learned about it in a section 9B meeting with a student."

"What kind of meeting is that?" Riley asked, looking at Fletcher.

"The professor is referring to section 9B of the school's honor code," Fletcher said. "It provides for a special meeting that students can initiate with professors when they're unsure of their duties under the code."

"Okay," Riley said. "Perhaps you could elaborate on that for us."

Fletcher sighed deeply. "Well, if you must know," she said, and then she began speaking as though she was giving a lecture she had given hundreds of times: "Our school's honor code not only requires students to conform their own conduct to exacting ethical standards. It also affirmatively requires every student to report the suspected misconduct of other students to me, the dean of students. But sometimes—"

"Wait a second," Frank interrupted. "Did you just say that this *honor* code requires them to be snitches?"

"Essentially, yes, Sergeant," Fletcher said. She sighed again and then returned to the lecture: "Students here at GTU Law are expected to police one another, just as they someday will have to do when they're licensed attorneys subject to a code of professional responsibility. The school fully understands, though, that sometimes a student isn't sure about how this reporting obligation applies to a particular situation. So there's a section in the honor code, section 9B, that instructs the uncertain student to seek clarification, confidentially, from someone on the faculty. In the context of that meeting—"

"Whoa, slow down, Dean Fletcher," Frank said. "Are you saying that students here can't even decide for themselves if there's really a need to snitch on someone?"

"Yes I am, Sergeant. I can't tell you how many times I've had to tell a student that 'I didn't know' is no excuse. They have a duty to inquire."

"Man," Frank said, "you people are—"

"Hold on, Frank," Riley said. She turned to Fletcher. "So, apparently Professor Caparo had one of these confidential meetings with a student who knew of some problem with this March Madness pool, something not publicly known, that went beyond just the technically illegal gambling?"

Fletcher nodded. "And whatever that problem was," she said, "the professor either advised the student that it didn't merit telling me, or that it did and the student unwisely chose not to. In either case, Professor Caparo has an obligation to keep his counsel confidential."

"What'd you just say?" Frank asked. "That the professor here has an obligation to stonewall us?"

"I suppose you could put his duty of confidentiality in those terms," Fletcher said. "But nonetheless, the inviolability of the student-teacher relationship must be preserved."

"Oh c'mon," Frank said. "Are you shittin' me? Do you really expect us to just—"

"Not now, Frank," Riley said.

"Seriously, Riley," Frank said. "You graduated first in your class from the academy. Did they ever teach you anything about this lame immunity that Professor Knucklehead here is trying to assert?"

Before Riley could respond, Frank stepped toward Caparo and, wagging his finger, said, "Listen, man, you better come clean with—"

"No, you listen, man!" Caparo shouted back as he stood up and got into Frank's face. "Despite a right to remain silent that every person has when dealing with bullheaded cops like you, I've cooperated as best I can here. But now I'm asserting that right, which I assure you is not the least bit lame. This interview is over, Sergeant."

Caparo was halfway to the door when Riley called out to him. "One moment, please, Professor. I'm not going to ask you to say anything. I promise." He stopped. "The form you showed us before," she said, "the form you submitted for the March Madness pool, I think it said something about a time and place for payment to the winners at the bottom of the page. Can I see it again, just for a second?"

He silently held out the form, and everyone leaned in to read the note at the bottom: "Winners will be paid at 9:00 a.m. on the Tuesday after the final game, at Lex Caffeina. Everyone is welcome to take a break from studies and join us."

Riley looked at her watch. It was 8:40.

"Lex Caffeina," she said. "That's the coffee shop just down the street, right?"

Caparo nodded.

Riley turned to her partner. "What do you say, Frank? You up for buying me a cup of coffee?"

"Oh, no, Detective, don't make the sergeant pay," Dean Fletcher said. "Professor Caparo and I will join you, and the professor can buy us all a couple rounds of specialty coffee drinks—with the ill-gotten windfall that he won behind my back."

C11

8:16 a.m., Tuesday, April 5.

Harlan sat across from Nikki at the kitchen table in the boys' townhouse. He noticed her starting to fidget with her engagement ring as they talked.

"When was the last time you saw Joe?" he asked.

"Yesterday afternoon, when he stopped by my cubicle at school on his way out."

"What'd he say?"

"That he and Leo would be going up to the cottage after they watched the game, and that he'd be sure to call me this morning before I went to work."

"Where'd they watch the game?"

"Some bar on the way to Omena Point. I don't know which one. Joe called me from there early in the second half. He said it was getting one-sided and that he and Leo were leaving for the cottage."

"Do you know if that's where they actually went?"

"I assume they did," Nikki said, her voice beginning to shake as it had when they spoke earlier over the phone. "That's the last time I talked to him."

"You know, Nikki, I can see that you're concerned right now about Joe. But it's not clear to me why."

Nikki stopped fidgeting with her ring. "Well, it's like I told you over the phone—it's not like him not to call me."

Harlan shook his head. "C'mon, Nikki, in all the time that you and Joe have been a couple, there must have been another morning or two when he didn't call."

Nikki paused and stared at Harlan.

"What is it, Nikki? I can tell there's something more going on with you."

"You really don't know, do you, Mr. Holmes?"

"Don't know what?"

"About the March Madness pool."

"What March Madness pool?"

"The one Leo's been running at the law school since the middle of March."

"What?" Harlan gasped. "That boy's been running a gambling operation at the school for weeks, and I'm just finding out about it now?"

"Apparently so," Nikki said, smiling despite the circumstances.

"How the hell did he manage that with me into his shit practically 24/7?"

"He was using Craig Davies as a front guy, Mr. Holmes. Have you ever met Craig?"

"Yeah, I've seen him during a few of my weekly visits with Leo, here at the townhouse. When you say he was Leo's front guy, just what do you mean?"

"Well, he's the one who distributed the entry forms at school and collected all the money—and who was supposed to keep the money until the winners were paid."

Harlan glanced down at the table top. Nikki was fidgeting with her ring again. "And do you have some doubts about how well Craig took care of the money?" he asked.

Nikki nodded.

"Why?"

"Because he's a dumb ass, Mr. Holmes, just the kind of guy Leo could dupe into giving him access to the money. I'm sure that's why Leo recruited him for the job."

Harlan leaned back in his chair and sighed.

"And Craig has serious anger issues," Nikki added.

"What do you mean?"

"He's capable of flipping out over the most trivial thing, like the time I saw him beat the shit out of two guys in a bar—a couple of mean-looking bikers in full leather regalia. And then he stepped right up to this booth where the rest of their gang was sitting and asked if anyone else wanted some, and none of 'em made a move."

"Holy shit. What set him off?" Harlan asked.

"Well, one of the bikers asked a girl at our table to dance, and Craig told him to take a walk. The guy said something back and called Craig '*college boy.*' And that's when Craig went after him."

"Being called college boy? That's what set him off?"

"Yep, and—"

"Wait a second," Harlan said. "I think I've heard Leo call him by that name—college boy—and he didn't seem to mind."

"Well, after the bar fight, everybody around the law school started calling him that," Nikki said. "The incident made him an instant hero, and that nickname has become a kind of honorary title that he seems to like."

Harlan thought for a moment and said, "So, are you're worried about College Boy going ballistic on Leo or Joe if they did something to piss him off?"

Nikki nodded.

"Like maybe Leo pissing him off by duping him out of the March Madness fund and then blowing it in a casino?" Harlan asked.

"Yeah," Nikki said. "Or like Joe pissing him off by ratting out the pool to someone at the law school," she added.

"And you think Joe would do something like that?"

"I don't *think* he would, Mr. Holmes. I *know* he did."

"Why did he do that?"

"The school has some asinine honor code that Joe takes seriously. And because of it, he went and told one of the profs, in some confidential meeting, about Leo secretly sponsoring the pool and how it was at risk because of his gambling issue."

"And Joe told you this?"

"Yeah, he told me before he met with the prof."

"Did you say it was a confidential meeting?"

"Yeah, some kind of secret meeting that a student can have with a prof to get advice about whether he really should rat out a classmate to the dean's office."

"Did Joe end up doing that?"

"I don't think so. If he did, he never told me. But still, ratting out a friend to a prof, even privately, was a stupid move on his part. I told Joe that if he really wanted to do the right thing, he should talk with *Leo*, not with some prof. Leo needs someone to sit his ass down and talk straight with him about his gambling addiction and his need for treatment."

Harlan nodded. Since the day he had become Leo's 24/7 babysitter, at this very kitchen table, he had held the same opinion about the kind of intervention Leo really needed. "You and Joe are pretty close with Leo and his family, aren't you?" he asked.

"Yes, very close. Joe and Leo are both gonna go to work in the Surocco family business after they graduate. And Joe and I have visited the family with Leo a lot over the years. They've become kind of like our own family, and it feels like we're betraying them when we just stand by and watch Leo self-destruct."

"So you two watched Leo and Craig put together this March Madness pool?"

"Yes, we did," Nikki said as she dropped her head.

"Just how big did it get?"

"A little over five thousand dollars."

"Shit," Harlan murmured to himself, shaking his head. "When are they supposed to pay that money back to the winners?" he asked.

"Nine o'clock this morning, at Lex Caffeina."

"The coffee shop on Front Street?" Harlan asked as he glanced at his watch. It was 8:40 a.m.

Nikki nodded. "Are you gonna go there?" she asked.

Harlan thought for a moment. "No, I don't have the time. I have to stop at my office to check on something and then go directly to the airport."

"Are you leaving town, Mr. Holmes?"

"No. I'm meeting someone who's coming into town. What about you, Nikki? Do you have time to go to Lex Caffeina?"

"I was planning on going."

Harlan glanced down at the business card sitting on the table between them. It was his card, the one Nikki had removed from the refrigerator when she called earlier. He reached for it and slid it across the table to her. "Would you call me from Lex Caffeina as soon as you learn anything there?"

"Sure."

C12

9:00 a.m., Tuesday, April 5.

At home in his office, Harlan listened to the conversation a second time. Other than Nikki's call from the townhouse that morning, it was the only call his landline phone taps had recorded in the past few days. The call had been made by Leo on the cottage phone at 2:37 a.m. The groggy recipient of the late-night call was his father, Angelo.

"Hi, Dad, it's me, Leo."

"Who... Leo?"

"Yeah, Dad. Sorry to call so late."

"What's going on?" Angelo asked.

Leo stammered nervously. "I... I'm not quite sure how to say this... but look, Dad... I'm a... a little short of money this week. Can you help me out?"

"What the hell did you do, Leo, get yourself into more gambling debt?"

Leo didn't respond.

"You did—didn't you?"

"Please let me explain, Dad. I was—"

"I don't want to hear it, Leo. I'm done cleaning up your messes. Whatever the hell's going on, it's your problem, not mine."

"I understand how you feel, Dad, but—"

Angelo hung up.

Several seconds of silence followed. Then came a deep sigh. And then Leo's voice. "Hi, Mr. Holmes. I know you've tapped the landlines here at the cottage and at the townhouse. Sometimes I wonder whether you've gotten to my cell phone. Anyway, I used the landline to be sure you got this message if my dad hung up on me the way he just did. Please share it with him as soon

49

as you can."

Another several seconds of silence, another deep sigh, and then Leo's voice again, more earnest than Harlan had ever heard it before.

"Dad, please, hear me out. I messed up worse this time than ever. Other people are at risk along with me because of what I did. I'm on my way to Chicago to ask you for money in person. It's money I really need, Dad. Look, I know I'm sick. I've actually spent a lot of time online lately searching for a good treatment program. And I found one, a wellness center in Virginia, where I'm thinking I'd like to go to for help after exams are done next week. They have a twenty-eight-day treatment program that I want to talk about with you and Mom. I'm really serious this time, Dad. I want to do everything I can not to repeat this. You know I love you both, and I hate like hell to be putting you two through this. I'm sorry. I'll see you soon."

C13

9:30 a.m., Tuesday, April 5.

Harlan sat alone in the terminal's waiting area, looking at his cell phone. He finally clicked "send" on an email that attached pictures he had taken earlier at the cottage. Also secreted from the cottage and ready for delivery was the briefcase that Angelo had requested.

A few minutes later, Angelo's private jet touched down, and he and three companions soon appeared at the terminal's opposite end. Their pace was serious as they approached. So, too, was Angelo's expression. His jet-black eyes locked onto Harlan.

What kind of crew did he bring along? Harlan wondered as he squinted back. From a distance, they didn't fit his preconception of the guys this capo would assemble for a significant assignment, except perhaps the one he couldn't account for.

To Angelo's right was the only member of the crew wearing a suit, a chalk-white man whose advanced age showed as he labored to keep pace with the others. *That must be Tommy MacPherson*, Harlan thought, *Angelo's attorney.* Harlan had never seen Tommy in person, but over the past few months Tommy had been his phone and email point of contact for almost all matters concerning Leo, including the pictures he had just emailed.

To Angelo's immediate left was, no doubt, Leo's older brother, Vincent Surocco. Harlan had seen pictures of Vincent at the cottage. With just one look at him in person, it was already becoming clear to Harlan how his younger brother, Leo, had displaced him as heir apparent to the family's business—the gambling issue notwithstanding. Vincent, age twenty-nine, looked like a preppy rich kid in his designer jeans and Polo sweater. He, too, labored to keep pace as the two bags he carried took turns banging against his legs.

To Vincent's left, also carrying two bags, strode the last of the crew, an African American man with an athletic build. Harlan knew nothing about this guy, and his choice of eyewear suggested that he might not be easy to get to know. Though indoors, he wore mirrored sunglasses.

Vincent and the stranger separated from the crew before reaching the waiting area and headed for the counter of a car rental agency. Harlan extended a hand toward Angelo, but the man passed him by and continued through a door leading outside, gaining speed. The door had barely swung shut behind them before Angelo had a cigarette lit.

"Gimme the briefcase," Angelo said through the smoke that streamed out of his mouth and nose. He let the cigarette dangle from his lips so that his hands were free to lay the briefcase on top of a trashcan and work its combination lock. "What can you tell us?"

Harlan reported what he had done that morning in search of Leo, though he glossed over the details of his meeting with Nikki Ybarra and he avoided entirely any mention of the recording of Leo's late-night plea to his father for help.

As he spoke, Harlan watched Angelo open the briefcase and push aside some documents. Beneath them, lining the bottom of the briefcase, were bundles of cash. Harlan caught only a glimpse before Angelo snapped the briefcase shut. The bills on top of the few bundles he saw were hundreds. If the rest were the same, there had to be at least ten thousand dollars per bundle.

Tommy barely looked up from his cell phone when Harlan introduced himself. "These pictures you took at the cottage," Tommy said, "I don't see one showing any sign of forced entry."

"I don't think there was," Harlan said. "The front door was unlocked when I got there, and the alarm system was shut down."

Tommy stopped at a picture of tire tracks and footprints in the driveway and turned so Harlan could get a look at it. "Well, do you know who Leo or Joe might have let in—who these tire tracks and footprints might belong to?"

"No," Harlan answered. He paused and then added, "But Ms. Ybarra offered a theory this morning."

"What theory?"

After sighing deeply, Harlan told them what he had learned from Nikki that morning. Angelo stood stock-still, staring at him, as Harlan described Leo and Craig's March Madness pool and the gambling proceeds it made available to Leo. By the time the account reached Nikki's concerns about Craig's volatile temper, Angelo was glaring at Harlan.

"What the hell have I been paying you five grand a week for, Holmes?" Angelo shouted.

"I'm sorry, Angelo, but—"

Harlan's phone rang. He didn't recognize the number on the caller ID, but he remembered that Nikki might be calling sometime soon. "I should take this," he said. Angelo continued glaring at him.

"Hi, Mr. Holmes."

"Nikki?"

"Yeah. I'm leaving Lex Caffeina now. The boys never showed up. But my boss and two cops did."

"What cops?" Harlan asked.

"Some detective, Riley something—"

"Summers?"

"Yeah, and her sidekick, a sergeant... uh—"

"Frank Tice."

"Yeah, and the two of them interrogated the shit out of me," Nikki said, "after telling me that... that—"

"What is it, Nikki? What'd they tell you?"

"It's about Joe," Nikki said. Her voice trembled. "He was found washed up on the beach this morning at Stony Point, nearly dead, all tangled up in weeds and a swim buoy and wearing nothing but his pajamas. He's in Butterfield Hospital right now. They say he's been talking in his sleep about Leo and the Bucknell Bison."

"The Bucknell Bison?"

"Yeah," Nikki said. "They say he's not making any sense yet. I'm heading to the hospital now. I think those two cops are too. I'll talk to you later, Mr. Holmes. I really have to—"

"Hold on, Nikki, please. You say the cops interrogated you. What'd you tell them?"

"Not much that they didn't already know."

"What do you mean?"

"My boss, Professor Caparo, had already told them about the March Madness pool. I guess he actually played in it. But he didn't tell them about Leo being the guy who was really running it, which blew me away. I can't believe that the professor didn't give up Leo."

"So the professor already knew about Leo running the pool?"

"He sure did," Nikki said. "He's the prof Joe squealed to in that confidential meeting I told you about."

"So the cops still don't know that—"

"Yes, they do, Mr. Holmes. I told them all about Leo and his gambling problem. They were already looking for him anyway—him and Craig Davies. And like I told you before, I've had enough of all this denial of Leo's problem."

"What'd you tell them about me?"

"Don't worry, Mr. Holmes. All I told them is that you're keeping an eye on Leo for the family and that you're looking for him too. We didn't get into any details about all that surveillance stuff you do."

"That was Nikki Ybarra," Harlan said after the call ended.

"No shit," Tommy said. "What cops was she talking about?"

"A couple state troopers assigned to Joe Rylands' case. The kid nearly drowned in the Grand Traverse Bay this morning."

After Harlan explained the few details he had learned about Joe's near drowning, Tommy asked, "Who's in charge of the investigation?"

"Detective Riley Summers."

"You know him?"

"You mean *her*," Harlan said. "And, yes, I know Detective Summers. I worked closely with her before leaving the force."

"What kind of relationship did you have?"

Harlan shrugged. "A complicated one," he said.

"What, were you sleeping with her?"

"No, not that complicated."

"Well, then what was—"

"I got laid off, man, and she took my fuckin' job."

"Well that explains a lot," Angelo said. "We got the reject working for us."

"Okay," Tommy said, "Let's just stay focused on—"

Harlan's cell phone rang again. *That didn't take long*, he thought as he glanced at the caller ID. "It's state police headquarters," he said, looking at Tommy, who, in turn, looked at Angelo.

"I think we should tell them about the evidence at the cottage and give them consent to search the place," Harlan said.

"Why the hell would I do that?" Angelo asked.

"So I can send Riley Summers there and maybe give us a shot at talking to Joe Rylands first."

Angelo paused.

"They're gonna get a warrant at some point anyway," Harlan said.

Angelo nodded.

"Charlie Bivens, you're still working the phones?" Harlan said. "How the hell are you?"

"Alright, Harlan. And you?"

"I'm having a real shitty day, Charlie. Thanks for asking."

"Well, I'm about to make it worse," Charlie said. "Summers wants to talk to you. She says you'll probably know why."

"I'm afraid I do, but go ahead and put me through anyway."

While he waited for the call to transfer, Harlan removed a small iPod and a set of earbuds from his pocket. "Something was picked up by the cottage phone taps last night," he said, extending the items to Angelo.

"The call to me?"

"Yeah, but some more was said after you hung up."

After Angelo took the items, Harlan walked down the sidewalk in front of the terminal until he was out of earshot.

"Harlan?"

"Hey, Riley."

"What are you into with the Surocco family?" she asked.

Harlan glanced back at Tommy and Angelo and casually took a few more steps away. "It's kind of a babysitting thing. I'm supposed to be keeping an eye on one of the kids in the family, Leo Surocco. But I somehow lost him. And just a few hours ago, I discovered evidence suggesting foul play, maybe a home invasion and assault, at the family's cottage."

"Where's the cottage?"

Harlan gave her the exact address.

"Can you or your client meet me there to let me in?" Riley asked.

"There's no need for that," Harlan said. "The door's unlocked, just the way I found it this morning. And my client's okay with you searching the place without us being there. Hell, I was just about to call you to tell you that myself."

"Yeah, right."

"Look, I just met my client at the airport, and cooperating with the police is one of the first things I insisted we do. I'm telling you, Riley, we're on the same team on this one, like old times."

Before anything more was said, he heard, through the phone, the screech of vehicle tires. Hopefully that meant she was headed for the cottage at Omena Point.

"If you intend to be so cooperative with the police, why didn't you call us immediately after you visited the cottage?" Riley asked.

"C'mon, Riley. How about cutting me some slack here? Like I told Charlie a minute ago, my day's gotten off to a rough start. I'm dealing with a client who's seriously stressed out."

She sighed. "Alright, just tell me what you know."

"I will, I promise. But this is not a good time for a long talk."

Harlan looked back over his shoulder. Angelo had finished listening to the iPod and a Cadillac Escalade with tinted windows was pulling to the curb alongside him. The man with the mirrored sunglasses stepped out of it. Behind him another vehicle, a Lincoln sedan, pulled to the curb. Vincent emerged from that one. The crew reconvened around Angelo. Soon they all were looking at Harlan.

"Harlan, are you still there?" Riley asked.

"Yeah, but I'm keeping my client and... uh... his family waiting here at the airport for me to finish this call. I'll call you back later, Riley, when there's more time to talk."

"I think we've got a clear shot at Joe Rylands," Harlan said when he returned to the crew.

"It's about time you did something right," Angelo said. He then gestured to Tommy and the two stepped aside for private conversation. Harlan used the intermission to introduce himself to Vincent and the guy wearing sunglasses, Phoenix Wade, whose gentle handshake contradicted everything about his appearance. He looked to be about six feet tall and a fat-free two hundred pounds. Every part of him was thick.

Phoenix had taken off his sunglasses for the introduction.

"So, what do you do?" Harlan asked.

Phoenix shrugged. "Whatever the boss wants," he said. He then put his sunglasses back on. Apparently the boss didn't want him to chat at length with Harlan.

Tommy and Angelo returned. "Harlan," Tommy said, "do you know this guy Craig Davies, the one they call College Boy for some reason?"

"Sure, the hockey player. I saw him at Leo's townhouse a couple times when—"

"I can tell you why they call him 'College Boy,'" Vincent interjected. "I met that gorilla once when Leo brought him to Chicago on a day trip and—"

"Vincent," Angelo said, "shut up and let Tommy talk with Mr. Holmes."

Vincent looked down at the sidewalk.

"Vincent's got a point," Harlan said. "Craig's an imposing guy, built just like Phoenix, but even bigger."

"Big enough to leave those footprints you found at the cottage?" Tommy asked.

"I don't know," Harlan answered. "I guess I never looked at his feet."

"What about those tire tracks?" Tommy asked. "Does Craig drive a car that might leave those?"

"Jeez, Tommy, those tracks were from some standard-sized tires. They could come from just about any ordinary sedan or economy car."

"Dammit, you're not answering my question, Harlan. Do you know what the kid drives?"

Harlan had to think about the question. "An old Pontiac... a Grand Prix or Grand Am... I think. Its tires might leave tracks like those on the driveway, just like the tires on a million other cars in northern Michigan."

"Do you know Craig's phone number?" Tommy asked.

"Not offhand, but I might have it at home."

"How about where he lives?"

Harlan almost said no, but then he recalled something and began to think out loud. "It wasn't candy... no, it was fudge... yeah, fudge—"

"What are you talking about?" Tommy asked.

"Craig was at Leo's townhouse during one of my visits," Harlan said, "and he offered me fudge. He had a big box of it—you know, the kind of box the tourists from downstate drive all the way up north for. He told me that he was able to get it for free at one of the shops downtown—Marbury's Fudge Shop, I think he said—because he rents an apartment above the business."

"Vincent," Angelo said, "you know where this fudge place is, don't you?"

"Sure, Dad, Marbury's Fudge. It's on State Street. I've been by it a thousand times, you know, when we're here visiting." Vincent had lifted his head and looked eagerly at his father.

"You take the Lincoln," Angelo said, "and see if this guy Craig is there."

Vincent began striding for the car.

"Vincent," Angelo said. "Where the hell are you going? I haven't finished talking to you."

Vincent stopped and turned. "Sorry, Dad."

"Just talk to him. Nothing else, you hear? We can't be sure whose footprints those are. So just ask him if he's seen Leo, and don't get cute with him. You understand?"

"Got it, Dad. I'll be cool."

Vincent started for the car again.

"Dammit, Vincent," Angelo said. "Get back here. I'm not done yet."

The unfortunate son returned for further instructions.

"If he's *not* there, go inside and have a look around. But be discreet. And call me as soon as you're done. Okay?"

"Got it, Dad. Check the place out, low profile, and keep you posted." Then he stood motionless, staring at his father.

"Well?" Angelo said. "What are you waiting for? Get going."

Angelo then turned to the rest of the crew. "Let's go see Joe."

Harlan was halfway across the street in front of the terminal, heading toward the parking lot for his Jeep, when Phoenix called out to him. "Mr. Holmes."

Phoenix stood beside an open door to the backseat of the Escalade, like a chauffeur awaiting his fare. Harlan returned to the car and climbed in alongside Tommy and behind Angelo. As the Escalade pulled away from the curb, he looked back at the parking lot through a deeply tinted window and watched his Jeep disappear.

C14

10:45 a.m., Tuesday, April 5.

Nikki Ybarra was sitting alone in a corner, visibly distressed, when Angelo, Tommy, Phoenix, and Harlan entered the ICU visitor's area at Butterfield Hospital. She stood up and launched herself at Angelo, who stumbled backward when she landed on him. Harlan recalled Nikki telling him about the close bond she had developed with the Surocco family. Apparently it extended to Angelo.

"They won't let me see Joe," Nikki said as a few tears rolled down her face.

"We'll do something about that," Angelo said. He guided her back to her seat and sat down next to her. "Have you heard anything about how Joe's doing?"

"Not much," Nikki said. "He's been out of it since he got here this morning, and they have no idea how long it'll be until he comes around."

Angelo nodded. "Harlan tells us you have a theory about what happened."

"I do, Mr. Surocco, and I feel so bad that Joe and I didn't do something to prevent it when we saw that March Madness pool getting so large, I mean, you know, with Leo's gambling issue and all, and that stooge of his, Craig Davies, supposedly handling all that money."

"So you really think that this guy Craig—"

"Excuse me," a woman's voice interrupted. "I'm Nurse Plessy. Are you the one that the police say is engaged to our patient, Joseph Rylands?" she asked, looking at Nikki.

"Yes. When can we see him?"

"What do you mean, *we?*" the nurse asked. "Are all of these gentlemen here with you?"

"We sure are," Harlan interjected. "We're the closest thing Joseph has to a family."

The nurse looked them over and paused when she reached Phoenix, the only nonwhite member of the crew. Phoenix removed his sunglasses and presented a forlorn expression. "Please, ma'am," he said, his voice seeming to struggle with anxiety. "Joe's like my little brother. You gotta let me see him."

Man, he's pretty good, Harlan thought.

Angelo's concerned expression was even better. His struck Harlan as genuine. "Joe goes to GTU Law with Leo, my son," Angelo said. "They're best friends and roommates, and Joe basically lives with my family in Chicago when they're on break from school. Please, if you could just—"

"The same Leo that Joe's been talking about in his sleep?" the nurse asked.

"Yes, ma'am."

"And you're his father?"

"Yes, I'm Leo's father, and I'm practically Joe's too. Those two boys have lived together for years. They're almost never apart. In fact, both of them are coming to work for me in my family business next fall."

Nurse Plessy nodded. "Come with me," she said. "Joe is still pretty out of it, but maybe some familiar voices and faces will help bring him around."

Outside the door to Joe's private room sat two state troopers, Officers Katko and Briney. They stood up and converged to block the crew's entrance but did not warn them off. "Harlan Holmes, great to see you," Katko said.

Vigorous two-handed shakes ensued between Harlan and his former colleagues. But when Harlan tried to step around them, Officer Katko extended a hand and shook his head. "You know," he said, "we're not supposed to let anyone in until Summers and Tice have had a chance to get this guy's statement. They're on their way right now."

"It's cool, you guys," Harlan said. "Headquarters called me earlier today as the case unfolded and it became clear that this guy Joe is essentially a member of my client's family. And I've already talked with Riley about the situation, just a little while ago. She's decided not to come to the hospital just yet. I think she's discovered a crime scene somewhere on the Leelanau Peninsula and is investigating it right now."

"I dunno," Katko said. "I should probably call her and see what she has to say."

"Look, guys," Harlan said, "my clients really are like family to the kid, and they're just here to visit. Certainly you can understand how worried they must be. Even the nurse here thinks this is a good idea, that it might help his recovery, don't you, Nurse Plessy?"

The nurse nodded.

"What do you think?" Katko asked, turning to his partner.

"I guess it's okay with me," Briney said. "But if the kid starts coming around, Harlan, you be sure to tell us."

"Of course," Harlan said.

The officers stepped aside.

C15

10:57 a.m., Tuesday, April 5.

Nikki sat on the edge of the bed next to Joe, caressing his head as he slept. She then leaned over him, kissed him on the cheek, and began whispering in his ear. Eventually Joe responded with a kiss to Nikki's lips.

Angelo stepped back from the foot of the bed and gestured to the rest of the crew to do the same. Presumably he thought the couple would want some space before discussing Joe's close call with death. But Nikki cut to the chase.

"Joe, what the hell happened to you?"

The crew scurried back to the foot of the bed.

Joe winced as he sat up. His expression went blank as he gazed across the faces that stared at him from the foot of the bed. He turned back to Nikki and said, "What?"

"C'mon, Joe, snap out of it," she said. "Someone found you washed up on the beach at Stony Point this morning. He saved your life and brought you here. Please, Joe, tell us—"

"Here?" Joe said.

"The hospital, Joe," Nikki said, sighing. "Would you just tell us what—"

"Mr. Surocco, is that you?" Joe said, squinting toward the foot of the bed.

Angelo stepped around to the side of the bed opposite Nikki. "Yeah, Joe, it's me," he said as he sat in a chair and scooted close. "Please, son, we need you to tell us what happened last night. Leo is missing. You've been talking about him in your sleep, like something went wrong. The two of you were at the cottage last night. What happened there?"

Joe looked down at his bandaged arm and then back at Angelo.

"Leo's missing?"

Angelo nodded.

There was a long pause before Joe responded. "I remember something waking me up in the middle of the night, a couple guys outside my bedroom door on the loft. One of them I could tell was Leo. The other guy was yelling and cursing. And then there was a crash against the wall."

"Who was the other guy?" Angelo asked.

"I don't know. I didn't hear him say much, just something about money. I think Leo offered the guy his watch, but the guy said he didn't want it. He just wanted money."

"What happened after the crash?"

"I ran to the door and opened it, and there was Leo, pinned to the wall by the guy. The son of a bitch was huge, and he was yelling like he was out of his mind."

"What was he yelling?"

"I'm sorry, Mr. Surocco, I don't know. It all happened so fast."

A tear rolled down Joe's face. "It's okay, Joe," Nikki said as she caught it with a fingertip. "Just tell us what you can. It'll do you good to talk about it."

"Can you describe this big guy?" Angelo asked.

"I only saw him from behind, sir. The hands he held Leo with were white, and so was the skin on his neck. I saw that when I jumped on his back."

"You jumped on him?" Angelo said.

"Yeah and... and..."

"And what, Joe," Angelo asked, leaning forward.

"We were by the stairs, and the big guy must have lost his balance. He must have fallen down the stairs with me on his back."

Joe placed a hand on his rib cage.

"I don't know what happened to Leo, whether he fell down the stairs too. But I know that the big guy fell right on top of me. It was like being crushed under a tank and... and then..."

Joe turned back to Nikki, his eyes filled with tears. Nikki snatched a box of tissues from the bed stand and began wiping Joe's face. He raised a hand and waved her off.

"Mr. Surocco, it was like a nightmare after that, like it might not even be real."

Angelo was on the edge of his seat. "I think it was real, Joe. Please, son, tell me as best you can."

Joe's breathing intensified. So did the speed of what he said next. "The fall must have knocked me out because I remember waking up later and... and it was so dark I... I couldn't see *anything*. And water was rushing in on me, ice-cold water. I started moving around, trying to get up, but I couldn't. There was something holding me down, like I was in a box, and it was keeping me from getting up. Everywhere I tried to move there were walls. I swear to God there were walls all around me, like I was in a big box filling with icy water in the pitch black. And... and..."

Nikki snatched Joe's left hand with both of hers. "Oh God, Joe!" she exclaimed, now crying along with him.

"I was running out of air when something... *someone*... pushed up against me and... and grabbed me. There was someone else in there with me trying to get out too. I couldn't see him... it was too dark... but... but for some reason I thought... I knew... it was Leo."

Angelo looked at the floor and froze. Tommy took over. "Do you remember anything else, Joe?" he asked.

Joe took a deep breath. "No, sir, I just remember running out of air and him grabbing my arm and... wait... something moved. One of the walls... I think... yeah... one of the walls moved while I was pulling away from him... kind of like a door on a hinge... and that's... that's actually the last thing I remember."

"Harlan," Tommy said, "you're certain that the GPS device would have malfunctioned if it was submerged in water, right?"

Harlan nodded.

Tommy turned back to Joe. "Please, Joe, try to compose yourself," he said.

Joe freed his hand from Nikki's two-handed grasp and used it to scrub his eyes and face. Tommy stared at Joe anxiously but gave him time to get his breathing back to something close to normal.

"Okay, Joe," Tommy said, "this box you've described, this thing you were trapped inside of, could it have been the bed of Mr. Surocco's pickup truck, the bed of the Avalanche pickup that he lets Leo use?"

"I suppose it could have been if the lid was fastened over it," Joe answered, his breathing continuing to slow.

"And the wall that you pushed through, the one like a door, could that have been a fold-down seat, you know, a seat that allows access between the cab and the bed of the truck?"

"Maybe it was, Mr. MacPherson, but I can't say for sure what I was trapped in."

"Well, I think that's exactly what you were trapped in. And once you were in the cab of the pickup, you must have gone through one of its doors or windows to get out. Do you remember that?"

"I'm sorry, Mr. MacPherson. I just don't remember anything after feeling that wall move."

"I understand," Tommy said. He paused for a moment. "Look, Joe, I know you didn't get a good look at the big guy on the loft, but I want you to think back as carefully as you can, okay?"

"Okay."

"Could he have been Craig Davies?"

"Craig? No way!" Joe shouted. "There's no way Craig would ever do anything like that to Leo or me."

"Joe, they know about the March Madness pool," Nikki said, "and how Craig probably let Leo have all the money in it."

Joe looked at Angelo, who nodded his head. He then squinted at the others beyond the side of the bed, all of whom were nodding.

"Well," Joe objected, "what does that have to do with me being thrown in the bay?"

Nikki sighed. "How badly did you hurt your head, Joe? Don't you see that some bad blood may have come between Leo and Craig if it turns out that Leo blew the money in the pool?"

"Maybe some bad blood, but you can't be thinking that Craig's capable of attempted murder," Joe said. He again looked at Angelo, who again nodded his head.

"Joe, I was at the cottage earlier today," Harlan said, "and a third person—a large person who drove an ordinary car, like Craig's old Pontiac—left tire tracks and big footprints in the driveway. There was no sign of forced entry, and no sign that Leo ever went to bed. Do you remember seeing Leo go to bed?"

"Well, no. I went to bed around midnight, I think, while Leo was still watching the postgame stuff on TV. I didn't see him again until I saw the big guy attacking him on the loft."

"So apparently," Harlan said, "Leo stayed up last night and let someone into the cottage, some big guy. Besides you, Joe, who else does Leo ever invite to the cottage?"

"Just Craig and me, as far as I know."

"And Craig is about sixty pounds heavier than you and about four or five inches taller, right?"

"I guess."

Harlan recalled the blood and hair he'd discovered on the cottage steps. "And Craig's hair is longer and lighter than yours and Leo's, right?"

"Well, yeah, but why does that matter?"

"Because it fits the description of the hair on the head of the big guy who attacked Leo, doesn't it?"

Joe's face flashed with realization. "You're right, Mr. Holmes, kind of, but this guy's hair was even longer than Craig's. Yeah, it was longish brown hair, styled like those guys with big hair in the eighties, like a big mullet hangin' off the back of his head. How do you know about his hair? I didn't even remember it until now."

Harlan ignored the question. "Okay, Joe, let's talk about the money," he said, stepping around the bed to get closer. "We need to know what happened to the money in Leo's March Madness pool. What can you tell us about it?"

Joe looked down at the bed and shook his head. Harlan repeated the question, but Joe remained shut down.

"C'mon, Joe," Nikki said, "answer Mr. Holmes' question."

"Dammit, Nikki, why are you telling me to rat out Leo?"

She shook her head. "Joe, you need to start thinking straight here. This isn't about ratting out your friend. Somebody almost killed you, and it sounds like they actually did kill—"

"Leo spent the money, I think," Joe said.

"On what?" Harlan asked.

"I don't know."

"Well, how do you know he spent it?"

"I can't believe this shit," Joe said, looking at Nikki.

"Please, Joe, just tell Mr. Holmes what you know."

"Leo and I watched the basketball game together last night," Joe said, "at some bar that was on the way to the cottage. He was in a great mood, certain that Bucknell would finish their run and beat Michigan State. But obviously they didn't, and when Leo started to realize that State was gonna blow 'em out, he got more than just upset."

"What do you mean?" Harlan asked.

"He was actually nervous, to the point where I could see him trembling. I've never seen him like that. Usually he's so confident, no matter what. We ended up leaving for the cottage way before the game was even over."

"And that's how you figured out he had spent the money," Harlan said, "because he was so nervous?"

"That, and something he said, Mr. Holmes."

Everyone in the room leaned in slightly, toward Joe.

"We watched the rest of the game at the cottage," Joe said. "As soon as it ended, Craig called. And I overheard something."

"What phone did the call come in on?" Tommy interjected.

"Leo's cell," Joe answered.

Angelo gave Harlan a look.

At some point early in the babysitting assignment, Angelo had specifically instructed Harlan to tap all phones that Leo had access to. Harlan was able to do that only with the landlines at the cottage and the townhouse. He knew of software that could be used to tap a cell phone, but it had to be downloaded onto the target phone, which required physical possession of the phone for at least five minutes. Gaining that kind of access to Leo's cell phone was impossible. The kid always had it with him.

Harlan shook his head and then resumed questioning Joe. "Okay, so what did you overhear?"

"Well, like I said, the game had just ended and I was sitting across from Leo, on the recliner in the great room, watching the State players cut down the nets. I don't remember everything Leo said, but it was pretty clear that he was telling Craig not to worry—*I'll get it covered'* was how he put it, I think."

"How was he going to do that?"

"I don't know. My guess was that he'd cover his losses the same way he did the last time he got in too deep: ask *you* for the money, Mr. Surocco."

Angelo didn't return Joe's look.

"How much money did he need?" Harlan asked.

"I don't know."

"Do you know if Leo was expecting a visit from Craig last night?"

"No, Mr. Holmes. And I'm telling you, it wasn't Craig on those stairs. The guy was just too damn big to be Craig, and I would have recognized Craig's voice."

"How can you be so sure?" Harlan said. "They woke you up in the middle of the night from a sound sleep. And you don't see so well without your glasses, Joe, which is pretty obvious given the way you keep squinting at anyone in this room who's beyond the side of your bed."

Joe said nothing.

"Well," Harlan pressed, "did you have your glasses on during the few seconds you looked at this guy—from behind?"

Joe remained silent.

"Does Leo owe money to anyone else?" Harlan asked.

"Not that I know of, sir."

Indignation then filled Joe's voice as he went on to scold Harlan. "With all due respect, Mr. Holmes, you're the only person in this room who might know of any irregularities in Leo's financial situation—with all your surveillance and weekly visits. Why do you think he pulled this March Madness stunt to begin with?"

Harlan nodded and then slowly retreated to the end of the bed.

"Joe, what's Craig's phone number?" Tommy asked.

"I don't know offhand, but if you get me online, I can get it for you."

While Tommy worked his cell phone, Nikki asked, "Where'd the swim buoy come from?"

"What swim buoy?" Joe said.

"The guy who found you on the beach said that a bunch of weeds got tangled around your neck in the straps of a swim buoy. It probably saved your life by keeping your head out of the water. Where'd it come from?"

"From the bed of the Avalanche," Angelo said, finally breaking his silence. "There was some fishing and swimming gear back there."

Joe looked bewildered as he reached for his neck. Moments after touching it, he gasped. "Nikki, my necklace... it's... it's gone. I must have lost it when... when..."

"You wore a necklace to bed, Joe?" Harlan asked.

"Yeah, it's the necklace Nikki gave me when we got engaged—a big titanium necklace—that I promised I'd wear until we were married."

"It's okay, Joe. I'll get you another one," Nikki said as she ran a hand along the base of his neck.

"And you have no memory of losing it?" Harlan asked.

Joe shook his head.

"And no memory of getting tangled up in the swim buoy and those weeds?"

Joe shook his head again.

"Okay, I've got a connection," Tommy said as he extended his cell phone to Joe. Seconds later Joe recited Craig's phone number.

Angelo rose from his chair and slowly paced the length of the bed while punching the number into his cell phone. Then he slowly returned, waiting for an answer. He stopped midway down the length of the bed when a woman's voice answered—

"Hello."

The volume on Tommy's phone was set so loud that everyone in the room could hear the voice clearly. Indeed, even from the one-word response, Harlan thought it sounded familiar.

"This is Angelo Surocco. Where is my son, Leo?"

"Mr. Surocco, this is Detective Riley Summers of the Michigan State Police. I'm sorry, sir, but I don't know where your son is. I'm at your cottage right now, speaking to you on a cell phone that was found inside the cottage under a bed."

C16

11:38 a.m., Tuesday, April 5.

"That son of a bitch Craig Davies went berserk," Angelo said after he ended the call, "and Leo sensed it coming."

"What do you mean?" Tommy asked.

Angelo reached into his pocket and withdrew the iPod and earbuds that Harlan had given him earlier. "It's a recording of a call Leo made to me last night," Angelo said, extending the items to Tommy. "There's also a message for Harlan at the end. Listen to the way Leo's talking. He's scared shitless."

"He left a message for Harlan?" Tommy said.

"You'll see. Just listen to the damn recording. Apparently, Leo's been more than a step ahead of our PI all along."

Harlan rolled his eyes and started for the door.

"Where the hell are you going?" Phoenix asked.

Harlan stopped and faced Phoenix. "Just out for some air, Mr. Wade. You got a problem with that?"

"Lighten up, you guys," Angelo said. "If you want to step out, Harlan, that's fine, but I'd rather you stick around to hear Tommy's take on this."

"I've already thought through the theory of College Boy's rampage," Harlan said. "I'm gonna see if I can learn something new from the cops outside."

"When did Leo make this call?" Tommy asked after the recording ended.

"It was about 1:30 in the morning, Chicago time, when I answered it,"

Angelo said, "an hour later here in Michigan."

"So around 2:30 this morning he was planning to drive to Chicago to ask you for money in person."

Angelo nodded.

"And when was payment to the March Madness pool winners due?" Tommy asked, looking toward Joe and Nikki.

"At nine this morning," Nikki said.

Tommy began to think out loud. "So the five grand in the pool was gone, and Leo had about six and a half hours to get to Chicago and get his father to wire that amount to Craig Davies for payment to the pool winners."

Angelo nodded.

"And the drive itself is at least five hours," Tommy said, "probably longer with the way traffic gets around Chicago in the morning. So he doesn't have much time. But with the way these kids are always texting and calling each other, I'll bet he takes a minute to share the development with his partner, Craig, before leaving."

Angelo nodded. Tommy continued. "Joe, what time did you say it was when he assaulted Leo and woke you up?"

"I didn't say what time it was, Mr. MacPherson. And by *he*, I assume you mean that crazed Neanderthal I saw last night for the first time in my life."

Tommy ignored the answer and continued to advance the theory. "So, shortly after Leo's call to his dad, Craig probably learns that there's not going to be a money wire, at least not anytime soon."

"And Craig has no way to come up with the money himself," Nikki interjected, "not the way that dumb ass burns through his student loans."

"Nikki," Joe said, "you're not buying into some lame theory that—"

"What about family?" Tommy asked. "Does Craig have anyone who can front him five grand?"

"You've been to his folks' place in the UP, Joe," Nikki said. "Could they have helped him out?"

Joe sighed. "They're simple people, working-class Yoopers. But I'm telling you, there's no way that—"

"Craig has to see Leo in person at that point," Tommy continued, "to talk face-to-face about the shit that'll be coming down—not on Leo, but on him—within just a few hours if he doesn't have the money for the winners of the March Madness pool that everyone thinks he's running."

Tommy began scrolling through the digital pictures that Harlan had taken earlier at the cottage. He stopped at the picture of the fresh tire tracks and big footprints in the dirt driveway. "And when he gets to the cottage, he's not just worried about money. Craig's whole career as a lawyer, which he's spent three years busting his ass for, is at stake. No law school in the country would ever graduate an outright thief, not with the all ethical restraints they put on their students."

Tommy then stopped at the picture of the front door to the cottage. "But Leo thinks he can talk to him and lets him into the cottage, which is why there was no sign of forced entry."

Angelo nodded.

Tommy moved on to the picture of the luggage on the end of Leo's bed and stopped again. "Leo tries to convince Craig that things will be okay after Leo gets to Chicago and sees his dad in person. But Craig knows all about the major fallout between Leo and Angelo in the past over Leo's gambling. So Craig figures there's no way Angelo will give him the money."

Tommy scrolled through some more pictures of Leo's bedroom and continued. "Leo eventually retrieves the Rolex watch from the wall safe in the bedroom closet, something to appease Craig. But he's not happy with that, and the altercation begins there, in the bedroom."

"Which explains how Craig's cell phone ended up under Leo's bed," Nikki said, again to Joe's chagrin.

Tommy scrolled past the picture of the cell phone and on to the picture of Leo's Rolex watch lying on the floor of the loft. "Then the altercation moves to the loft, where Craig discards the watch."

Nikki nodded. "And that's when Craig totally loses it. He slams Leo into the wall and—"

Angelo's cell phone rang.

"Yeah," Angelo said. As he listened, his expression grew angry. "What the hell did you do, Vincent?" he shouted into the phone.

"Here," Angelo said, extending the phone to Tommy. "You take this. I can't deal with this kind of shit right now."

"What is it?" Tommy asked.

"It's Vincent, dammit. He got his ass thrown in jail!"

73

Tommy sighed as he held the phone to his ear and listened to Vincent explain his situation. "I don't know how they caught on to me so fast, Tommy. I couldn't have been inside Craig Davies' apartment for a minute when the cops came down on me."

"How'd you get in?" Tommy asked.

"Well, I kind of busted the door down."

"Shit, Vincent, don't you realize that the cops are following the same leads we are?"

"Oh, yeah."

"What's been happening at the station?"

"They've been totally bustin' my chops, man, like they think I know something about what happened to Leo and Joe. But I've been cool, Tommy, not telling them anything, except that I know my rights and... and... Tommy? Are you still there?"

"For crying out loud, Vincent, stop making things worse for yourself and just cooperate with them. Tell them that you just flew in from Chicago to look for your missing brother, and you don't know what's going on with these boys."

"Got it, Tommy, cooperate, but don't let on."

Tommy rolled his eyes and shook his head as he ended the conversation. "I'll catch a cab over there right now," he said to Angelo.

Harlan re-entered Joe's room shortly after Tommy left. Phoenix apparently had asked Joe some questions about events that Joe had earlier said he couldn't recall.

"I'm telling you, Mr. Wade, I just don't remember. Getting out of the truck, reaching the surface, washing up at Stony Point—I have no memory of any of it. My next memory was waking up here at the hospital, looking at all of you."

Phoenix nodded. "It's the trauma," he said. "You're blocking it out. My guess is that your assailant opened the driver's side window or door to reach in and steer the truck while pushing it into the bay, and that gave you a way out once you got into the cab."

But where along the coast did he push it in? Harlan thought, recalling the solid wall of trees blocking access to the bay.

Angelo stood alone, his back to everyone, looking out a window.

"I have some news from the officers outside the room," Harlan said.

Angelo spun around to face Harlan, looking like he expected to hear the best, or worst, news of his life.

"It's nothing like that, Angelo, nothing about Leo's whereabouts. It's about an incident at the law school's library. The cops outside the room say that there was a fight in the library stacks, around 2:30 in the morning. It may have nothing to do with this assault on Joe, but the police are considering the possibility of a connection, so I thought you should be aware."

"How'd you get those cops to tell you something like that?" Phoenix asked.

Harlan shrugged. "I'd tell you, Phoenix, but I'd rather stay a couple steps ahead of you."

Angelo shook his head and turned his attention back to the window.

"And there's one other item of news," Harlan said, "which you'll also want to know about."

Angelo turned back.

"Detective Summers has called for a water search and rescue off Omena Point, near your cottage."

C17

1:12 p.m., Tuesday, April 5.

The Escalade passed through Peshawbestown, northbound on M-22.

"I really think we should continue on to Omena Point," Harlan said, "to see what police search and rescue might find."

Ignoring the suggestion, Angelo instructed Phoenix to turn right onto the dirt drive leading into Pontiac Park. Midday became twilight as Phoenix completed the turn into the cave-like entrance created by the tall evergreens surrounding the park. He stopped the car alongside a picnic table. Nobody else was there.

Once on foot, Harlan led the way to the beach. Phoenix followed as they hiked down a narrow footpath that cut through the bayside wall of evergreens, pushing through weeds and tree branches that blocked the path as they headed for the water.

"You see what I mean?" Harlan said. "There's simply no way to get a pickup truck down here."

Harlan stepped onto the beach, squinting at the bright afternoon sunlight after the darkness of the path. "Where's Angelo?" he asked as Phoenix joined him at the water's edge.

"I don't know. Maybe he stayed back for a cigarette."

They both studied the wall of evergreens extending north and south along a lengthy stretch of the coastline. Phoenix removed his shoes and socks to wade into the water for a better vantage point, but he quickly changed his mind.

"Damn, that water's freezing cold. It's amazing Joe survived in that."

"Sheer luck, I guess," Harlan said.

"Well, I guess I don't know the science of hypothermia either," Phoenix said. "But I suppose the swim buoy and the weeds tangled around his neck kept his head out of the water enough for him to retain some core body temperature."

As he watched Phoenix put his shoes and socks back on, Harlan wondered, *What the hell kind of chauffeur did Angelo—*

His cell phone rang.

"Harlan, it's me, Angelo. What's the phone number for that detective—what's her name—Summers?"

"Angelo? Where are you?"

"I'm looking right at you, for crying out loud. Now, what's that cop's number?"

Harlan peered into the trees, toward the center of the park.

"Behind you, dammit," Angelo said, "out in the water."

Harlan turned around and scanned the bay. About a hundred yards southeast, well into the bay, was Angelo. He seemed to be standing on the water's surface.

Angelo dropped his cell phone to his side and yelled, "Dammit, Harlan! What's that detective's phone number?"

Phoenix removed his sunglasses and rubbed his eyes. "That just can't be happening," he said, shaking his head.

As Angelo returned his phone to his ear, Harlan did the same. "I don't know her phone number offhand, but I can give you the dispatch number and they can transfer you."

Before Harlan gave him the number, however, he had to ask: "Angelo, how are you doing this... this thing, walking on the water that way?"

"What the hell are you talking about? I'm not walking on water. I'm standing on the wall of the GTB Marina."

Harlan struggled to make sense of what he was seeing. He had never heard of a GTB Marina. It certainly wasn't on any of the maps used by his GPS program. And he was having trouble making it out even as Angelo claimed to be standing on it. But as he stared out, Harlan eventually discerned the surface of a marina wall on which Angelo stood. He was at the very end of the wall, where it ramped up several feet out of the water.

"What are you doing out there, Angelo?"

"Never mind what I'm doing, Harlan. Just give me that cop's—"

"Well, how'd you get there?"

"Oh for Pete's sake—the two-track off the park's driveway. Now, are you going to give me the phone number, or do I have to swim over to Omena Point to tell that detective where she needs to send her search team?"

Harlan recited the number and then he and Phoenix hurried on foot up the park's driveway to find the two-track. They eventually emerged from the park onto the shoulder of M-22 and exchanged blank looks.

Backtracking slowly along the driveway, they carefully surveyed the bank of trees along its south shoulder. At a point where the tree branches were more sparse and elevated than anywhere else, they stopped and studied the ground.

And there it was—the remains of a two-track road barely visible beneath dead pine needles and encroaching weeds.

C18

1:36 p.m., Tuesday, April 5.

Phoenix had joined Angelo at the end of the marina wall while Harlan remained onshore in the marina's tiny harbor, which was tucked into an indentation in the coastline.

In the harbor was a small, lone vessel with a deeply rusted hull. It looked far from seaworthy. Harlan stood beside it, staring at his cell phone, reading about the GTB Marina online.

According to an obscure website, Harlan was standing on the bank of an old tribal marina located on reservation land that belonged to the Grand Traverse Band of the Ottawa and Chippewa Indians. But they hadn't used the marina in decades, and it didn't show up on any of the usual online mapping sources.

Harlan looked up from the phone and walked along the bank, stepping over dense, knee-high weeds. *No wonder we couldn't see this place from the park next door*, he thought. Wondering how Angelo knew of it, he recalled Leo once telling him that his dad had grown up in the area and spent a lot of time on these waters.

Harlan stopped at one of the marina's two walls that enclosed the harbor and stepped off the bank onto it. The wall was made of massive stones that extended about seventy yards into the bay, barely above the water's surface. His online source had said that over the years the massive stone walls had sunk into the floor of the bay, leaving their topsides barely above the water's surface after the typical spring melt-off.

He paced the wall's width, trying to determine whether it was wide enough for a pickup truck to roll along the top. It seemed so, but there'd be

79

little margin for error to the sides of the vehicle. Then he looked toward the other end of the wall, well into the bay where Angelo and Phoenix stood, and imagined what it looked like from their vantage point—the edge of an underwater cliff.

As Harlan stood on the wall thinking the worst, his cell phone rang. It was Detective Riley Summers.

"Harlan, I'm at Pontiac Park. Where's the two-track road to this hidden marina that your client's talking about?"

Harlan directed her as best he could and soon afterward Riley's car pulled into the marina's boat-launch area, scraping through low-hanging evergreen branches.

She slammed the door after getting out and headed toward him on foot, tromping through the weeds. Harlan braced himself. He'd been a step ahead of her all day—to the cottage, Nikki Ybarra, Joe Rylands, and now this marina—and obviously she was livid about it.

"Hi, Riley. Where's Frank?" Harlan said, trying to deflect her.

"None of your damn business, Harlan. Just tell me why Angelo Surocco is so certain that we need to search this area."

They both glanced at Angelo. He was yelling at Riley and pointing at a specific spot in the water.

Harlan told Riley about the GPS device he had planted on Leo's truck and how it went dead at 4:47 that morning in the vicinity of the neighboring park.

Riley immediately contacted her search team and directed them to the new location.

"So, Harlan Holmes, what else are you keeping from me?"

"Look, Riley, I can't think of anything else that you wouldn't already know by now."

"Why don't you start by telling me who your client is."

Harlan glanced at the distant end of the marina's south wall. "Well, you know, the guy out there in the water yelling at you, Angelo Surocco."

"No shit, Harlan. And what does he do when he's not in Traverse City searching for his missing son?"

Harlan briefly described Angelo's Chicago-based import-export business, of course skipping over any mention of his likely connections with trafficking contraband in the Great Lakes region.

"Oh, I see, Harlan. You'd have me believe that he's just an ordinary businessman from Chicago. Do you remember who trained me for this job?"

Harlan smiled. "My goodness, Riley, I think you just complimented me."

"And I think you better start talking."

"I'm telling you, Riley, as far as I know, he's just a regular guy. And right now, with his son missing, he and the rest of the Surocco family are worried sick."

"Is that what they're called, Harlan—the Surocco *family*?"

"Okay, maybe that was a poor choice of words. But merely being a Chicago businessman of Italian ancestry doesn't make him a mobster."

"So who's the muscle-bound African American guy at the businessman's side right now—just another worried member of the Surocco family?"

"His name is Phoenix Wade. I'm not sure what to make of him. He's kind of the understated, cerebral type. About all I've seen him do is drive Angelo around."

"Oh, I see. Angelo brought along an especially sensitive chauffeur—who just happens to look like Evander Holyfield."

"Gee, Riley, you seem to have an issue with the guy just because he's black and buffed, kind of like the issue you have with businessmen of Italian ancestry. It sounds to me like you're one of those cops who's into racial profiling."

"What I suspect that chauffeur is has nothing to do with his race," Riley said, glaring at Harlan.

"Well, what do you suspect he is?"

"A soldier of sufficient rank to be at Angelo Surocco's side right now and at the hospital for an interrogation of Joe Rylands—after you diverted me to that so-called cottage at Omena Point."

"Look, Riley, I wasn't trying to... uh—"

"What, Harlan, obstruct my investigation, like you did at the hospital when you weaseled your way into Joe Rylands' room and then lied to Officers Katko and Briney about his physical condition while probing them for information about the case?"

"Oh... you heard about that."

"Shit, Harlan, I've been hearing about you all day, like how you removed evidence from that cottage before sending me there. Tell me, right now, what are you hiding?"

"What are you talking about?" Harlan asked.

"The fingerprints you left on the handles of those wall safes, and the broken spider web on the one in the master bedroom. You went into those safes and removed some things before you sent me there, didn't you?"

"You're fishing, Riley. You know that's not enough to make a case of tampering with evidence."

"But you know I'm right, don't you?"

"Off the record?" Harlan asked.

Riley nodded.

"Okay," Harlan said, sighing. "I got some things out of the safes that Mr. Surocco regards as private."

"So you removed evidence from a likely crime scene."

"Yes, I did."

"What was it?"

"I'm sorry, Riley, but I owe a duty of confidentiality to my client on this one."

"Dammit, Harlan, you tampered with evidence. Now tell me what it was."

"I can't do that, Riley. In the state of Michigan, confidential matters that a PI learns about his client in the course of employment are privileged. If you don't believe me, just Google Michigan's PI licensure statute."

"Are you serious, Harlan? Do you actually think you can hide behind an obscure provision of state law that some corporate elites got on the books to cover the antics of their sleazy private eyes?"

"I'm just saying—"

"Okay," she said, "maybe you don't have to tell me *what* you learned was in those safes, but I expect you to tell me *where* it is now because your PI code of conduct cannot possibly privilege you to hide tangible evidence. So *where* is it?"

Harlan thought about the current location of the briefcase, in the back compartment of the Escalade, which was parked only about a hundred yards from where he and Riley were standing at the moment.

"Look, Riley, I didn't conceal any evidence relevant to your investigation. And I'd appreciate it if you'd simply trust me on that point and let this thing go. You're off target on this. Mr. Surocco, more than anyone, wants you to figure out what happened to Leo. Please, Riley, I'd like a little professional courtesy on this one."

"Professional courtesy!" Riley shouted. She then burst out laughing. "You are one serious piece of work, Harlan Holmes. I thought that maybe you had strayed just a little ways off the reservation. But now I come to find out that you're living in an entirely alternative reality, complete with people who actually think they can trust you."

C19

2:50 p.m., Tuesday, April 5.

"Please Detective Summers, tell them to search the area just beyond the end of the marina's walls," Angelo said as soon as he joined Riley and Harlan onshore. The man had been on the wall for an hour and a half, with the water splashing at his feet and lower legs all the while. His pants were soaked.

The search team had moved to the vicinity of the GTB Marina but had begun their work about a quarter mile south, in a small inlet known as Suttons Bay. Harlan looked in that direction. The team was working its way along the mouth of the inlet toward a buoy that marked a point about halfway between the GTB Marina and Stony Point, where Joe Rylands had washed ashore that morning. The buoy also marked the forty-fifth parallel north. Harlan briefly imagined Joe's ordeal as he crossed it.

"I think he's right," Harlan said, turning back to Riley.

"Why?"

"Because those marina walls look wide enough to support Leo's pickup truck, and I don't see any other point of vehicle access to this bay along this stretch of shoreline. Do you?"

Riley nodded her head, stepped away, and made a call on her cell phone.

Twenty minutes after the search team arrived at the spot, a tow truck pulled an Avalanche pickup out of the bay. There was no stopping Angelo from venturing back onto the south marina wall as the pickup truck emerged alongside it. Harlan accompanied him.

Angelo's face was expressionless as the driver's door flopped open, revealing Leo's upper body. It was sticking into the cab. His lower body was still in the truck's bed, the top of which was sealed with a locked lid.

In between the cab and the bed of the truck, with Leo draped over it, was a fold-down seat that allowed interior access between the two compartments. It was the moving wall that Joe had described back at the hospital. Leo had failed to get all the way through it.

Harlan crouched down beside the vehicle to get a better look inside. Some of the swimming and fishing gear from the bed had spilled into the cab. Also in the cab, on the floor, was a large boulder. It must have been knocked loose from the wall when the truck plunged into the bay and then drawn in through the open door as water gushed in.

The police removed the lid that covered the truck's bed shortly after the truck was onshore. Harlan and Angelo, ignoring an officer's command to step back, got a good look inside the bed of the truck. Some of the swimming and fishing gear had impeded Leo's escape. His left foot was tangled in fishing line and, ironically, the straps of a life jacket that hung up on a tie-down clamp mounted inside the rail of the truck bed.

"I said get back," the cop repeated.

Angelo turned and began walking toward the two-track leading back to the park next door. Along the way, he let Phoenix join him. The moment Harlan caught up, however, Angelo shouted, "Leave me the hell alone!"

Harlan picked the worst way to do that. He returned to the scene and managed to get another look inside the truck.

The same cop who twice had warned Harlan off approached him and said, "How many times do I have to tell you to—"

The command suddenly became unnecessary. Harlan had investigated many crime scenes back in the day, but at that moment this one hit him like no other. Someone had rolled Leo over and revealed his water-bloated face.

Harlan physically cringed at the sight, so severely that he stumbled backward and nearly fell. The trigger was not a wave of shock or grief, however. That would come later. At the moment, it was shame. He was having the primal reaction of one struck with a sense that he was a deeply flawed person, undeserving of being counted among men. It came with an irrational train of thought that he couldn't stuff down. If only he had been a good PI, or a good state trooper who never had to become a PI in the first place, this would have never happened.

The train of thought ended with the image of Leo's lifeless body lying on its back. Harlan's stomach turned. He was bent over at the waist, suppressing the urge to throw up, when Riley approached—the last person in the world from whom he'd want condolence.

"Are you okay, Harlan?" she asked.

He straightened up, swallowed hard, and shrugged, uncertain of what strange sound might come out if he tried to speak through his constricted throat.

"It's not your fault. You know that, right?"

Of course it's my fault, he thought, turning away. *It happened right under my nose on a computer in my house.*

There was a long pause before she stepped around him to make eye contact. "Look, Harlan, I know this is a terrible time to ask, but I really need to have access to that GPS program of yours as soon as possible."

Rather than turn away again, he looked straight into her eyes. She was the same cop he had mentored just a couple years ago, a rising star in those days, and someone he had come to respect.

"I'll be going home soon," he said, finding his voice. "Just send over your CSI people and I'll let them download everything I have."

"I'll make sure they have a proper warrant."

"Don't bother, Riley. There's nothing on that program you can't have."

"That's very thoughtful, Harlan," she said. She offered an awkward smile.

Harlan saw something in her expression, something more than discomfort. Over the past two years he'd seen the same thing during encounters with other cops whom he used to work with on the force. He construed it as an expression of guilt they felt for having survived the departmental downsizing that cost him his job.

"What about you, Riley. Are you doing okay?"

She shrugged.

C20

9:27 a.m., Wednesday, April 6.

Joe's only expected visitor, Nikki, had left half an hour ago and didn't plan to return until lunchtime, so he figured the knock on the door probably meant something unpleasant, like a nurse coming to ease his pain with the poke of another needle. They never waited for him to say "come in."

"Hi, Joe, how you feeling?"

"Mr. Wade?"

"Please, Joe, call me Phoenix."

"Okay, what brings you—"

"May I?" Phoenix asked, nodding at a chair beside Joe's bed.

Phoenix dropped into the chair before Joe could answer, scooted close, and said, "I came here to talk with you about Craig Davies. I'm sure you've thought about places where he might go into hiding. What can you tell me?"

"Why are *you* asking? Why not Mr. MacPherson or Mr. Holmes?"

"You're not answering my question, Joe, and that makes me wonder about your loyalties."

"Loyalties? What are you talking about?"

"I hear you've accepted a job with Surocco Imports."

Joe nodded.

"Well, welcome to the company. The boss wants you to work with *me* on this one. So let's get started."

"I'd like to know who I'm working with, first," Joe said.

Phoenix shrugged. "Fair enough," he said, and he went on to explain the work he did as in-house investigator for Surocco Imports. The way he described it, the job seemed fairly innocuous.

"I mostly look for problems that prospective clients may create for the company, clients who want to contract with us for the transport of goods. And sometimes I investigate internal matters, like company employees suspected of stealing or mishandling inventory."

The explanation jogged Joe's memory. "So you're the guy who Leo worked with on that thing he did for the company... that... that—"

"Data mining," Phoenix said.

"Yeah, that's what Leo called it. He tried to explain it to me a couple times, but I never understood the lingo, all that stuff about algorithms, analytics, and—"

"Leo mostly did something called subject-based data mining," Phoenix said. "He was like a wizard at searching huge databases and finding nonobvious relationships between people. I might give Leo the name of a prospective client or employee, and he'd find all kinds of people from the guy's past, maybe someone he roomed with in college, or someone he sold a house to or used as a job reference. And if a search turned up a suspicious relationship—maybe a fed or someone on a watch list—he'd pass it along to me."

"Did you guys work pretty closely?" Joe asked.

Phoenix nodded. "It's a hell of a thing, what happened to him. Now, you gonna answer my question? Where do you think—"

"Can I just ask you a couple more of my own, Phoenix? Like how you got started at Surocco Imports?"

Phoenix sighed. "Same as you. I got steered to the company by one of the Surocco kids."

"Vincent?"

"Yeah, he and I became good friends in college. We were on the school's wrestling team and used to room together on the road."

"Oh yeah," Joe said, "I remember Leo saying something about Vincent being a wrestler in college. I can only imagine what his scrawny body must have looked like in one of those skimpy wrestling singlets."

"He may have been scrawny," Phoenix said, "but he was a beast in his weight class. Now, are you gonna answer—"

"What about you, Phoenix, were you a good wrestler?"

"Well, yeah, I was an All-American. My athletic scholarship was the only reason I could afford to go to college at all."

"Wait a minute," Joe said. "Leo once told me about a guy at Surocco

Imports who almost made the US Olympic team. Was that you?"

Phoenix nodded. "I came up just short of making it as an alternate."

"You're not much older than me, Phoenix. How come you're not still pursuing it?"

"Because it doesn't pay the bills."

"And what they pay you at Surocco Imports is pretty good?"

"It's real good."

Joe's interrogation stopped. He paused for a moment and then nodded his head. "Okay," he said, "I'll work with you, but you have to work with me."

"What do you mean?"

"I'm positive that the assailant was *not* Craig."

"Look, Joe, even if that's true, we—"

"But I totally get where the elders, and now you, are coming from. You guys see a mountain of circumstantial evidence, not to mention College Boy's volatile temper. I take it you know how he earned that nickname."

"Yeah."

"Did you know he went into hiding for a week after that bar fight because he was worried about getting arrested?"

"No."

"Well, he did. And he once told me where he hid."

Joe paused for a moment to let the point sink in.

"And you think he might have gone back there this time?" Phoenix said. Joe nodded.

"But wouldn't that be a stupid move on his part?"

"Obviously, you've never met College Boy."

"Okay, so where'd he go that time?"

"You'll find out when we get there."

"What do you mean," Phoenix said, "when *we* get there?"

"What's the matter, Phoenix? I thought we were working together on this."

"Yeah, but... but you're in no condition to do this. I mean, just look at you, all busted up and suffering in that bed. You can't—"

"Oh yes I can," Joe said. He eased himself out of bed and started making his way across the room to a suitcase that Nikki had dropped off earlier.

"But what about the doctors and nurses around here," Phoenix said, "and that cop outside your room who made me sign some approved visitor list? At the very least, she's gonna follow you."

"I'll deal with her."

"And just how are you gonna do that?"

"What are you driving, Phoenix? And where will it be in thirty minutes or so?"

"Why do you ask?"

"Because thirty minutes after you leave, that's where we're meeting."

"You mean we're not leaving together?"

"Nope."

"Well then, how can I be sure that you'll actually—"

"What's the matter, Phoenix? Do you still doubt my loyalty?"

C21

10:58 a.m., Wednesday, April 6.

Angelo was sitting alone in a coffee shop's outside seating area, waiting for his crew, when Harlan showed up.

"It's kind of cold out here," Harlan said. "Why don't we go inside?"

Angelo ignored the question and lit a cigarette. "What do you have," he asked.

Harlan sat down at the table. He was struck by the man's stoic manner the day after discovering his son's dead body. "Not much on Craig Davies," Harlan said. "Right now, the police consider him a person of interest, but they can't find him either."

"They've tried Joe Rylands and the school?"

"Yeah."

"And family?"

"Nobody's heard from him," Harlan said.

Angelo nodded at a newspaper sitting on the table between them. "Why isn't there anything about this in the news?" he asked.

"The police want it under the radar to keep the assailant off guard."

"If that's the case, who on the force is giving you inside information?" Angelo asked, looking directly into Harlan's eyes.

Harlan stared back and said, "The same cop who says DNA analysis on the blood at the cottage and law school library should be done soon, if it's not already."

"And you'll get that?"

"I think so."

Harlan looked away and sighed before sharing a final bit of information.

"What is it?" Angelo asked.

"Probably nothing, at least nothing relevant to... to Leo's..."

"Just tell me, Harlan, what else do you have?"

The son of a bitch will probably blame me for this, too, Harlan thought. "Well, it looks like Leo was cheating on his law school exams."

"What!" Angelo exclaimed.

"I found copies of a bunch of law school exams that he had stashed away."

"Where?"

Harlan removed a USB flash drive from his pocket and held it in front of Angelo. "It's one of the things I removed from the cottage yesterday," Harlan said.

Angelo glanced at the device. "Why'd you do that?" he asked.

"Because yesterday morning you told me to get stuff like this out of the cottage."

"Is that the flash drive Leo used for all those passwords you got hold of?"

"Yeah, and one of them leads to his remote access desktop with your company and all that data mining stuff he was doing for you. I didn't think you'd want me to leave that in the cottage."

Angelo nodded. "So what's the exam issue you're talking about?"

"Well, it turns out Leo wasn't just mining data on your clients and employees. He was also mining data at GTU Law. Last night I went into the flash drive and found a password on it that I'd never seen before. It got me into a cloud-based account where he backed up a bunch of files downloaded from secure sites at the school."

"Are you saying that he hacked into the school's system?"

"Big time, Angelo. He had a shitload of GTU files in that cloud. I was about a third of the way through them last night when I came across this."

Harlan removed a piece of paper from his pocket, unfolded it, and set it in front of Angelo. It was a printout of an index to some files with a footer bearing the path and filename "Documents/GTU/Exams." Listed on the page were links to nine documents.

"The links take you to final exams given at GTU Law," Harlan said.

"Well, maybe the school lets students have copies of exams after they take them," Angelo said defensively.

"I'm afraid they don't. I checked the school's website. It has a database with old exams that have been released to students for use as study aids, and I couldn't find any of these exams there."

"Maybe you didn't look hard enough."

"Trust me, Angelo, I searched the whole damn thing. And then this morning I called the school and got ahold of the librarian who manages the old exam bank. I told her that I was a law student and asked her about a couple of these exams specifically. She said they weren't released. She says that most professors stopped releasing their exams years ago because they don't like creating new ones all the time."

"Besides," Harlan added, "the last exam on the list hasn't even been given yet. It's scheduled for next Monday for a class Leo finished just last week."

Harlan watched Angelo's eyes scan down the page. The exams were listed chronologically, dating back to Leo's first semester, nearly three years ago. Angelo then looked up. His stare was penetrating.

"Why the hell didn't you discover this problem sooner?"

Harlan felt defenseless. *That kid really was ahead of me—way ahead of me—the whole time.*

"Do the cops know about this?" Angelo asked

"I don't see how they could."

Angelo's angry look mellowed as he took a long drag from his cigarette. It was like watching the man trying to anesthetize himself from the angst his son continued to cause even after death.

"By the way, Angelo, I'm out of pocket quite a bit to the cop I mentioned before, the one who's been so helpful."

Angelo withdrew an envelope from a pocket inside his jacket and handed it to Harlan. Inside was some cash that Harlan would count later. It would barely cover his expenses.

Harlan was on his third cup of coffee, and Angelo his last cigarette, by the time Tommy joined them at the coffee shop. "It's about time," Angelo said. "What took you so long?"

Tommy was returning from a visit with Dean Fletcher at the law school. He and the dean had been classmates at the school several decades ago. They barely knew each other back in those days, but he'd hoped that the alumni connection might open the dean up to sharing information that could lead to Craig Davies.

Tommy shook his head. "I had to walk here from the law school. Phoenix never picked me up, and he didn't return my call. Where is he?"

"Well gee, Tommy," Harlan said, "the school's only a half mile away. Certainly you didn't spend all that time walking."

"You guys have no idea what I've been through this morning," Tommy said as he sat down at the table. "That Dean Fletcher's a stick in the mud, man. First she insists on giving me a tour of our old stomping grounds, showing me every single thing about the place that's changed over the years. And when we finally get to her office, she insists on brewing fresh coffee on this old-fashioned percolator of hers. The damn thing took forever."

"Well, you didn't just sit there while she made coffee," Angelo said. "What'd you get on this Craig Davies kid?"

"Nothing."

Harlan couldn't prevent himself from laughing. Angelo scowled at him and then at Tommy. "You were gone for damn near two hours," he said. "What the hell did you talk about?"

"I swear," Tommy answered, "that brainiac schoolmarm droned on about every waking moment of our law school careers—about shit I don't even vaguely remember."

"Did you question her at all about Craig Davies?" Harlan asked.

"Sure I did. But every time, she found a way to avoid the question and continue rambling on about our good ole law school days. I'm telling you guys, I was in hell over there."

"And I suppose I should be grateful for your sacrifice," Angelo said. He took out his frustration on the empty cigarette pack, which he crushed tightly into his fist. "I need some smokes, dammit. Let's get out of here."

"In what car?" Tommy asked. "Where's Phoenix?"

"Beats the hell out of me," Angelo said. "I'm only the guy's boss."

"I'm right here," Phoenix said, emerging from around a corner of the coffee shop.

"What are you doing sneaking around like that?" Angelo said, glancing up and down the street in front of the shop. "Where's the Escalade?"

"In the alley around back," Phoenix answered, "parked behind a dumpster."

"So you *are* sneaking around," Harlan said.

"Just playing it safe after the cop at the hospital saw me coming and going from Joe's room."

Phoenix then led them to the alley and explained a new lead on the possible whereabouts of Craig Davies.

They suffered through the stench of a dumpster as they approached the Escalade, listening to Phoenix.

"So, based on Craig's prior run from the police," Phoenix said, "Joe thinks he may know where he went into hiding this time. But there's a little catch to Joe's willingness to help. You see—"

One of the Escalade's tinted back windows rolled down, interrupting Phoenix and bringing them all to a halt.

"Hi, Mr. Surocco," Joe said through the open window. "Are you coming with us?"

Phoenix then quickly summed up the terms of Joe's offer to help find Craig. "He won't tell me where we're going until we get there—with him."

"How about you, Mr. MacPherson?" Joe asked. "And you, too, Mr. Holmes, you guys are coming too, right? I want all of you guys to come along."

"What the hell kind of circus is this?" Angelo said. "Why don't we just swing by the law school and ask Dean Fletcher if she'd like to join us too? Then we could all share in some of the old biddy's riveting conversation."

"Be careful," Phoenix said. "Don't give the kid anymore ideas."

C22

12:30 p.m., Wednesday, April 6.

The group had traveled about sixty miles east out of Traverse City and then north a few miles on Old U.S. 27. After they passed through a small town named Frederic, a sign indicated that the next town, Waters, was three miles ahead.

"Slow down," Joe said. "The place comes up just before Waters."

Harlan glanced out the window and recalled this stretch of road from his childhood, back when his family traveled it on the way to their hunting cabin near Wolverine, Michigan.

Back then, Old U.S. 27 was a major artery for Michigan travelers. But over subsequent decades the old two-lane blacktop had come to more closely resemble one of Mad Max's post-apocalyptic highways on the Australian outback due to the siphoning effect of the modern interstate highway, I-75, which ran parallel to it. *Not a bad idea for a place to hide out*, Harlan thought.

"Right there," Joe said. "You just passed it."

"Passed what?" Phoenix said.

"That sign back there. I think it says the name of the place. Turn around and go back."

Phoenix returned slowly to a tiny white sign inscribed with the words, "Mort's Dock & Cabins." Beyond the sign, tucked into a patch of woods alongside a lake, was a row of seven small cabins. One had a manager's sign on the door. A lone vehicle was parked beside it.

Phoenix drove past a dirt drive leading to the manager's cabin, opting instead to maneuver over the highway's shoulder and through a shallow ditch, toward the last cabin. He stopped alongside its south wall, where the Escalade couldn't be seen from the other cabins to the north.

After instructing the others to stay in the vehicle, Phoenix got out and disappeared into the woods. A few minutes later he returned.

"There's a white Grand Am parked behind an interior cabin," he said, "third one south of the manager's."

"That's what Craig drives, right?" Harlan asked Joe.

"Yeah," he answered.

Phoenix disappeared into the woods again while the others exited the Escalade and headed for the cabin. Harlan stopped before reaching the front door and positioned himself to see both its front side and the woods beyond its south wall.

When Angelo got to the front door, he gave it a close-fisted pound with one hand while trying to turn the doorknob with the other. "Open the damn door," he said, pounding faster and harder.

"Hold on, Angelo," Harlan said, stopping the man midswing. "Phoenix has him."

"Take it easy, College Boy," Phoenix said as he led Craig along the south wall while keeping him secured in a wrestling hold.

"Where'd you catch him?" Harlan asked.

"Just out back. He climbed out a window and made a run for the woods."

Harlan marveled at Craig's twisted configuration and the ease with which Phoenix seemed to maintain it. *That can't feel good*, he thought. Both of Craig's arms were pinned behind his back, his big frame was bent ninety degrees forward at the waist, and his feet shuffled through the dirt and weeds as Phoenix ushered him along.

"Craig, everything's okay," Tommy said. "We just want to talk."

"Who are you?" Craig asked from his stooped-over vantage point.

"He's Mr. Surocco's lawyer," Joe said, stepping in front of Tommy. "He's here with Mr. Surocco and a couple other guys."

"Joe? Is that you?" Craig asked.

"Yeah, Craig, and everything's okay here. It's like Mr. MacPherson says. These guys just want to talk with you—right, Phoenix?"

"Of course," Phoenix said. "We just want to have a little chat. Are you okay with that, College Boy?"

"Yeah, man, sure."

"When I let you go, you're not going to make me chase after you into the woods again, right?"

"I'll be cool, man. Please, just let me go."

After obtaining his release, Craig straightened up and rolled his head and shoulders to realign himself.

"Open the door," Angelo said.

Craig reached into a pocket, but his hand came out empty. "Oh shit, I left the key inside."

"Harlan," Angelo said, "go make yourself useful."

"Hi, Mr. Holmes," Craig said. Harlan nodded and then headed around the side of the cabin to look for a back window. He found the one that Craig had left open.

"What am I doing here?" Harlan muttered to himself as he flopped head first toward a toilet. His legs, knees, and feet scraped over the window sill before he tumbled to the floor. Using the toilet bowl's edge for support, Harlan pulled himself to an upright position on his sore knees. The effort placed his face directly over the open bowl, where he resisted the urge to take a deep breath.

Harlan hobbled from the bathroom through the only other room in the cabin, which combined sleeping, living, and eating quarters all in one. "Where's Tommy?" he asked after letting the others in.

"Off seeing the manager," Phoenix said. "Do me a favor and keep a lookout at the front window while I talk to Craig, okay?"

While you talk to Craig? Harlan thought. He was about to object, but a look from Angelo confirmed that the chauffer was his choice as lead interrogator.

Phoenix directed Craig to the cabin's tiny kitchen area, where Craig eased himself into the seat of a spindly legged wooden chair beside a small table. Joe seated himself in the only other chair at the table.

Angelo opted to remain standing, propped against one of the cabin's discolored walls. He also opted to remain silent, smoking, as the interrogation proceeded.

"Alright, College Boy," Phoenix said, "how about you save us all a lot of aggravation and just tell us what happened to Leo?"

"Well, I... I don't know. I haven't seen him for a while. Is he okay?"

"He's fucking dead, College Boy! What did you—"

"That son of a bitch—Tank Lochner—I'll kill him myself!" Craig shouted as he exploded to his feet.

"Sit your big ass back down, College Boy!" Phoenix shouted back.

Craig did as he was told.

Phoenix waited for what seemed a long while. Craig's breathing eventually slowed. "Alright," Phoenix said, "let's both of us try to stay calm here, you and me, okay, Craig?"

"Okay."

"So just who is this guy, Tank Lochner?"

"He's the bagman for Leo's bookie," Craig said.

"And Leo was in trouble with this bookie?"

Craig nodded.

"For an unpaid gambling debt?"

Craig nodded again.

"Okay," Phoenix said, "let's start there, with everything you know about this gambling debt."

"Well," Craig said, "Leo placed the bet on the night before the State-Bucknell game, after I came to the townhouse for a visit..."

C23

5:10 p.m., Sunday, April 3.

The townhouse door opened and there stood Leo, shouting—"The dog is with us, College Boy!"

Craig was surprised by more than just the frenzied greeting. Leo had invited him there for a meeting with a few classmates to prepare for their final exam in bankruptcy law. But nobody from the study group was there. Preparing for their exam, it seemed, was not on Leo's agenda.

Leo's choice of words also confused him. "What do you mean?" Craig asked. "What *dog* is with us?" He swiveled his head to check out the surroundings, as if he thought that perhaps Leo had acquired a new puppy that might be somewhere in the townhouse.

Leo laughed. "Not that kind of dog, man. I'm talking about the *underdog*, the Bucknell Bison. They're with us, College Boy. And they're gonna make us rich—you and me, partner—five large lining our pockets after they spank Sparty's little ass and we cash out the March Madness pool."

"Yeah, partner! Go Bison!" Craig cheered.

Craig's excitement continued to rise as Leo broke down the key factors that had carried the Bison through five rounds of elite opponents and now had them standing at the threshold of a national championship, with only one more opponent to go, the Michigan State Spartans.

"Tomorrow night, partner, I'm gonna be there," Craig breathlessly said, "right there at Langdell's Draft House with all our classmates, watching the Bison take ole Sparty out to the woodshed, and watching our classmates cry in their beer as Craig 'College Boy' Davies walks off with all their money."

Leo smiled at his volatile friend and continued to build his excitement.

"So tell me, College Boy, what are you gonna do with your share of the cheddar?"

Craig shrugged. He couldn't remember what it felt like to have spare cash. His student loan money for the semester was long gone, and he was living on what little margin remained on the last of his credit cards. "I think I'll go out and have me a big steak dinner," he said.

"Well, I've got bigger plans," Leo said.

"What do you mean?"

"Follow me, Craig. There's something I want you to see."

Leo escorted Craig out to a balcony that overlooked a segment of the Boardman River, which ran behind Leo's midtown Cass Street townhouse. A laptop computer sat on a table on the balcony. "It's kind of cold," Craig complained. "What are we doing out here?"

Leo spun his head around quickly as he rebooted the computer. "Just playing it safe," he said. "For all I know, that damn PI, Harlan Holmes, has got some bug planted inside."

"Are you shittin' me? You think he'd do that?"

"Oh, yeah," Leo said. "I gave the place one of my usual sweeps before you came over, but I can never be sure."

After he rebooted the computer, Leo turned it toward Craig. It was logged onto the website of a top sportsbook in Las Vegas. "Check out the Vegas line on tomorrow's game," Leo said.

The line read: "MSU Spartans –7."

"You know what that means, right Craig?"

"Yeah, that Sparty's a seven-point favorite."

"Which, of course, means," Leo added, "if you get down on Bucknell with this mainstream sportsbook in Vegas, you'll win even if Bucknell loses, as long as they lose by less than seven points."

Craig nodded.

Leo raised his eyebrows and smiled. "But that's Vegas, College Boy. What do you suppose the local line is among bookies around here, in Michigan?"

Craig thought for a moment and shrugged. "I don't know. Wouldn't a smart bookie around here just follow what the Vegas experts suggest, the Spartans minus seven?"

"We're in Sparty's backyard, Craig, and you know what that means, right?"

"Does that somehow affect the line?" Craig asked.

"It sure does."

"Why?"

Leo stepped closer, leaned forward, and spoke in a hushed tone, as if he were letting Craig in on some kind of inside information. "Okay, partner, here's how it works. Most bookies actually aren't gamblers themselves. They just book bets between people who *do* gamble, and they make their money by charging the losing gamblers a commission—usually ten percent—what they call the bookie's juice or vig."

Trying to keep pace, Craig said, "So if I bet a hundred bucks on the Spartans and they don't cover the spread, I'd owe a hundred and ten."

Leo grinned. "That's right, partner. So the key to running a profitable book is to keep the bets equal on both teams. That way the bookie never has to cover any of the bets. But to do that here in Michigan, where a lot of folks want to bet on the home team Spartans, the bookie has to—"

"Oh, I get it," Craig said. "The bookie has to spot the Bison more points, something more than seven, to even out the action."

Leo smiled. "Right on, my man," he said. "The bookie's only alternative is to hold the line at seven, where the experts say it belongs, and lay off the excess home team action on another bookie, maybe one from out of state. But you can see why many local bookies don't want to do that, can't you?"

Craig thought about the question for a while. "Oh, I see," he eventually said. "Because they don't want to give up the juice."

"That's right, partner," Leo said, beaming. "So just a phone call away, at this very moment, some local bookie is spotting Bucknell more than seven points—I guarantee it. And you and I know that, in fact, the underdog Bison is going to give Sparty a real battle, maybe even take 'em straight up."

"Leo, you're not thinking—"

Leo's beam brightened as he nodded.

"Are you kidding?" Craig exclaimed. "After all the losses you piled up in the casinos last fall, your dad would have your ass on a platter."

Leo laughed. "That's not really what happened last fall, Craig. I didn't lose any money in the casinos. I was actually a little ahead in that department."

"What are you talking about, Leo? I thought you got hammered for thousands of dollars there."

Leo shook his head. "No, not there. Where I got hammered was on sports betting, which of course you can't do in Michigan casinos."

"You can't?" Craig said.

"Nope. For sports betting around here, you either have to go to an online gambling site or to an old-school bookie. And I found a local book who was real cool about carrying my markers, until I started losing big."

"How'd that happen?"

"Well, I was what you call a Chalk Player or Favorite Freddy, somebody who likes to play the favorites. I don't know how well you remember last fall's college football season, but it seemed like every week there were all kinds of upsets."

"I remember," Craig said. "It was an exciting season because you never knew who was gonna win any given game."

"Exciting," Leo said, "tell me about it. Week after week I got pummeled by those dogs, more and more when I started doubling down to try to get back to even."

"But if you were placing your bets with an old-school bookie, how did your losses show up at the casino?"

"Because of the way I used to pay down my markers after I ran out of money. I paid the bookie—actually his bagman—at one at one of the local casinos with casino chips that I bought with my credit cards. I told the bookie that I was laundering the payments for tax purposes, you know, to make them look like casino losses that offset taxable casino winnings. The bookie was cool with that because all his bagman had to do with the chips was walk over to a cashier's counter to convert them to cash."

"His... uh... b-bag..."

"His bagman, College Boy, you know, the guy who collects for the bookie."

"And you can buy casino chips with a credit card?"

"Generally you can't," Leo said, "not beyond your cash advance limits. But I found a local casino that would go all the way to my credit limits, as long as they got a little kickback."

"Isn't that some kind of fraud?"

"Could be," Leo said with a shrug. "I'm sure the credit card companies don't wanna be paying cash rewards for that kind of thing."

"So that's why you had to call on your dad," Craig said, "and why he thinks that your losses happened at the casinos."

Leo nodded. "And now, partner," he said, his voice rising and the beam returning to his face, "you can see why this reformed Favorite Freddy, more than anyone, believes in the underdog, the Bucknell Bison. I want to get on the dog, and I want to get on him right now, for real, my man. I want vindication. And we've got just the dog—you and me, baby—to make that happen."

"But... but... Leo—"

"There's no buts about it, partner. I need a beard, and you're my man."

"You need a what?" Craig asked.

"A beard," Leo said, "a cover guy, a front man, a partner who knows the score. I can't make this play without you, College Boy, not with all the PI surveillance I'm under."

"I... I dunno, Leo, this might not be—"

"Our five-thousand-dollar March Madness payoff is chump change, College Boy. Let's make a real play, a real score, you and me. What do you say, man? Are you in the game?"

"Well, I... I—"

"You're in the game, right?" Leo shouted.

"I—"

"The dog is with us, right?" Leo shouted, as loudly as he could.

Craig erupted, "Yeah, Bison!" And then he let loose a primal yell that reverberated down the river to the outskirts of Traverse City. On its heels, Craig shouted again, "I'm in the game, partner! I'm in the game!"

As Harlan peeked through a part in the curtains to the front window, he saw Tommy approach the cabin's front door. Harlan stepped over to the door and opened it. "What'd you learn?" he whispered to Tommy as soon as the door closed behind him.

"Well, the guy said—"

Tommy stopped. His gaze drifted toward the interrogation and began tracking Phoenix, who was pacing the room like a big cat, growing restless.

"I'll tell you later," Tommy eventually said. He then stepped over to Angelo and leaned against the wall beside him. Angelo offered Tommy a cigarette. He took it and began adding to the ashes accumulating on the cabin's floor.

C24

5:32 p.m., Sunday, April 3.

"C'mon, man, I need your cell phone," Leo said for a second time.

Craig's exhilaration finally settled enough for him to reply. "Why?"

Leo looked around quickly, as if he thought someone might be watching the two of them on the townhouse balcony, now seated at the table. "I can't trust any of my phones, man."

"Do you actually think that PI's tapped 'em?"

"Well, I know he's tapped the landlines here and at the cottage. I don't think he's gotten to my cell, but I can't risk it."

"And you want to use my phone to..."

"To do the deal, partner."

Craig handed his cell phone to Leo, who then quickly dialed the number. Leo put the phone on speaker mode and set it on the table between them.

A voice answered: "Carl."

"Hey, Carl, it's me, Angel's Demon. What's happening, bud?"

"Demon!" Carl exclaimed. "Where the hell you been, kid? I thought maybe you finished school and blew this sorry town."

"Not yet, man. I still have a few things to do here, including a little hoops play."

"Go ahead, kid. What's your play?"

"No offense, Carl, but I think this one should be pitched directly to the man. Is Jimmy around?"

"I thought you said you had a *little* play."

Leo smiled at Craig and then at the phone.

"Well," Leo said, "maybe it's not that little."

Carl laughed. "Hold on. I think Jimmy's up front."

While they waited, Leo covered the phone and told Craig that he had placed a call to a wire room and was talking to one of a handful of writers, Carl, who took bets over the phones and did some basic tallying for the bookie, a guy named Jimmy.

"What's a wire room?" Craig asked, eager to learn all he could from his experienced friend.

Leo smiled. "Well, in this case, it's the back room of a bar in Williamsburg, a place called Jimmy's Pub. Its setup is old school, wired with landlines that Jimmy's writers use to process calls. I'm sure they're busy today, handling a lot of action on tomorrow's game."

"So Jimmy is the bookie?" Craig asked.

"Yeah."

"And this pub of his, Jimmy's Pub, that's the front?"

Leo nodded and smiled again.

"What's with this name you're using, Angel's Demon?"

"Oh, that's just an alias I use with Jimmy's writers, mostly for fun, in honor of my old man, Angelo, and his love of my gambling ways. I actually got the idea from something a shrink once told me about the psychology of my gambling problem."

"So this guy Jimmy, the bookie," Craig said, "what's he all about?"

"What's Jimmy 'the Leg' Dillon all about?" Leo said.

"Jimmy who?"

"Jimmy 'the Leg' Dillon," Leo repeated. "He lost a leg in Vietnam, so some people call him Jimmy 'the Leg' because he has only the one left. To tell you the truth, I've never felt comfortable calling him that. I usually just call him 'Jimmy' or 'the man.'"

"Hey, kid, what's going on?" a voice called out from the phone.

Leo put his hand up to wave off Craig's next question. "Jimmy! How you doing, man?"

"Alright, kid. Hey, where the hell you been lately? Are you a lawyer yet?"

"Not yet, but pretty soon."

"So why have you been MIA?"

Leo grinned the way he sometimes did when spinning a lie. "I had to take some time off to do some things for my old man, back in Chicago," he said. "Of course, I also used some of that time to shake down some Chicago books. But I'm back now, bankrolled, and ready to shake down your ass, dude."

Jimmy laughed. "I love you too, kid. What can I do for you?"

"You can get me down on some hoops, man. What's your line on tomorrow's game?"

Leo picked up a pen. On the table in front of him was a pad of paper, beside the laptop. He jotted down Jimmy's line after he said it: "Sparty minus twelve, kid." Craig beamed at the number, –12, as it poured from the tip of the pen. He glanced back at the –7 Vegas line, which still appeared on the computer screen. *Bucknell is going to take State straight-up*, Craig thought. *With State laying twelve, this thing's a lock.*

"And what's your limit on the dog?" Leo asked.

Craig was confused. He used another pen on the table to jot a note on the pad of paper: "Limit on the dog?"

"Shit, Leo, are you serious?" Jimmy asked. "Just what kind of gig did you have going in Chicago, anyway?"

"It was quite the gig, Jimmy. And yes, I'm serious—dead serious."

"Look kid, I'm getting a lot of action on this game, actually a hell of a lot more than I've ever taken on any game. The number's pretty big."

"Just let me hear it, Jimmy."

After Jimmy said the number, Leo wrote it down on the pad, followed by a note: "40K—the max bet before the line drops."

Craig could feel his heart racing.

"I want it all, Jimmy—on the dog."

There was a long pause on the other end of the line. Finally, Jimmy spoke up. "Look, kid, you've always been one of my favorite players, but I haven't seen you for a while. And now you're calling me—like you're back from the dead or something—with the biggest play I've ever seen you make."

"It's not that big, Jimmy, when you consider what you've booked for me in total over the past few years. Customer loyalty must mean something here, doesn't it?"

"Sure it does, and your marker's always been good. But this is pretty steep for a one-legged old man like me. How would you feel about doing something up front?"

"What do you need?"

"I hope this doesn't offend you or anything."

"Just tell me what you need, Jimmy, and let's do this."

"Alright, kid, I want to see the juice up front, just a token of good faith, a refundable token, of course, if you win. And then you're on."

Craig understood enough to know that Jimmy's request deviated from the usual practice of booking bets without payment of anything in advance. Leaning forward, he jotted another note on the pad of paper: "Why not just take your marker?"

Leo shrugged at Craig and jotted down another note: "4K down."

"Not a problem," Leo said, "and no offense taken. I'll get it to you, say, tomorrow morning at ten, in the usual way, at the Chancery Casino. It'll be like old times."

"Tank will be happy to see you," Jimmy said.

Tank? Craig thought. *He must be the bagman.*

"That reminds me," Leo said, "Tank will actually meet with a longtime partner of mine, a guy who goes by the name College Boy."

"Me?" Craig silently mouthed as he pointed at himself.

As soon as Leo nodded, Craig realized, *Oh, yeah, I'm the beard Leo needs to avoid Harlan Holmes.*

Jimmy was silent as Leo briefly described Craig's physical features, and he remained silent for a few moments after Leo was done. "Who's this new College Boy character?" Jimmy eventually asked. "This isn't some kind of fraternity stunt, is it, Leo?"

"Hell no. College Boy has been with me since you've known me. He's a player, man, my partner. Let me tell you something, Jimmy. I did well in Chicago, like I said. But College Boy is backing half of this play, like he's done many times with me in the past. He just wants to see who he's dealing with."

After a long pause, Jimmy said, "Your old man, back in Chicago, what were you doing for him these past few months?"

The lie kept spinning smoothly. "I'm joining his import-export business permanently in the near future, and he wanted me involved in closing some deals with new clients so they know who they're working with down the road."

There was no response from Jimmy.

"Look, Jimmy, if you're really worried about this, take a minute right now and Google my dad's business online—Surocco Imports, Incorporated. Go ahead, man, check it out. I'm not jerking you around here."

"I'm sure you're not, Leo," Jimmy finally said. "I'll tell you what, we can do this, but I want to deal with cash only, none of that casino chip nonsense."

"No problem," Leo said.

"And I want early settle up," Jimmy added.

Settle up? Craig wondered. *That must mean the time of payment.*

"An early settle up is actually our preference," Leo said, "in fact, the earlier the better. The game should end tomorrow night around eleven. How about a couple hours later, 1:00 a.m. sharp, again at the Chancery Casino?"

"Another old-time visit with Tank," Jimmy said, "except I suppose he should be expecting College Boy once again, rather than you, right?"

"Exactly, Jimmy. But just tell him for me that if he's so much as one minute late with my money, I'll personally hunt him down and kick his three-hundred-pound ass to tomorrow."

Jimmy could barely speak through his laughter. "Okay, kid, you just closed another deal. You're on, you and your partner."

Leo hung up the phone and sighed deeply. "We're on the dog, College Boy, you and me, for forty large. We're in the game now, for real."

Angelo tore the seal from a new pack of cigarettes and pinched two out, the second for Tommy, who was now matching him smoke for smoke. The smog they produced should have choked the men in these cramped quarters. But everyone in the room was fixated on Craig's story—so fixated that none noticed Harlan, over by the window, texting someone. A particular detail in the story had inspired Harlan to reach out to a former client, a man named Carl Trimarco.

C25

1:42 p.m., Wednesday, April 6.

"Okay, Craig," Phoenix said, "so you're the one who met with this bagman to make the four-thousand-dollar deposit, right?"

"Yeah. After the phone call with the bookie, Leo told me how the deal would go down. The next morning, I'd get the five thousand in cash that I had stashed at my apartment, in my sock drawer, and I'd put four of it in an envelope that I'd give Tank Lochner at the Chancery Casino."

"The five thousand stashed in your sock drawer—that would be the money you collected at school for the March Madness pool, right?"

Craig's head dropped. "Yes," he whispered. His anxiety was palpable. After three years of legal study and with less than two weeks to go, the embezzlement probably would cost him his law degree and license to practice. He had also betrayed over two hundred classmates, many of them friends, who trusted him with their money.

"How could you do that?" Joe interjected. He was still seated at the table with Craig. "That money was entrusted to you for—"

"Joe," Phoenix said, "let me ask the questions."

"So how did the transaction with Tank go?" Phoenix asked, turning back to Craig.

"It was simple, I guess, just like Leo said it would be. There's a small lounge in the casino, off the main floor, with a couch and a couple chairs and a fireplace, no slots or tables, and no casino employees. I went in there a little before ten in the morning and sat down on the couch, and I put the envelope of cash on a coffee table in front of me. Some old guy was in there too at the time, just sitting in a chair, drinking a beer. I shot the shit with him for a while, waiting for Tank... and... and then..."

"And then what?"

"Well, this enormous guy who practically had to turn sideways and duck to get through the doorway walked in. I knew instantly he was Tank Lochner. And he recognized me from Leo's description. So he came over and sat on the other end of the couch from me. We talked a little, mostly small talk, until the old guy left. Then he asked me a few questions, you know, to check me out, just like Leo said he would."

"What kind of questions did he have?" Phoenix asked.

"The kind that Leo said he'd have," Craig said, "like where I was getting the money to back half of a forty-thousand-dollar wager."

"And what'd you tell him?"

"Just what Leo told me to tell him: that I was a spoiled rich kid with a trust fund from my old man that vested a few years back, when I turned twenty-one. Tank seemed satisfied with that. Then I walked out of the lounge, leaving the envelope of cash on the table in front of him and... and... wait a minute... Oh, man, I don't' believe it."

"What'd you just remember?"

"I... I told that son of a bitch where he could find me if I missed the drop after the game!"

"You did what?" Phoenix asked.

"He asked me about law school, whether it's as hard as people say it is. I told him that whatever he'd been told, it's at least ten times worse. And then I told him where I spend practically all of my time during dead week, the week before exams, which is where he found me after I missed the drop."

"Where's that?"

"The library."

"Which floor?"

"The fourth floor, deep in the stacks."

"That's it!" Joe exclaimed. "That totally explains—"

"Joe! Shut the hell up!" Phoenix shouted. "You're only here because we have such a nice fucking working relationship—remember?"

Up to this point, Phoenix actually had been fairly nice, even with Craig, considering the circumstances. At this moment, however, something about him changed.

"How long have you been here in this cabin, all by yourself, College Boy?"

"I... I guess since yesterday morning."

"And what have you been doing besides ignoring those law books over there," Phoenix said, nodding at an overstuffed backpack in the corner, "and playing with yourself?"

Craig's face went blank. Phoenix glared at him and continued, "You've spent hours alone in this rat hole, with nothing to do but concoct a bullshit story about how you were duped into backing a marker for forty grand with a one-legged bookie and then how his enormous bagman hunted you and Leo down for payment, tortured Leo and Joe, but just let you go."

"But I... I'm telling you the truth."

"And let me guess how you'd describe this evil bagman of yours. He's what, six and half feet tall, weighs three hundred pounds in the raw, and has the face of a Neanderthal, am I right?"

"Well, basically, yeah, except I'd say he weighs more like three and a quarter and looks like a Sasquatch, with those huge feet and that big hair of his, long brown hair hangin' off the back of his head."

"Are you trying to get cute with me, College Boy?"

"No. I wouldn't—"

"Show me your injuries," Phoenix said.

"What?"

"Your injuries, College Boy, or would you rather I call you Craig?"

"Yes, please, call me Craig."

"Alright then, *College Boy*, you say you had a run in with this Sasquatch bagman, the guy you claim beat the shit out of your friends and pitched them into the bay. Show me something, an injury or bruise, something that this beast did to you before he just let you go."

"But I wasn't... I mean... he didn't..."

"I'm sure he didn't hurt you, College Boy, because he's a product of your twisted imagination. But what the hell, why don't you tell us what happened after you left your make-believe boogeyman in the casino lounge with your money."

"What?" Craig said, shaking his head, as if that would help him track the disjointed line of questioning.

"I want to hear some more of your bullshit story, man. What did you do after you left Tank Lochner with that envelope full of cash?"

"I... I played some blackjack."

Phoenix rolled his eyes.

"I'm serious," Craig said. "Look, Leo thought that Tank might follow me for a while to check me out, and so Leo said that I should act like a real player, you know, do a little gambling after meeting with Tank. So that's what I did. I used some more of the March Madness money—some of the thousand that was left—to play a little fifty-dollar blackjack, like Leo told me to."

"So tell me, Mr. High Roller, what's your play when you're dealt seventeen and the dealer's showin' paint?"

"What?" Craig said.

"Hit or stand, man—what the hell do you do?"

"I... I don't understand..."

"Shit, man, how'd you get through three years of law school?"

"I... I..."

"Alright, College Boy, tell me where you were and what you did when Sparty finished spanking Bucknell's ass."

"I watched the game at Langdell's Draft House, with some classmates. And as soon as it ended I called Leo to ask him what to do."

"What phone did you use?"

"I borrowed a cell phone from a friend, a classmate, who was there watching the game too."

"Why didn't you just use your own cell?"

"Because Leo kept my phone after using it to place the bet. He gave me his phone but told me not to use it for any calls relating to our March Madness pool."

"So, you're saying that Leo was so paranoid about Mr. Holmes' surveillance that he—"

"Oh my God!" Joe exclaimed. "That's why the phone at the cottage under the bed was—"

"Dammit, Joe!" Phoenix shouted. "You see that window over there by Mr. Holmes?"

Joe nodded.

Phoenix stuck his face, teeth clenched, in front of Joe's face. "I'm gonna throw your scrawny ass through that window if I hear another sound out of you. Now get the hell out of that chair and out of my sight."

Craig apparently sensed that something about what he had just said had somehow helped his case, as did something he said the first time Joe spouted off. He straightened up in his chair and looked squarely into the eyes of his examiner, who picked up on his sudden bravado.

At that moment, Phoenix grabbed Joe's now-empty chair and flung it across the room. He did the same with the kitchen table, so there was nothing between them. Then he stepped closer.

"When you called Leo after the game, what was said about the financial crisis he had created for you?"

"Well shit, man," Craig confidently replied, "it's not like either of us had a stash of forty large just lyin' around. Leo told me that he'd have to hit up his old man for the cheddar and that I should lay low until it was wired."

Phoenix stepped closer. "You must really want me to think you're a total dumb ass, College Boy—that you really were duped into betting forty *large* on some *dog* when in fact you didn't have a shred of *cheddar* to pay a Sasquatch collector who knew right where to find your ass because you told the beast ahead of time exactly where you'd hide."

Craig's head began to sink and apparently along with it his fleeting confidence.

"Or maybe you think *I'm* the total dumb ass, College Boy, that I might actually be duped into believing this shit." Phoenix stepped in close and leaned forward, his face within inches of Craig's, and asked again, "Is that what you think of me, College Boy, that *I'm* the total dumb ass here?"

"No, sir," Craig whispered.

"Well then, who is, if it's not me?"

Craig said nothing. His head remained down.

"Answer me, dammit," Phoenix said.

One of Craig's hands began to tremble. "Me, sir," he said, still staring at the floor.

"Well, in that case, maybe *I* should tell *you* what happened that night. You did in fact go to the library after the game, to your usual spot, deep in the fourth-floor stacks. And later, around half past two, Leo did in fact call his father to ask for money, because you two had somehow managed to piss away the March Madness fund. But his father refused to bail him out this time. So Leo did what any decent guy would do. He immediately told you, his partner, the bad news. I don't know what the hell phones the two of you were using, but not long after Leo talked to his dad, he got word of the bad news to you—didn't he, College Boy?"

"Yes, sir... but... but..."

"Shut up, dumb ass. I'm not done yet. After you got the bad news, it eventually dawned on your lame brain that you'd probably get kicked out of school, just a couple weeks before finishing three years of grueling legal studies. Hell, maybe you'd even get your sweet little booty thrown in the joint with all those horny felons. So there you were, deep in the library stacks, all alone, ruminating about how Leo had ruined your life. At some point, your ballistic temper engaged, the same temper that got you into that bar fight with those bikers last year, and you started yelling and busting things up right there in the stacks, all by yourself, College Boy, until you decided to go to the cottage and direct your rage at the person who ruined your life."

Craig looked up, tears now streaming down his face. "I swear, Mr. Wade, I'm telling the truth. That's not what happened."

Phoenix folded his arms and shook his head. "Okay," he said. "Let's hear your version of what happened that night in the library."

C26

2:34 a.m., Tuesday, April 5.

"Well look at you, doing your homework like a good little college boy."

Craig shot to his feet, spun around, and then froze. Out of the shadows stepped Tank Lochner. His head nearly scraped the low ceiling of the secluded study area. As he stepped forward, it felt to Craig as though the surrounding shelves of ancient law books also closed in on him.

The only light in the area came from a lamp on Craig's desk. Its glow reflected up from the desktop onto the underside of Tank's face, casting a shadow over his upper features. His eyes were invisible.

"Where the hell's my money?" he said, seething.

Craig's heart pounded and his speech faltered. "Mr... Mr. Lochner, I... I..."

Tank stepped closer, further into the angular lighting, revealing eyes that glared from sockets carved deep into an oversized brow. "What kind of loser did Leo bring along on this bullshit play?"

Craig patted his empty pockets and tried to think of something to say. "I... I don't have any..."

"Where the hell is Leo?" Tank asked, raising his voice.

"He's... he's..."

"You give up Leo, you son of a bitch, or I'll fuck you up worse than him!" Tank shouted, completely disregarding the possible presence of others in the library around them.

Surging from within was an irrepressible urge for flight or fight. To be sure, flight was his preference, but Craig had nowhere to run.

The unorthodox right hook that Craig led with was bigger than any punch he'd ever landed on anyone's face, on or off the ice. When it crashed into the meat of Tank's left jowl, a protruding ring on Craig's tightly closed fist tore into flesh. Blood sprayed from the gash as Tank's head snapped to his right. But immediately his head snapped back to its original position.

From the look on Tank's bloody face, the blow had only made him angrier.

Craig followed with a straight left aimed at the tip of Tank's nose. The blow, however, didn't get there. Tank caught it in one of his big mitts, squeezed it, and then used it to fling Craig into a wall of books and back again toward the desk.

Craig's 220-pound frame landed on the desktop and smashed it to the floor. Immediately following the crash, Craig found himself pinned beneath the bagman's knee, backed by his full weight. Craig's ribcage buckled.

"Where's Leo?" the beast shouted.

"Leo, you gotta get out of that cottage now!" Craig begged into a payphone, his heart racing from his fight with the bagman and then his dash down five flights of stairs.

"What the hell's going on?" Leo asked.

"I just got into it with the bagman, Leo."

"You mean a real fight?"

"Yeah. And then after he whipped my ass, I gave up your location, man."

"You told him where my dad's cottage is?"

"I'm sorry, Leo. But I was scared out of my mind. The guy's a monster!"

"Okay, try to calm down, Craig. When did this happen?"

"Just a few minutes ago," Craig said, still breathing heavily.

"Where?" Leo asked.

"In the library, man, right in the fourth-floor stacks!"

"At school?"

"Yes. I'm in the basement right now, on the phone in the student lounge."

"What the hell are you doing at school? And how the hell did Tank Lochner find you there?"

"It's a long story, Leo. I'll tell you later. Right now, you need to get out of that cottage, you and Joe."

Craig could hear Leo sigh into the phone. "What is it, Leo?"

"Another long story, I just called my dad a few minutes ago, and he hung up on me as soon as he realized I was asking for money. I'm packing right now for a trip to see him in person to ask again, and I need to get going."

"Oh shit," Craig said, breathing heavily again. "What are we gonna do?"

"Well, it looks like I'm stuck here until after I deal with the guy you invited to my dad's cottage."

"Hold on a second," Craig said. "I know what to do. You take off now and I'll haul ass over there to the cottage and see if I can smooth things out with Tank before he wakes up Joe."

Leo laughed out loud, notwithstanding the gravity of the situation. "No offense intended, partner, but that's probably our worst option. I think you need to get the hell out of town. Go to some obscure place far away, and don't tell me where. You still have my phone, right?"

"Yeah."

"Okay, be sure to take it with you, but don't make, or take, any calls. Just lie low until you get a call from me, maybe in a day or two. I'll be using your phone, so the caller ID to pick up on will be obvious."

"But then who's gonna handle the money wired from Chicago and do the drops, man?" Craig complained.

"Sorry, partner, but I really think we need a new front guy, going forward."

"Who?"

There was a pause before Leo answered. "I'll recruit Joe."

"Joe? But he didn't even involve himself in the pool as a player."

"Which makes him the perfect stakeholder for the March Madness money if there's any delay with getting it wired," Leo said.

"And what about the drop with Tank, to get Jimmy his money?"

"I'm sure my dad will want to handle that one himself," Leo said, "along with a crew he'll no doubt bring up from Chicago. But that's not what I'll tell Tank. I'll also tell him he'll be dealing with Joe."

"So you actually think you can negotiate with that guy?"

"Sure, after he's done kicking my ass."

"What? You know he's gonna mess you up if you stay. Why not just collect Joe and get the hell out of there?"

"I'm sure he won't hurt me too bad. You're okay, aren't you?"

"I guess."

"Trust me. He wants money, not trouble. But he also has to show some muscle, you know, show me that he's someone to be taken seriously. That's just something any bagman has to do before hearing you out."

C27

2:40 p.m., Wednesday, April 6.

"What'd you do after you got off the library phone with Leo?" Phoenix asked.

"Just what Leo told me to do," Craig said. "I swung by my apartment and grabbed the rest of the March Madness money and some clothes and other stuff. Then I left town, headed east on M-72. Around Kalkaska I stopped for gas and thought a little about where I should go and decided to come here."

"What time did you get here?"

"It was a little after four in the morning, 4:20, to be exact. I know it was because I checked the time on Leo's cell phone and decided to just crash in my car, outside the manager's office, until he opened for business."

Phoenix glanced at Harlan and tilted his head. Harlan nodded back. Craig must have seen the exchange. "Mr. Holmes," he said, "do you know what time Leo... uh—"

"I'm asking the questions, College Boy," Phoenix said. "Now tell me, how long were you asleep in your car?"

"Not long. The manager knocked on my window just after five."

"In the morning?"

"Yeah. He wanted to know what I was doing there. I told him I wanted a room."

"The manager just happened to get up at five in the morning and—"

"He was going bass fishing that morning. At least that's what he told me when he checked me into this cabin. He said he had set his alarm clock for five so that he could be on the lake by daybreak."

Phoenix shook his head. "And I'll bet that's exactly what he told my associate over there, Mr. MacPherson, when he went to see him."

"Actually, that *is* what he told me," Tommy said.

Phoenix rolled his eyes. "And how much of the March Madness money did you pay the manager to tell that story, College Boy?"

"I didn't—"

"Oh c'mon, Phoenix," Tommy said. "Why keep busting the boy's chops when obviously—"

"Because that's what I pay him to do," Angelo said. "Let him do his job, would you? This isn't some law-office deposition subject to your damn *civil* procedures."

Phoenix smiled. "I don't mind being civil," he said, "but answer me this, Tommy—what were the manager's *exact* words?"

"Exactly what Craig just said—that he set his alarm clock for five so he could go bass fishing at daybreak. And he noticed Craig's car outside the office while he was getting ready to go."

"He specifically said all that," Phoenix said, "the exact time the alarm clock was set for, the exact species of fish he was going to catch, and the exact time he was going to catch them."

"Well, yeah. So what?"

"And you don't find that the least bit suspicious?"

"Why should I?"

"Because neither of them simply said that he woke up early to go fishing—period. Why do you think they both include all those identical, extraneous details about him setting an *alarm clock* for *five* so he could fish for *bass* at *daybreak*?"

"Well I find it suspicious," Angelo said. "And I'd like Phoenix to—"

Harlan's cell phone rang. "I really should take this call," he said.

Angelo nodded and Harlan stepped out of the cabin.

"Phoenix, I want you to go check out this manager yourself," Angelo said. He then peeled off a few bills from a stack of cash, extended it to Phoenix, and added, "But don't get rough with the guy. Be nice and civil, like Tommy, so he doesn't call the cops."

Phoenix took the money but paused before heading for the door. "You want me to go right now, Angelo, with Harlan also outside the cabin? You sure?"

Angelo nodded.

122

"Hey, College Boy," Phoenix said, "don't even think about pulling any shit with Mr. Surocco while I'm gone."

"I would never pull any—"

"Shut up, Craig," Angelo said. "I have a few questions of my own for you, and I want straight answers, understood?"

"Yes sir," Craig said.

"Have you ever been to the GTB Marina?" Angelo asked as he stepped toward Craig.

Phoenix had reached the door but paused again.

"Yes. Leo took Joe and me there a couple times to drink a few beers and do some fishing. He scared the hell out of us by driving his truck onto the marina wall, all the way out to the end, where he liked to fish."

Angelo's eyes widened. "So you knew that the wall could support Leo's truck," he said, as he stepped closer to Craig.

"Alright, Carl, you take care," Harlan said into his phone before dropping it to his side. He then looked up at Phoenix, who had just stepped out of the cabin.

"Who's Carl?" Phoenix asked.

"A former client of mine. I texted him a little while ago when Craig told us about the guy who—"

Harlan's phone rang again. He glanced down at the caller ID. "It's Riley Summers. I have to take this."

Phoenix nodded and headed off toward the manager's cabin.

C28

2:51 p.m., Wednesday, April 6.

"How's it going, Riley?"

"Not well, Harlan, and I think you know why."

"What do you think I know?"

"That your client is continuing to present a problem for me and my homicide investigation."

Harlan was standing just outside the cabin's front window. He glanced through a slight part he had left in the curtains before stepping out to take the prior phone call. Through the opening he caught a glimpse of Angelo wagging a finger in Craig's face.

"What's the problem?" Harlan asked.

"I'm sure that you're aware of Mr. Surocco's first phone call to me yesterday," Riley said, "you know, the call that he made to Craig Davies' cell phone, which I answered at that cottage."

"Sure."

"And now, today, I've just learned that your client's lawyer, this Tommy MacPherson fellow, went to the law school and met with Dean Fletcher, and he tried to get information about Craig's whereabouts. I'm sure you're aware of that too."

"Yes, I am. But try to put yourself in Mr. Surocco's shoes for a second, will you?"

"Oh, I am thinking about his intentions if he catches up with Craig Davies, and that cannot happen. I want you to control your client—keep him away from Craig Davies—do you understand?"

Harlan looked back through the window. At that moment, Angelo stood about three feet in front of Craig and was growling something at the boy.

"That might be kind of difficult to do," Harlan said. "I mean, Mr. Surocco is pretty suspicious of Craig at the moment."

"I'm telling you, Harlan, your client has already gotten to one material witness before me, and I can't let that happen again. Keep him the hell away from Craig Davies. Is that clear?"

Harlan looked again through the window. Angelo had stepped closer and leaned toward his seated suspect. His face—now within inches of Craig's—beamed red.

"I can try to intervene, Riley, but I can't make any guarantees. Please understand my situation here for a second. Mr. Surocco is pretty adamant about these suspicions he has of Craig Davies. It's not going to be easy to keep him from trying to get in the boy's face."

"Alright," Riley said, "if I give you something—some information that might help you control your client—could you please try to get him to stand down and let the police handle this?"

"I'll definitely try, Riley. What do you have?"

Riley sighed. "I'm only doing this because I appreciate your candor yesterday about that GPS data and the access you gave CSI to it. It's been very helpful. I'd like to think that I can trust you to do the right thing with what I'm about to tell you."

"Certainly."

"It's about the blood and hair found on the cottage stairway," she said. "Forensics says that it doesn't belong to any of the boys—it's not from Leo, Joe, or Craig. It's from someone else."

"So there was someone else at the cottage," Harlan said, "who may have left the big footprints and tire tracks too."

"Yes, someone else who also left blood at the law school's library that night."

"You mean to say that the blood at the library and the blood at the cottage are from the same person?"

"Yes."

"Who?"

"We don't know yet, and frankly, I'd like your client to be the last to find

125

out. I want him to stand down, Harlan."

"So you haven't been able to get a match in any of the DNA databases?"

"No, not yet. But after we do track him down and get him into custody, I'll let you know who he is. Until then—"

"I know, Riley. Until then, I'll do everything I can to keep my client away from Craig Davies."

"Thanks, Harlan. And there's something else you might be able to help me with."

"What's that?"

"It's about Joe Rylands. He walked out of the hospital earlier today, without even checking himself out. The kid actually gave one of our officers the slip by cutting through an employee-only area in the ER."

"Wonder why he'd do that," Harlan said.

"I don't know for sure, but I've been told that your client's other associate, that chauffeur or whatever he is, Phoenix Wade, visited with Joe a little while before he left the hospital. I take it that Mr. Wade hasn't said anything to you about where Joe may have gone, has he?"

"Well, Phoenix didn't tell me much about what was said during his hospital visit, but I'm expecting to see him soon and can ask whether... hold on, I see him coming right now."

Phoenix was returning from the manager's cabin with his head down, poking at his cell phone with a finger.

"Hey, Phoenix," Harlan whispered after covering his phone. "Joe didn't actually leave the hospital with you today, did he?"

"Well he kind of did. Thirty minutes after I—"

"I mean literally," Harlan said.

"What?" Phoenix said.

"Did you two *physically* leave the premises together, at the same time?"

"Well, no, I left first, and he met me a half hour later, outside, a few blocks away."

Harlan uncovered his phone. "Riley, apparently Phoenix went to the hospital to ask Joe about Craig's possible whereabouts. But Joe got evasive about the topic, and Phoenix left. Phoenix thought that Joe might actually have some idea. You don't suppose that the kid went off looking for Craig, do you?"

"It's entirely possible."

"Man, with an unidentified suspect still loose, that's not a good thing."

"Tell me about it," Riley said. "Between losing Joe Rylands and coming up empty on Craig Davies, I'm not too popular with the captain right now."

"Sorry to hear that, Riley."

C29

3:01 p.m., Wednesday, April 6.

"It wasn't Craig," Harlan called out over the heated questioning still in progress when he and Phoenix returned to the cabin.

Angelo stopped questioning Craig and turned to Harlan. "What are you talking about?" he asked.

"I just got off the phone with Detective Summers. They've finished testing the blood and hair at the cottage, and its DNA is from someone other than Leo, Joe, or Craig. And it matches the DNA from the blood found in the library."

Angelo looked away, into space. He seemed indifferent to the news.

"Did you hear me, Angelo?" Harlan asked. "Someone else was at the cottage, someone who also got bloodied at the library. This is significant corroboration of Craig's story, don't you think?"

Angelo looked at Phoenix. "What'd the manager say?"

Phoenix shook his head. "He wasn't in. The guy's probably off fishing somewhere."

"Well, what do *you* think about this DNA stuff that he's all worked up about?"

"Actually, Angelo, I agree with him," Phoenix said. "It's significant corroboration of what Craig's telling us. And even before Harlan learned about it, I was going to tell you that I believe the kid, every word of his bizarre story."

"You do? Why?"

"He never tripped up. No matter how I came at him, the kid's story was consistent in every detail, and many of its specifics are consistent with other facts we know to be true."

"Like what?" Angelo asked.

"Well," Phoenix said, "even putting aside the DNA analysis for a moment, there's the simple fact that there was fresh blood evidence in the library that night, right where Craig says he bloodied this bagman. I don't see a scratch on the kid, and he couldn't show me one when I challenged him to show me any injury he suffered that night. So where'd the blood come from?"

Angelo nodded.

"And there's his description of the guy. He called him a Sasquatch and said he had long brown hair hangin' off the back of his head. That's just how Joe described the guy's hair, and it's also consistent with the hair Harlan found at the cottage."

Angelo nodded again.

"Joe," Phoenix said, "what size shoe do you wear?"

"Size ten," Joe answered.

"Have you ever tried on a pair of Leo's shoes?" Phoenix asked.

"Yeah, they're a little loose on me, maybe a size too big."

"Go over by Craig and put one of your feet next to his for us."

Joe did as Phoenix asked. "Look for yourself, Angelo," Phoenix continued, "Craig may be a lot bigger than Joe, but his feet aren't much bigger—maybe a twelve or thirteen." Craig nodded.

"If you look at the picture that Harlan took of the footprints outside the cottage, the big guy's prints dwarf the others. Craig didn't know about those footprints when he described the bagman's big feet, and Craig's feet couldn't leave prints that would dwarf Leo's and Joe's that way."

"And if that's not enough," Phoenix added, "there's his account of the cell phones that he and Leo had—"

"Enough," Angelo said, shaking his head and raising a hand.

Harlan jumped in anyway. "I also got further corroboration from a former client, the guy who Craig told us—"

"I get it already, goddammit!" Angelo exclaimed. "My son—Angel's Demon—got whacked by a Sasquatch bagman who works for a one-legged bookie because he lost some crackpot parlay he played on the Bucknell Bison."

The room went silent for what seemed a lengthy interval. Tommy broke the silence. He turned to Phoenix and said, "So you were over there busting

129

that boy's chops, and the whole time you knew full well that—"

"Where did he say that bookie does business?" Angelo asked.

"A place called Jimmy's Pub in Williamsburg," Phoenix said. "By the way, Angelo, the place actually exists. I checked it online just a few minutes ago."

Angelo gave Phoenix in an intense look, followed by an almost imperceptible nod of his head. But Harlan saw it, as well as the slight nod Phoenix returned before heading for the door. Upon reaching it, he paused and looked back.

"Hey, Craig, don't get down on yourself, man. Leo was one of a kind, a guy with more savvy than anyone you'll ever meet. He was flat gifted at playing people. Just ask that wily old PI over there."

Man, don't you guys ever let up? Harlan thought.

"You know, Craig," Angelo added, "Phoenix is right about Leo. The kid was hell on wheels."

Craig shook his head. Intense grief showed on his face. "Phoenix was also right about me being a dumb ass," he said. "Leo would be alive right now if I had just used my head. It's my fault that he's—"

"Listen, Craig," Angelo said, glancing briefly at Harlan, "there's plenty of blame to go around here, much more for some of us older guys than for you."

Is that it? Harlan thought. *That's as close as you'll come to admitting that you screwed up too?*

Angelo reached into his pocket, pulled out a wad of cash, and started thumbing through it. "Tommy," he said, "go out to the car and get a couple more envelopes from my briefcase."

Then Angelo looked at Craig and Joe. "Okay, guys, there are a few things I want you to do. First of all, Craig, I want you to take this money—it's about six grand—and use it to pay the kids who won that March Madness pool of yours. And use the extra money to treat them to something, like some beer and pizza—you know, to make up for being late with their money."

Craig's eyes bulged as he accepted the wad of cash. "Oh my gosh, Mr. Surocco, I don't even know what to—"

"You know where that money came from, don't you?" Angelo asked.

"Well, obviously from you, Mr. Surocco. You just handed it to me, sir."

"Wrong answer, Craig. It came from your sock drawer, where you stored the March Madness money that everyone at school gave you."

Craig looked confused. "Look, son," Angelo said, "the four-thousand-dollar payment to Tank Lochner—you know, that deposit you made with him—it was made with *other* money, Leo's money, and you have no idea where he got it. Do you understand, son? The only reason you didn't pay your school friends on time was because Leo got you involved as the front guy with a wager secured with *his* money, and things went so bad with *his* bet that you had to run from a crazed bagman. Got it?"

Craig nodded slowly and then looked at his friend. "You'll back me up on this, won't you, Joe?"

Joe paused and looked down. Then he looked up at Angelo, nodded his head, and answered, "Yeah... uh... sure, Craig. I got your back on this one."

Tommy returned and handed Angelo two thick envelopes. Angelo gave one to each boy and continued giving instructions. "When you two get back to Traverse City, I want you to finish getting your law degrees, you hear, and then I want you to buckle down and study all summer for the Illinois Bar Exam. There's plenty enough money in those envelopes to do that without having to borrow or work. Just focus on that exam, and kick its ass."

"Holy shit, Mr. Surocco," Craig said. "I don't even know what—"

Craig stopped himself and said, "Did you say the Illinois Bar Exam, sir?"

"Maybe I'm getting ahead of myself," Angelo said. "Do you have a job lined up after graduation, Craig?"

"No, sir."

"Well, how would you like to come to Chicago and join my crew this fall?"

"Are you kidding?" Craig exclaimed. "That would be awesome!"

"You sure, Craig? Even after the way we busted your chops here today?"

"I got no problem with what happened here today, Mr. Surocco. After all this, you're the one who should be thinking twice about *me*."

"What I'm thinking, kid, is that you've got lots of potential. I don't know many guys who'd try to fight their way through a three-hundred-pound bagman the way you did. And I see your loyalty to Leo, and that goes a long way with me. Do you know why?"

Craig shrugged.

"Because of all the things you need to get ahead in this fuckin' world, what matters most are the people around you. They gotta be loyal to the core, like family. Leo must have thought you were that kind of guy, Craig, the kind of guy who stands by his own no matter what—to the wall. So tell me, was he right?"

"He sure as hell was, sir."

Harlan looked over at Joe and thought he might be thinking the same thing. *First Leo dupes this poor guy. Now his old man is taking a turn.*

"That's good to hear, Craig," Angelo continued, "because this goddamn game of Leo's isn't over yet. I'm in it now, and I'm gonna finish his play. And I'm counting on you to have my back, the way you had Leo's. Can I do that?"

"Hell yeah," Craig answered, "to the wall—right Joe?"

Joe nodded tentatively. Then Angelo instructed them to continue lying low at the cabin in Waters, Michigan, until he got word to them that they could come out of hiding. "It may take a day or two, but I need you boys to..."

"Angelo, what the hell are you doing?" Harlan said. "They should call Detective Summers right this minute and arrange for a police escort back home. In fact, if they're not going to do that, I will."

Harlan grabbed his cell phone from his pocket and—

"Hold on, Mr. *Ex*-cop," Tommy said. "Don't forget who you're working for."

Harlan slid the phone back into his pocket and opted instead to jot the phone number for state police headquarters in Traverse City on a piece of paper and set it by the cabin phone. "Okay, boys, then as soon as we leave here you need to call—"

"There's no need for alarm," Tommy said. He stepped over to the cabin phone, picked up the note, and stuffed it into his pocket.

"Think about what you're doing, man," Harlan said. "That bagman knows who these boys are and that they're material witnesses to what he did. Don't tell them to take chances."

Angelo and Tommy ignored Harlan's plea, and Tommy took over instructing Joe and Craig. "You boys are plenty smart enough to understand what's going on here. Craig, I'm sure you understand why Mr. Surocco had to talk with you today, and why he'd like to talk to this bagman, Tank Lochner, before the police do."

"I hope you do a hell of a lot more than just talk with that son of a bitch," Craig said.

Harlan shook his head and started for the door. "I can't be a part of this, Angelo. This is becoming much more than the usual obstruction of justice you ask of me."

C30

3:20 p.m., Wednesday, April 6.

Harlan stepped out of the cabin and stopped when he overheard Phoenix end a phone conversation. The two men stood only a few feet apart on a dirt drive, alone.

"Who was that?" Harlan asked.

"Vincent."

"What are you guys up to?"

"Like you don't already know."

"All I know, Phoenix, is that I want nothing to do with whatever you're planning for Tank Lochner."

"That's unfortunate."

"Why?"

"Because you're central to the plan."

"No fucking way."

"That's what I said the first time. But you'll do it, just like I did."

"Do what?"

Phoenix removed his sunglasses and scowled. "Oh c'mon, man, wake up and smell the deep shit you've gotten yourself into. You know what has to be done here. And you know who has to do it."

"You can't possibly think that I'm going to—"

"Yes you are, and I'll tell you why—old man."

Harlan's heart pounded. He stepped closer to Phoenix and straightened up. The two locked eyes.

"The way Angelo sees it," Phoenix said, "you fucked up big time. And now you owe him—and Leo."

Harlan couldn't disagree. He'd been telling himself the same thing since yesterday afternoon. He let Leo down. He let him die. But now, more than just Harlan's mental health might depend on working through it. He needed to know exactly what these guys had in mind for him.

"So what's your plan?"

"It's simple," Phoenix said. "We've just sent some spotters to Williamsburg to try to track down Tank Lochner. And Vincent is working on getting us a couple of clean, VIN-cloned cars that we can use for the job. You and Vincent will take one of the cars to some remote location that Vincent knows about. And I'll take the other car and join you guys later, after I go to Williamsburg and bag the bagman, assuming our spotters can find him."

"I don't get it," Harlan said.

"What? Don't you know what a VIN-cloned car is?"

"That's not my question," Harlan said. He was familiar with the relatively recent technique used by some thieves to mask the identity of a stolen car. They get a vehicle identification number from another car of the same make and model, from out of state, and use it to make a counterfeit VIN plate for the stolen car.

"What I don't get is the big production," Harlan said. "Why not just do the guy on the spot, in Williamsburg, where you plan to nab him? Why drag him off to some remote location? That just creates more exposure."

"I thought we'd talk first, you know, give Tank Lochner some due process."

"Due process? What are you planning, Phoenix? Some kind of midnight hearing out in the woods somewhere?"

"Well, yeah, you being an ex-cop and all, I thought you'd want to give the guy his day in court—before you whack him."

"What? Listen, man, there's no way in hell I'm going to—"

"Enough!" Phoenix said. "Just gimme your gun."

"I don't carry one."

"Bullshit. Give it to me right now, old man."

Harlan turned and put his hands behind his head. "Go ahead, check for yourself."

Other than Harlan's wallet, keys, and cell phone, the only things revealed by the search were a small pocket knife and a pocket-sized first aid kit.

"This is what you carry?"

"Well, I do keep the knife pretty sharp."

Phoenix shook his head as he opened the first aid kit. As he rummaged through bandages and medical supplies, he came across a USB flash drive. It was the one Harlan had taken from Leo's safe back at the cottage. "What's this for?"

"It contains medical information about me—you know, just in case."

"Well, of course, who'd leave home without that?" Phoenix scoffed. He handed all of the items back to Harlan, except the cell phone. He then reached into one of his own jacket pockets for the keys to the Escalade, making sure to open the jacket wide enough for Harlan to see the gun he was carrying. "Here," he said, handing the keys to Harlan. "It's time for *you* to drive."

C31

9:33 p.m., Wednesday, April 6.

Tank Lochner had been so distracted by recent events that he overlooked a text message from his boss sent several hours ago. It said, "Get your big ass to the pub ASAP!" He hurried to Jimmy's Pub as soon as he read it.

"What's happening, Boss?" Tank said as he entered Jimmy's office.

"Why don't you tell me? Why the hell haven't we heard from Leo?"

Tank shrugged. "I dunno."

"Really? I think you do. What aren't you telling me about the other night?"

"You know I never hold anything back from you, Jimmy. Like I said before, things got a little rougher than I expected with College Boy and, well, with Leo and that other kid. But College Boy was fine when I left him. And things settled down at that place on the bay after me and that kid fell down the stairs. I'm telling you, Leo was cool with everything when I left."

"Then why were the cops here today asking me if I know the whereabouts of any of those boys?"

"Here today?"

"Yeah. Some chick detective was in my face with all kinds of questions this afternoon, like why a call to the pub on Sunday shows up on College Boy's caller ID, and why the number isn't a public one for the business."

"Oh man, Jimmy. Do you think she knows about the operation here?"

"She never said. But she's clearly trying to track down someone—some three-hundred-pound guy—who she thinks is chasing after these boys."

"What'd you tell her?"

"Never mind what I said."

"Look, Jimmy, if I somehow blew your cover here, I'm really sorry."

"I don't think that's happened, not yet anyway. The cops didn't search the place, and they haven't been back since this afternoon. But some guy I've never seen before has been out front nursing a couple beers for nearly two hours now."

"What's he look like, Jimmy?"

"Just some bald-headed guy sitting in a booth by the pool table."

"You want me to go up front and check him out?"

"No, let him be. I'm just jumpy right now."

Tank started to sit down on Jimmy's couch, but then popped back to his feet. "Wait a second," he said. "How does that detective know what calls have been made on College Boy's cell phone, if he's gone missing?"

"I've wondered that too. I've also wondered about Leo. Even if he's on the run, it's not like him to go silent on us. The kid's a talker. He should have called by now with some compelling story about why he missed payment again today and another plan he has to get us the money."

"You think something's happened to him?" Tank said.

"You're askin' me? What the hell are you gonna tell the cops when they track down your big ass? The same story you keep telling me?"

"It's the truth, Jimmy. You gotta believe me, man."

"It doesn't matter what I believe, Tank. I have to act on the basis of what others believe."

"You mean the cops?"

"Yeah, the cops, and maybe Angelo Surocco."

"Who's he?"

"Leo's dad. I take it you know nothing about him."

"Nothing at all, except maybe one thing. If he owns that place on the bay, he sure as hell can cover Leo's marker."

"Oh, I'm sure he can cover that," Jimmy said. "Or take some other measures to make it go away."

"What are you talking about, Jimmy? What other measures?"

"The kind that extinguish the debt by extinguishing the creditor."

"What do you mean?"

"The son of a bitch is a made guy," Jimmy said.

"You're shittin' me."

Jimmy shook his head. "When Leo placed the Bucknell bet, he said something about some Chicago books he'd shaken down recently. I called every book I know down there after things here went sideways. I found one who knows Leo—and all about his dad." Jimmy looked up at Tank and added, "He's a made guy, alright, and I think he's made you."

"What?" Tank said. "Are you sayin' that I laid the lumber to the son of a full-on wiseguy, and he knows who I am?"

Jimmy nodded. "What do you know about a private eye named Harlan Holmes?" he asked.

"Never heard of him."

"Well, he's heard of you," Jimmy said. "The sleuth called Carl Trimarco earlier today. Carl says he asked about you by name and wanted to know whether Carl knew where you were on the night of the State-Bucknell game."

"Why was he asking?"

"Get this. The PI tells Carl that some dude says you hooked up with his wife at a motel that night."

"Me? I can't even remember the last time I got any."

"Now that I believe, you big ugly bastard. Obviously, this PI was trying to place you somewhere else that night, my guess is Angelo Surocco's place on the bay, and I'd bet this pub he was doing that because he works for Surocco."

"So what'd Carl tell him?"

"What could he tell him?" Jimmy said. "Don't you remember how drunk Carl got at the pub that night, watching the game?"

"Oh yeah. Didn't he pass out here in your office before it was even over?"

Jimmy nodded. "And he was still sleeping it off on my couch when I came in the next day at noon. He doesn't know about anything that happened in between."

"But how could this PI even know to ask Carl about me," Tank said, "unless he knows something about our operation?"

"You mean *my* operation," Jimmy said.

"Listen, Jimmy—"

"No, Tank, you listen. I've always liked you a lot, but—"

"Are you firing me, Jimmy?"

Jimmy nodded. "I have to. In fact, I have to shut down the book for a while, probably a long while, and maybe even clear out of here myself."

"You saying I should leave town?"

"I'm saying you don't work for me anymore, and I don't wanna see you around here for a long time, maybe never again."

"What about my home, Jimmy, the apartment upstairs? Man, I've lived there for I don't know how many years."

Jimmy had been sitting at his desk throughout the meeting. Neither of them had looked away from the other for more than a few seconds until this point. Jimmy grabbed his cane and rose awkwardly while working it into position.

"Believe me," he said, glancing at his prosthetic leg, "I know what it feels like when you think you've lost everything. And I hate like hell to be the source of that for a guy who's been so loyal for so long. But I don't see any alternative here. It won't be long and I'll be too old and feeble to handle the action. I just don't see you figuring into anything I might do down the road."

"I get it, Jimmy. It's just business."

Jimmy reached into a pocket for some cash. "Severance pay," he said as he handed it to Tank.

"Thanks," Tank said. "You think it'd be okay if I stay in the apartment one more night and clear out in the morning?"

Jimmy nodded.

"And would you mind if I stop up front and have a drink with friends before I leave?"

"Of course, take your time. Whatever you want, it's on me."

C32

10:00 p.m., Wednesday, April 6.

When Tank reached the bar he placed a hand on the shoulder of one of the regulars at Jimmy's Pub. "How you doing, Floyd?" he said, looking directly at the man. Floyd gasped on a sip of beer as Tank's big hand swallowed his shoulder. Apparently he wasn't used to physical affection coming from Tank. Nobody at the bar was. Everyone there noticed the exchange.

Samantha Boadle, the bartender, also couldn't help but notice Tank's sullen expression. She knew about the police visit earlier that day and their interrogation of Jimmy about a player who'd been visited by some big bill collector the other night. Just then Jimmy appeared in the doorway from the back room and stood there, watching. The chain of events spoke for itself. *He just got canned*, she thought.

She offered Tank his usual. "Can I buy you a schooner of Bud, big guy?"

"Thanks, Sam, but I think Jimmy's got my tab tonight. Let's make it a schooner of Forty-Five North Riesling."

"That's twenty-two ounces of wine, Tank. Are you sure?" He nodded. She glanced at Jimmy, and he nodded as well.

Tank slugged down half the schooner in one drink. Sam sighed deeply and then shouted, "Yo, Bernie, drop a couple loads of bird!"

A crackling crash reverberated into the bar from the kitchen's deep fryer as the order of chicken hit the grease and sank in. On the heels of the crash, billows of smoke and steam blocked out the kitchen's service window at the end of the bar.

Sam wiped down the bar but kept an eye on Tank as he drank down most of what remained in the schooner. The man looked to her like he could use the kind of counsel that one might seek from a favorite bartender. She came over and tried, but any desire he initially had to visit with friends had passed.

Tank ignored her and began staring at something in the direction of his lap. She leaned over to the other side of the bar for a look. It was a small yin-yang symbol tattooed on the inside of his left forearm.

"I didn't know you had a tattoo," Sam said. "Isn't that some kind of spiritual thing?"

He shrugged and returned his stare to the tattoo. This behavior, too, was very different for Tank, Sam thought. It looked like he was trying to achieve some kind of meditative state.

"So why'd you get that tattoo in the first place?" she asked.

He sighed.

"Well, why?" she asked.

"To restore balance, dammit!"

"Oh, I see. And how's that working for you right now, big fella?"

"Just pour me some more wine, Sam."

She balked.

"More wine, dammit!"

Jimmy nodded at her from the doorway, so she poured the few ounces that remained in the first bottle, then topped off the schooner with most of the wine in a second.

Soon after the refill, a large pile of deep-fried chicken appeared on a platter in the service window. Sam brought it over to Tank. "You need to put something besides that Riesling in your gut," she said.

Tank made short work of the chicken and the rest of the second bottle of wine. During the feast, the bald-headed guy by the pool table messed with his smartphone and then left.

C33

10:47 p.m., Wednesday, April 6.

Tank pressed a hand to his stomach as he walked unsteadily through the alley behind the pub. He looked up when he reached a set of stairs that led to his second-level apartment.

Suddenly struck by an illusion of the stairwell extending skyward and spinning, he doubled over and puked up a pound of undigested chicken soaked in a mix of wine and gastric juices.

The attack came from behind while he was still doubled over—multiple blows to the back of his head and neck with what felt like some kind of blunt impact weapon.

Before he went down, however, Tank managed to turn and give back what he could, including another half-pound of barf. Then everything went black.

C34

11:49 p.m., Wednesday, April 6.

Harlan's body dripped with sweat, and his hands, arms, and back ached. He had spent the last several hours digging a hole in a remote place rarely seen by people. For him, however, the off-road journey to this area of state forestland had been through familiar turf.

They turned off the marked highway on their way to a destination about seventy miles northeast of Traverse City, deep into Lower Michigan's northern interior. The first off-road segment was a dirt drive that dead-ended into a small parking area for visitors to a nature preserve.

Vincent, however, continued through the parking area and headed northeast through state forestland along a serpentine dirt trail intended only for specialized, all-terrain service vehicles and barely wide enough for their SUV.

After pushing deep into the forest, Vincent branched off the service trail onto a two-track and continued further north for some distance beyond the two-track's disappearance.

"Where the hell are we?" asked a backseat passenger when Vincent finally stopped the SUV. Vincent looked into the rearview mirror. "My best shot at the middle of nowhere," he answered.

Harlan, seated in the front passenger seat, glanced back at the passenger. The man sat directly behind him. There had been no introduction, and there would never be one. The guy was just there, waiting in the backseat, when Harlan joined up with Vincent in Traverse City earlier that day. Harlan had tried to introduce himself, but the guy just looked out the window. His role was pretty clear. He had a handgun holstered openly on his hip.

"Sit tight," Vincent said to Harlan as he popped the rear cargo door. The guy in the backseat stepped out, retrieved something from the cargo area, and then turned to face the passenger side of the SUV. Harlan glanced out the window at him. The thing he had retrieved from the cargo area was a high-powered rifle. "Let's go," Vincent said.

Harlan stepped out and surveyed the area. He knew exactly where he was: ten miles due west of a hunting cabin that had been in his family for decades, located near Wolverine, Michigan.

He zoomed out on a map in his head and imagined where on the mitten that comprises Lower Michigan he'd be standing if it had fingers—right at the top joint of the middle one. He paused over that image apropos his current predicament.

Vincent retrieved a lantern and a shovel from the rear of the vehicle and then led the party for a quarter-mile hike. Harlan followed close behind. Bringing up the rear, but never too far back, was the guy with the rifle.

They worked their way through dense woods until they reached a clearing. Vincent instructed the guy with the rifle to stop and then led Harlan a little further, into the center of the clearing.

"Start digging," Vincent said, as he tossed the shovel to the ground at Harlan's feet.

"What, my own grave?"

"Not if you give Leo his due."

Vincent's cell phone rang. "Yeah, we're ready," he said into the phone.

Harlan continued to hack his way through tree roots and rock-hard clay for few minutes after the phone call ended. "That'll have to do," Vincent eventually said.

Harlan removed himself from the grave. He let the shovel fall to the ground as he glanced back at the excavation in the full glow of the lantern. After all that effort, it seemed like it shouldn't be so shallow.

The three men trudged back to the spot where Vincent had parked their SUV. Minutes later another SUV pulled up.

C35

11:59 p.m., Wednesday, April 6.

Harlan and Vincent stood beside the SUV and watched as Phoenix eased himself out, wincing. Phoenix looked back at them with only his right eye. His left one was swollen shut.

"What the hell happened to you?" Vincent asked.

"He gave me a little trouble," Phoenix said.

"No shit."

Phoenix exhibited none of his usual self-confidence while describing the back-alley confrontation with the bagman. "The way I beat on his skull with that blackjack, before he even knew I was there, it should've killed him on the spot. But it's like he's not human, like he's some kind of beast."

"What's that smell?" Vincent asked.

"The son of a bitch was stumbling drunk and puked all over me."

Harlan resisted the urge to smile as he watched Vincent struggle to process what he was seeing and hearing. Vincent held his lantern up to the passenger window and studied the massive face of their squinting hostage. "But Phoenix," he said, "you're supposed to be the beast in a street fight. How the hell could this guy mess you up if he was shit-faced and you suckered him from behind with a blackjack?"

"I don't wanna talk about it," Phoenix said.

"But if he could do this to you," Vincent said, "can you even imagine what he did to my little—"

Vincent suddenly dropped the lantern and drew a pistol. As he flung the door open, he shouted, "Get out of that car, you fucking freak, or I'll shoot your ass right now!"

"What are you doing?" Phoenix shouted as he grabbed Vincent's wrist and pointed the gun at the ground.

"He was my brother, man! Let me do this! Now get out of that car you…"

"He can't get out of the car," Phoenix said.

Vincent wheeled to face Phoenix. "Why?"

"Because he's duct-taped to the seat, man."

"Oh."

"Now just give me the piece. You know how your dad wants this done."

Phoenix shoved the gun beneath his waistband and then leaned into the SUV with a knife and cut Tank free of the seat. Tank stepped out awkwardly. His feet and hands remained bound and tethered with duct tape in the manner of a shackled prisoner in a courtroom.

"How'd you get the tape to do that?" Vincent asked.

Phoenix shrugged and then tipped his head back and turned the palm of a hand skyward. It was beginning to rain. "Let's just get this done," he said.

Vincent grabbed the lantern and led the group back to the clearing, their pace slowed by the tethered bagman.

As he had done before, the guy with the rifle stopped when they arrived at the edge of the clearing. The others proceeded to the center. The moment the glow of the lantern revealed the shallow grave, Phoenix charged at Tank from behind and drove a shoulder and arm into the middle of the man's back. Tank fell forward into the grave, his face slamming into its floor. He quickly turned his head to free his mouth and nose from mud that had been formed by the steady sprinkle of rain.

What followed next bore no resemblance to any "due process" that Phoenix had earlier suggested Tank Lochner would receive. Questioning from Phoenix and Vincent was but a series of hostile threats and accusations, ill-suited for eliciting any kind of testimony from the accused, who said nothing until Vincent finally made clear what they expected of him.

"My old man wants the truth, you son of a bitch!"

"Oh, the truth," Tank said. "Well why didn't you just say so?" His tone was menacing. "Tell your old man that after you guys killed me, I went straight to hell and cleared out all the demons, so that when he gets there, I can have his ass all to myself for the rest of time."

Vincent screamed as he snatched up the shovel and raised it over his head. But before he could bring it down on Tank, Phoenix grabbed the handle and wrestled it away. "Lighten up, man!"

"Lighten up? Are you serious? This freak of nature locks my brother in a truck and pushes it into the bay, and now he has the balls to say—"

"That's not how he got the truck into the bay!" Harlan shouted.

To that point, Harlan's presence had barely been felt. But now he had everyone's attention, including Tank Lochner's. Harlan crouched down alongside the grave to make eye contact with the accused.

"You know Carl Trimarco?" Harlan asked.

"Yeah," Tank said. "He's one of Jimmy's writers."

"Well I know him, too," Harlan said, "and I talked with him just today about what he did on the night of the State-Bucknell game. Carl says you were right there with him. So you know what happened to him that night, too, don't you?"

"Yeah," Tank said. "We watched the game at Jimmy's Pub, along with a bunch of other people—so what?"

"And Carl had too much to drink, didn't he?" Harlan said.

Tank nodded.

"And then he crashed in Jimmy's office," Harlan said, "you know, on that couch in the office. I'm sure you've seen it."

"Yeah," Tank said, "but what's that got to do with—"

"Because that's where Carl was sleeping—until you woke him up."

"What? I never—"

"Bullshit, Lochner. You came bustin' into the office around six in the morning, and it pissed Carl off because he had a massive hangover."

"I don't know what you're talking about," Tank said.

"What *are* you talking about?" Phoenix asked.

Harlan stood up and turned to Phoenix. "Something I learned back at that efficiency cabin, while you were interrogating Craig Davies. Do you remember Craig telling us about Leo's call to Jimmy's wire room?"

Phoenix nodded.

"The name of the writer who answered the phone was Carl," Harlan said. He paused until Phoenix nodded again.

"I realized then that Craig was talking about a former client of mine," Harlan said, "a guy named Carl Trimarco. I did some work for Carl about a year ago when he was going through a divorce. He once told me something about a job he had on the side at some book in Williamsburg. So I texted him, and he called me before we left the cabin."

Phoenix thought for a few seconds. "That guy you were talking to when I left for the manager's office?" he asked.

"Yeah."

"The guy you tried to tell Angelo about later?"

"Yeah."

Phoenix nodded. "Okay, so what'd this guy tell you?"

"Like I said, that Tank showed up at Jimmy's office around six that morning. He wasn't wearing a jacket or outer shirt, just a tank tee undershirt, and his pants were clinging to him, like they were wet and sticky."

"It's pretty damn cold around here that early in the morning, isn't it?" Phoenix said.

Harlan nodded. "I checked. It was thirty-eight degrees. Definitely not the kind of weather to go without a jacket and—"

"I don't get it," Vincent said.

"He fell in the bay," Phoenix said.

"When he pushed the truck in?"

"No," Harlan said. "I'm telling you, that's not the way the truck went into the water. It couldn't be launched from the wall that way, not by somebody just pushing it on foot, not without it—"

Harlan paused.

"Getting stuck," Phoenix said, realization dawning.

"That's right," Harlan said. Vincent still looked confused. Harlan turned to him and spoke slowly. "Just imagine someone trying to push the truck in, probably from behind, because that wall was barely wide enough for the truck to begin with. At some point, a wheel or two slowly slips off the edge of the wall's top surface and... and..."

Phoenix interjected again, "It would have hung up right there, and—"

"Oh, I get it, like a turtle on a fence post!" Vincent exclaimed, the insight finally getting through.

"Exactly," Harlan said. And then he stepped closer to Vincent and stared into his eyes. "You heard about the boulder that was found inside Leo's pickup, didn't you?"

"Yeah, sure," Vincent said. "The one that came loose from the wall and ended up inside the truck."

"That's not how it got in there," Harlan said.

"Well, how—"

"He put it in there," Harlan said, nodding toward the bagman.

"But why would he—"

"He stood outside the truck," Harlan said, "and used the boulder to floor the gas pedal so that the truck would drive itself off the wall. But when the truck accelerated—"

Harlan paused again.

"He had to step back fast," Phoenix interjected. "And like you said, the wall of the GTB Marina was barely wide enough for just the truck alone, so when he suddenly stepped back—"

"I don't know nothin' 'bout no fuckin' ABC Marina!" Tank shouted.

"The hell you don't!" Harlan shouted back as he jumped into the grave and dug his left foot into the side of Tank's face, deep into the big man's massive jowl.

Pressing Tank's face into the mud, Harlan shouted again, "You thought that boy was dead at the bottom of those stairs, and you panicked—you murderous bastard!"

Tank gagged on muddy water, unable to respond, as Harlan leaned more of his weight into his left foot.

The rain clouds had passed and the moon shone bright. Its glow lit up Harlan's glaring eyes. "Those boys were alive when you hauled them out to that marina and... and..." His voice cracked and tears welled. "And I watched you do it, you son of a bitch, on a computer in my own house!"

The glare intensified to something near demonic as the first tear ran down Harlan's face, the pain of so many misfortunes converging—losing his job, his wife, and his... his...

"Leo! Why did you kill him? You saw that cottage. You knew he could get the money."

Tank choked on a mouthful of mud, trying to respond. "But I... I didn't..."

"The hell you didn't! You tortured Leo, you fucking animal!"

Harlan reached a hand toward Phoenix. "Now, dammit! Gimme a piece!"

Phoenix stood transfixed by the meltdown. "Not so fast, partner," he eventually said. He then reached slowly inside his jacket and withdrew a 480 Ruger double-action revolver. After another pause, he tossed the high-powered handgun a few feet away from the grave and raised a hand toward Harlan.

"You stay right where you are until Vincent and I get all the way back to the guy with the rifle, understood?"

Harlan nodded.

"That guy's got you dialed in right now, and he's gonna keep you dialed in the whole time, understood?"

Harlan nodded again.

"Okay. The Ruger's got three rounds. On my signal, get it and use every one, or the guy with the rifle starts using his. Let's go, Vincent."

After Phoenix and Vincent were underway, Harlan moved his foot down to Tank's back to give him some breathing space. He then turned slightly away from the direction that Phoenix and Vincent were going and whispered, "So how am I doing, Tank?"

"What?"

"From your perspective, down there in the mud, do you think those guys believe I'll actually kill you?"

"Who the hell are you, man?"

"Harlan Holmes."

The name clicked with something Tank remembered Jimmy saying earlier that day. "The PI?"

"Yeah."

"Who you working for?"

"Right now, you."

"Look, man, if you're messing with my head—"

"Shut up and do what I say if you want a chance to live."

After giving some quick instructions, Harlan glanced back. Phoenix and Vincent had already joined the guy with the rifle. When their eyes met, Phoenix gave Harlan a quick nod.

Harlan scampered out of the grave and grabbed the Ruger. Meanwhile, Tank had rolled over to his back, sat up, and struggled as though trying to get to his feet. Harlan jumped back into the grave and drove a foot into the big man's chest, screaming— "Where the hell are you going?"

Tank allowed the kick to slam his body back down to the floor of the shallow grave. Harlan immediately pointed the Ruger and fired off two shots—both into the ground about three inches from Tank's gut. Harlan then pounced forward in the grave toward Tank's head, leaned in, and, before pulling the trigger, whispered, "Stay still." The final shot tore a chunk of flesh from Tank's shoulder. He didn't flinch.

Harlan scraped a hand through the gush of blood coming from the wound and scooped up a handful. He then jumped out of the grave and snatched up the shovel. Standing over Tank at the side of the grave that faced his audience, Harlan triumphantly pumped the shovel overhead, slathered the handful of blood across his face, and turned loose something inhuman—some kind of barbaric war cry that erupted from a dark, primal place deep within.

His thoughts, all along, remained on Leo—*his* 24/7 ward, tortured and killed on *his* watch, right before *his* eyes. He again thrust the shovel in the air and turned loose another primal blast—tears and blood dripping from his face as he stood in the glare of the nearly full moon.

None of the four men subject to the spectacle had ever witnessed anything like it.

And then, just as quickly as the spectacle erupted, Harlan calmly turned to the task of shoveling dirt back into the grave. He began by dumping a few shovel loads on Tank's wounded shoulder to slow the bleeding.

Phoenix was the first to break through his catatonic state. "What the fuck just happened?"

Vincent opened his mouth to respond, but nothing came out.

Phoenix then took a few steps in Harlan's direction and gestured for Vincent to follow.

"I... I'm not so sure..." Vincent stammered as he took a step backward.

"He's right," said the guy with the rifle. "You know," he added, "I've heard stories about guys coming unhinged on the first hit. But this... shit, man... this goes way the hell beyond any of that madness. You better give that guy a few minutes to cool off."

C36

1:02 a.m., Thursday, April 7.

Harlan spoke under his heavy breathing while moving dirt. He explained what had to be done if someone from the crew watching over them came to visit. Tank's expression was blank. No doubt he, too, was overwhelmed by the barbaric graveside ritual that had preceded the burial currently in progress.

"Have you heard anything I've said?" Harlan asked.

"I got it," Tank answered.

"And you have no questions at all?"

"I guess just one."

Harlan stopped moving dirt for a quick glance back at the crew. The guy with the rifle had just lit a cigarette. Harlan, an ex-smoker, knew all about the triggers that surround smoking. Just as there were triggers for lighting up, the act of putting out the smoke was often itself a trigger for some new activity. *We might have only the time it takes him to finish that butt*, he thought. He was back into moving dirt when Tank got to his question.

"That thing you did—that war-dance thing with the blood and the shovel—that was acting, right?"

"Some of it," Harlan answered. He then struggled with the question begged by his response. "The other night at the cottage," he said, "I'm sure that wasn't your first encounter with Leo Surocco."

"Are you kiddin'? I've dealt with that kid as much as anyone in the last few years. He's one of Jimmy's main players."

"Then maybe you have some idea what it'd be like to surveil the little son of a bitch, 24/7, and try to keep him from gambling."

153

"That was your job?"

"Yeah, and yet the damn kid—that royal pain in my ass—somehow got to me. Somehow that kid and me... we... we..."

Harlan couldn't say it because he hadn't yet fully realized just what it was about Leo's death that pained him so personally. But this much he knew for sure: "The boy was my responsibility. I was supposed to keep him safe. Those Surocco guys over there are right—I owe him. And I'm gonna get the son of a bitch who dumped him in that bay."

"And you don't think that's me?"

"We'll talk about that later, after we get through this."

"You actually think we're gonna survive this?" Tank asked.

"We might."

The guy with the rifle eventually finished his cigarette and flicked off the butt. He then looked at Phoenix and said something. Seconds later, Phoenix started walking toward the grave.

"Be ready, Tank, one's coming," Harlan whispered.

At that point, every square inch of Tank's body above his left knee and right ankle was well covered with dirt—except for a small gap around his face through which he breathed.

Shortly after the initial warning, Harlan whispered again, "Three, two, one—hold."

Tank sucked in a load of air during the countdown. The hold command was followed with several shovel loads of dirt and clay aimed at his face.

Phoenix stopped on the other side of the grave. Harlan continued shoveling dirt and clay into it, his head down but angled so that he could watch Phoenix peripherally. Phoenix's eyes scanned back and forth over Tank's buried body and finally paused in the direction of his unburied feet, the enormity of which were exaggerated by their isolated exposure.

"Man, that son of a bitch really was like a Sasquatch," Phoenix said.

Harlan continued moving dirt, head down.

"You alright, Harlan?"

He kept his head down and the shovel moving, like a robot performing a repetitive function according to a set of coded instructions.

"Harlan! Are you okay?"

His seemingly mindless, droid-like effort continued repeating itself.

"Look, man, I need to know if everything is going to be o—"

Harlan stopped moving dirt and picked up his filthy, blood-stained face, eyes glaring.

"... kay..." Phoenix said.

"Just leave me alone," Harlan said through clenched teeth. A grunt followed as he stabbed the shovel into some dirt and returned to his droid-like state.

Phoenix sighed deeply. "Look, I've been where you're at right now—well, not exactly where *you're* at. But I know how the first hit can mess with your head, apparently yours a hell of lot more than most."

Harlan watched peripherally, head down, as he continued moving dirt.

"Oh c'mon, man, snap out of it!" Phoenix shouted. Then he went silent for a few seconds.

Harlan preferred the shouting. The more still the air, the more he could swear he saw vibration in the dirt caused by the bagman's beating heart.

"Would you just put down that damn shovel and talk to me?"

Again the air went still. Harlan thought for sure that the bagman's beating heart was what had caused some dirt to slide down the sides of the pile.

"Alright, if this is how you want it," Phoenix said. He reached into his jacket, withdrew a few items, and tossed them to the ground. Harlan recognized the cell phone. It was his. There was also a wallet and a set of car keys.

"The wallet's his," Phoenix said. "There's some cash in it. Consider it a bonus. The keys are to one of the SUV's. We're leaving it for you. Just wipe it down when you're done with it."

Phoenix paused one more time before leaving. "Nice getting to know you, killer."

C37

1:37 a.m., Thursday, April 7.

"Will you come with me?"

Harlan had no idea where Tank was inviting him to go. And at the moment, he wasn't concerned with finding out. They had unearthed most of Tank's upper body, and Harlan was attending to the gunshot wound. He did what he could to clean and dress it with what was available in his pocket-sized first aid kit.

"Did you hear me?" Tank said.

Harlan nodded. "Where do you want to go?"

"After what those guys put us through, I say we go after 'em."

"Do you know who those guys work for, Tank?"

"Yeah, I've heard about their boss, Angelo Surocco, being a made guy. But right now, with him thinking that you just killed me, we've got the element of surprise. We won't have that if he ever learns I'm still alive. I say we strike now."

"What do you have in mind?" Harlan asked.

"Well, I'll be honest, I've never whacked a guy, but I'm—"

"Whoa, big fella! We're not whacking anybody."

"Then what *is* the plan, Boss?"

Harlan looked away from the wounded shoulder and into Tank's big face. *Boss? What's up with that?* he wondered, until he saw something in the man's eyes that reminded him of his dog, Dozer. "Well, I'm not sure what the plan is," Harlan answered. "I guess it'll depend on what you can tell me about the night you fell down those stairs with Joe Rylands."

"Okay, back up," Harlan said when Tank finished his account of the night in question. "You said that at some point before you left the cottage, after Joe started coming around, Leo tried to explain *the situation* to him. What *situation* was that?"

"Well, Leo was telling Joe the same thing he already told me while Joe was still groggy—you know, that the money wire from Chicago would come to him, to Joe, and that he'd have to handle the drop with me later because College Boy was on the lam."

Harlan paused to reflect on something College Boy had said the day before.

"I'm sure this sounds like total bullshit, Harlan, but I swear—"

"Actually, it doesn't."

"So you believe me?"

Harlan ignored the question. "How did Joe Rylands react to the news that he was going to be the new front guy?"

"Well, he didn't seem too happy about anything at the time. I mean, the kid had just been, you know, kind of traumatized by the fall, which I'm telling you was an accident. I really didn't mean to hurt that kid. Hell, I didn't even know he was there until he jumped on my back."

"I understand," Harlan said.

"But the way it must look, with those boys getting locked in that truck and pitched in the bay, and me being at that cottage right before it happened, whuppin' their asses."

By the time Tank was completely unearthed and free from the duct tape, the exchange had become surreal. The two were up close as Harlan adjusted the dressing he had applied to the shoulder wound. He could feel the man tremble and began imagining what it might be like if he had to put an arm around the three-hundred-pound beast to console him.

"Look, for what it's worth, I don't think you killed Leo," Harlan said as he was about to snap shut his first aid kit. Before doing so, he glanced at the USB flash drive inside.

"Who do you think did?" Tank asked. "Do you think it was College Boy? I'll tell you what, man, that dude's a loose cannon."

Harlan shook his head.

"Well then who?"

Harlan sighed deeply. "The real question is, how am I gonna prove it?"

"Well, is there anything I can do to help?

Harlan nodded.

"Just say the word, Boss, and I'll get it done."

"You need to vanish, completely, for at least a few days."

Harlan took the keys to the SUV out of his pocket. "Those guys left me a car. I want you to use it to go into hiding. But stay in-state. The car is supposed to be VIN-cloned. If that was done right, an SUV just like it in another state has the same VIN number, and you don't want to be driving the clone in whatever state that is."

"But I don't want to just go hide somewhere. I want to help you, man."

Harlan ignored the plea and gave further instructions. "Find a motel somewhere, maybe in the UP, and make just one call from the phone in the room to my office number. I'm listed. Leave a message with a number where I can reach you. Then wait for my call. It'll take a while, so be patient."

Harlan gave Tank the wallet that Phoenix had dropped on the ground. Among the items inside of it were Tank's driver's license and his severance pay from his prior boss.

"Take the cash, but get rid of the wallet and everything else in it," Harlan said. "I don't think the police have linked you to Leo's death yet, but I'm sure it won't be long until they do. If you happen to get pulled over by a cop, you're better off saying you're from out of state, here visiting relatives, and you lost your wallet while traveling."

"But then who am I supposed to—"

"There should be some clean documentation of title in the glove box, in-state registration and proof of insurance. Those are duplicates of documents actually filed with the state listing the cloned VIN number and the name of a fictitious owner."

"How the hell does a fictitious person get into the state's database?" Tank asked.

Harlan shrugged. "I guess that's what happens when skilled car thieves and counterfeiters put their heads together," he said. "But never mind that. You just need to memorize the name and hometown of that owner. That person is a close relative of yours, an aunt or uncle who loaned you the car while you're visiting. You have the same last name, and any first name you want, other than Tank."

"But—"

"And do something to change your appearance."

"Like what?"

"Start by shaving your head."

"But I like my hair."

"I can tell," Harlan said, unable to resist an urge to critique Tank's outdated mullet. "You must be the only guy on the planet who still wears big hair like that, like you're some kind of hard rocker from the eighties. You're already freakish in size, man. You don't need to make yourself stand out more with that big mullet on your head. Shave it, Tank, down to the skin."

Tank frowned, but nodded his head.

After he gave Tank directions back to the highway, Harlan went over his mental checklist of things he wanted to cover before they split up. He had covered everything, and in the process of aiding the fugitive before him, had added some items to another list he was keeping track of—a growing list of felonies he'd committed in the last couple days. *Man, when this is over, I'm history.*

"What about you?" Tank said. "I'm just supposed to leave you here in the middle of nowhere without a car? Where will you go?"

Harlan looked up at the night sky, which was now clear and packed with stars. His face was still stained with blood and dirt. He slowly brought his head back down, looked ahead, and pointed at a spot in the pitch-black woods beyond the clearing.

"I'm going that way."

C38

7:32 p.m., Thursday, April 7.

Angelo stepped away from Leo's closed casket and left his wife with the arduous task of greeting family and friends arriving for a rosary service. Everything about the situation sickened him, especially the smell. It worsened with the influx of visitors whose perfumes, aftershave, and body odor created that distinctly funeral home stench when combined with the aroma of embalming fluid.

Dispersed among the mourners was the equivalent of Angelo's secret service—men in black suits with tiny microphones and earpieces—patrolling the funeral home. Angelo had decided to deploy them as a precaution after hearing about the enigmatic behavior of Harlan Holmes the night before.

Two members of the security team suddenly converged on a spot next to Angelo to block the path of a rapidly approaching man.

"He's okay," Angelo said.

The two stepped aside. It was Tommy MacPherson. "Sorry to bother you, Angelo, but I have to show you something as soon as you're able to free yourself up for a minute."

Angelo welcomed the opportunity to step outside for a smoke. Phoenix and Vincent were already there waiting. Neither made eye contact with Angelo for more than a glance before dropping their heads. "What's the matter with you guys," Angelo asked as he lit a cigarette.

"They've already seen this YouTube recording," Tommy said as he finished tapping the screen to his cell phone and held it before Angelo.

At the moment, Angelo was taking a long drag from his cigarette. The smoke, however, never cleared his windpipe. He choked when he saw the recording of some enormous guy manhandling a flailing police officer in broad daylight. Even though he had never seen the assailant before, Angelo could guess his identity in light of the circumstances.

"What the... Is that the son of a bitch who whacked my son?"

"Yes, Angelo, that's Tank Lochner," Tommy said.

"When did this happen?"

"About two hours ago."

"But how?"

Tank had done as Harlan instructed and fled deep into the Upper Peninsula after leaving the state forestland. He had been going on nothing but junk food until he reached a pizzeria in downtown Iron River, where he stopped for a big meal. Upon his return to the SUV, he punched the remote access button on his car keys—and then he noticed a police officer crouched down beside the vehicle's right front tire.

The sound of the SUV unlocking and a flash of its headlights caused the cop to look up, directly at Tank.

"Excuse me, Officer, is there a problem?"

"So this here is your car, eh?"

"Well, actually no," Tank said. Fortunately, he had followed Harlan's earlier advice and was ready for the situation. Unfortunately, the registrant name that he had committed to memory was quite unusual. "The car... uh... belongs to my uncle. I'm just borrowing it."

"Your uncle's, ya say, eh. Is he gonna pay for your parking ticket too?"

"Parking ticket? For what, Officer?"

"For this right here," the cop answered as he stretched a tape measure from the curb to the sidewall of the tire. "Ya see that, don't ya?"

"You mean the space between the curb and the front tire?"

"I mean the seventeen and three quarter inches between there. That's pretty near six more inches than the limit allowed by city ordinance."

"I'm sorry, Officer. I guess I didn't know about the—"

"Ignorance of the law ain't no excuse in this town, fella. You're still lookin' at a twenty-dollar citation, ya know. Now, let me see your driver's license, eh."

"I'm sorry, Officer, but I'm afraid I lost my license while traveling. You see—"

"What do ya mean, you lost it? How could ya do that?"

"Well, you're not going to believe it, but—"

"I already don't believe it—ya flatlander."

"What'd you just call me?" Tank asked.

"Oh, yeah, that's what you are alright—one of those big-shot flatlanders who comes upstate to the UP with his fancy SUV and thinks he's above our Yooper laws and the Yooper cops who enforce 'em, eh."

"Me, a big shot what? Listen, man, you got this all wrong. I'm just a—"

"What's your uncle's name, flatlander?"

"Well... uh... it's Learned Hand."

"Leonard what?"

"No, officer, I said *Learned*. His name's *Learned Hand*."

"What the hell kind of name is that?"

"Actually, Officer, my uncle's named after a very distinguished historical figure, a man who served honorably on the United States—"

"Oh, I see," the cop said. "You got connections with important people, but ya got no driver's license."

"Please," Tank said, "just check the registration for yourself and you'll see. It's right in the glove box, Officer... what'd you say your name is?"

"Carduzi's the name there, flatlander, Benjamin Carduzi, and I think I will have a look at that registration—you bet ya, I will."

As the officer started toward the passenger door of the SUV, Tank murmured something under his breath, or so he thought. "What kind of backwoods Yooper-cop bullshit is this?"

Officer Carduzi stopped and spun around. "What'd ya just say, buster?"

"Me? Nothing, sir, really. I didn't say—"

"Alright, both paws on the hood of that snow tank—right now!"

"I'm sorry, sir, but I really don't get what you want me to do."

"Now, buster, both *hands* on the hood of that *car* where I can see 'em, eh!"

Tank did as he was told. The officer then backpedaled to the passenger door of the SUV, opened it, and retrieved the registration from the glove box. The car was indeed registered to a "Learned Hand," and the VIN number on the registration certificate matched the one on the car's VIN plate.

"So this Uncle Learned of yours, whereabouts does he live?"

"Cadillac, Michigan, sir."

The officer nodded and then retreated to his vehicle.

"Got me a roadside situation with a scary lookin' troll, wouldn't ya know," Officer Carduzi said into his handset. "Need a check on his VIN and license plate numbers."

"Alright, Benny, I'll get that going," the dispatcher said. "How about the guy's name and D-L number?" he asked.

"Haven't gotten that far yet," Benny said.

"Well, when you do, let me know. We just got an all points on some person of interest in connection with a homicide—a Tank Lochner, from downstate. The guy's described as—"

"What the—" the dispatcher said. "Say, Benny, can you read that VIN number back again?"

Benny read the number again.

"Holy crap!" the dispatcher shouted.

"What's wrong?" Benny asked.

"There's an SUV of the same make and model with the same VIN number, registered to a Dr. DeMay in Roscommon, Michigan."

"And I'll bet that Dr. DeMay has a driver's license," Benny said.

"Sit tight, Benny, backup's on the way."

A police siren could be heard in the distance. As it drew near, Officer Carduzi returned to the SUV. "Ya picked the wrong town to visit with that stolen car, flatlander, yeah, that's for sure, eh."

"What makes you think it's stolen, Officer?"

"Oh, I got my reasons, flatlander, you bet ya I do. By the way, just what is your name?"

Tank cleared his throat and spit on the ground. "Lochner's the name there, flatfoot, Tank Lochner," he answered as he turned from the SUV and faced the officer, whose gun was still holstered. Towering over the scrawny man, he added, "And I've had enough of your shit—you bet ya I have, eh."

"Answer me, dammit! How did this happen?" Angelo shouted.

"Well," Vincent said, "the way I heard it, the cop had his dash and body cameras running, and the authorities released the video right away because for once it wasn't one of a cop abusing a motorist. And the thing went viral."

"For crying out loud, Vincent, I don't give a damn about the video," Angelo said. "I want to know how the hell—"

"Because I fucked up," Phoenix said. "I'm the one who checked on Holmes after the shooting. The son of a bitch duped me with all that psycho shit he was doing."

"So you were conned by a broken down ex-cop," Angelo said.

Phoenix nodded.

"And let him set free the man who tortured my son."

"Look, Angelo, I don't know what else to say here. There's no excuse for it. But please, how about letting me make up for it? Let me take some guys up north and hunt that bagman down."

Angelo paused to light another cigarette off the butt of the first one. "No," he said through the smoke. "Let the cops have him. If they don't do him after what he did to one of their own, we'll get him in the joint."

"What about Holmes? That son of a bitch failed Leo and betrayed us too. Please Angelo, turn me loose on him."

"Remember those guys from Philly?" Angelo said, looking at Tommy.

"Yeah," Tommy answered, "the guys who did that exotic thing for us that time."

"Turn *them* loose on Harlan Holmes, and tell them to do it exactly the way it was done to Leo."

Tommy nodded.

Angelo turned back to Phoenix. "There is something you can do to help clean up your mess. I want you to find this con man, Harlan Holmes. But when you do, you're not to touch him. You hear me? Don't go near him. Just spot him for these guys from Philly, and then step aside and let them do the job. Got it?"

Phoenix nodded and then hung his head. His job had been outsourced, and he had been demoted to spotter.

C39

7:30 p.m., Sunday, April 10.

Harlan turned on the radio and cut into a recording of the feature interview on NPR's Weekend Edition.

"What a lot of people don't understand, Rachel, is that this instant hero is a thug from the underworld who's wanted in connection with the brutal murder of a young man. He certainly shouldn't be celebrated as some kind of champion of the people because he beat up a police officer during a traffic stop."

Hey, I recognize that voice, Harlan thought. *That's—*

"But in all fairness, Detective Summers, he's merely suspected of that homicide. I mean, the man's presumed to be innocent until actually proven guilty in court, isn't he?"

"Of course."

"And certainly you can see how—given the rash of police violence recently captured on video—this enormous bagman who turned the tables has endeared himself to millions of Americans, can't you?"

Wait a minute, are they talking about—

"Oh please, Rachel, let's be clear about who this bagman, Tank Lochner, really is."

"Holy shit, they are!" Harlan shouted. He was alone, driving back to Traverse City in an old pickup truck that had been stored at his family's hunting cabin near Wolverine, Michigan.

After he and Tank had split up back in the state forestland, Harlan had hiked to the cabin and then spent a few days there studying various websites made accessible by some new passwords on Leo's flash drive. From those sites he culled bits of information that he hoped would help nail Leo Surocco's killer. The effort was tedious and time consuming and, along with catching up on some sleep, essentially sequestered Harlan from everything going on in the outside world. This NPR program was his first exposure to anything resembling news.

"Let's bring in our correspondent, Chase Samuels, on location in Iron River, Michigan, where this dark-sided hero fought his way through a police manhunt and into the hearts of many."

"Indeed he did, Rachel. I'm standing here with Officer Benjamin Carduzi, a central figure to the story, in front of the pizzeria where it all happened. On the street before us, perhaps in response to us and another news crew here today, there are still occasional fans of Tank Lochner carrying signs and shouting out words of support to him and his Uncle Learned."

"Oh please, give me a break," Riley interjected. "Don't people realize that this so-called *Learned Hand* is the product of some car thief's imagination?"

"Hold on, Detective, we'll come back to you in just a minute. Right now, let's give our correspondent a chance to ask the officer on the scene for his thoughts about the situation."

C40

8:04 p.m., Sunday, April 10.

"I don't know about you, man, but all this sitting and waiting for some guy who's probably fled the state, maybe even the country, is pissing me off to no end," Vincent said to Phoenix.

For several hours straight, the two had been sitting in the front seat of a car parked a few houses down the street from Harlan's house. And this wasn't their first shift. Angelo had made a point of requiring that they shoulder almost the entire burden of this particular assignment.

"What's pissing me off is being stuck in this car with your nonstop complaining," Phoenix said.

"Hey, man, we wouldn't have this shit duty if—"

"Don't go there, Vincent."

"I'm just saying—"

"And I'm just telling you not to."

Phoenix dropped his head back into his headrest and sighed. "You're right," he said. "I'm the one who got bested by that broken-down ex-cop and got us saddled with this shit duty."

"That's not what I was about to say."

"But that *is* what happened," Phoenix said. "That old man got into my head and actually unnerved me."

"C'mon, man," Vincent said. "Don't you see what's happening here?"

"What are you talking about?"

"I'm talking about you, Phoenix, and the way you've been getting down on yourself ever since that bagman damn near whipped your ass in that back alley."

"But he was stumbling drunk, and I jumped him from behind with a—"

"Just stop it already!" Vincent shouted.

After a pause, Vincent sighed. "I'll tell you what's really pissing me off, a whole hell of a lot more than this stakeout," he said. "It's knowing that those guys from Philly are just sitting around on their fat asses in some five-fucking-star hotel, ordering room service and watching porn on TV, waiting for us to call them and step aside so they can come along at their leisure to close the deal."

Phoenix offered a barely perceptible nod as Vincent continued. "We're talking about a guy who made fools of both of us—you *and* me—and set my brother's assassin free. I mean it, man, if this son of bitch Harlan Holmes shows himself, I'm closing that deal. And nobody but you is doing it with me."

This kind of unrestrained talk was typical of Vincent, no matter the circumstances. He must have known how seriously ill-advised it would be to blatantly disregard his father's orders and usurp the role of his specially chosen contractors.

But Vincent is the man's son, Phoenix thought. *He can get away with that kind of defiance. There's no way I can, unless...*

"I'm sorry, Vincent, I was caught up in my own thoughts and missed almost everything you just said."

"How could you do that? You're sitting right next—"

"I'm telling you, man, all I caught was something about you hoping that Harlan Holmes will show himself. And it got me to thinking about how hard it would be for me to control the impulse to jump out of this car and chase his ass down."

"Hold on. You didn't hear me say—"

"And then I remembered what your dad said, how serious he was, and the impression that made on me. So I'm pretty sure that I'll be able to control myself if we see that son of a bitch, Harlan Holmes. My real concern, I just realized, is you. I mean, if you were to impulsively charge out of this car so fast that I couldn't stop you, well, I couldn't just sit back and watch you go mano a mano with that wily ex-cop."

"I would hope not," Vincent said. A hint of a smile showed on his face.

"Of course not," Phoenix said. "I would have no choice but to follow after you and help you do the very thing your dad told us not to do."

"Well, yeah, we're partners after all."

"And the worst part would come later, after we did the thing your dad told us not to do, when we're telling him that we did it. I'd have to tell him the truth, you know, because he's my boss and all, which means I'd be throwing you, my partner, under the bus."

"Well, I guess I'd have that coming, you know, after putting you in such a predicament in the first place," Vincent said, his smile broadening.

"So I guess what I'm trying to say, Vincent, is that I need you to promise that you won't put me in that predicament because the last thing I want to do is the thing your dad told us not to do and then have to throw you under the bus for making me do it."

Vincent smiled fully. "Rest assured, partner, I'd never put you in such a predicament," he said. He then extended a tight fist toward Phoenix, who returned the gesture for a fist bump much like the ones they used to share before taking to the mat back in their college wrestling days.

C41

8:27 p.m., Sunday, April 10.

"Hey, Boss, I had... uh... a little trouble up north and needed somewhere to stay. Hope you don't mind me using your place. When you get this message, call your office and hang up after two rings. Then call again right away and I'll pick up. Make sure to call first before coming. Someone's staking out your house."

Harlan sighed deeply when the voicemail message ended. He was about twenty minutes from Traverse City, pacing around outside a gas station off the highway with his cell phone in hand. Eventually he did as Tank suggested.

"What's happening, Boss?"

"Why don't you tell me, beginning with what you've been doing since your cinematic debut in Iron River."

"You know about that, huh?"

"Is there anyone on the planet who doesn't?"

"Sorry, Boss, but it really wasn't my fault. I tried to be cool, but that Yooper cop was—"

"Let's talk about that later, Tank. Obviously, you got through the police dragnet in the UP. How'd you manage that?"

"I slipped by 'em at the Straits."

"The Mackinac Straits?"

"What other straits are there around here?" Tank said.

"But the cops must have been stopping every vehicle crossing the bridge."

"I didn't use the bridge. I swam."

"You swam?"

"Yeah, at night, about a mile west of the bridge."

"Through five miles of frigid water?"

"Sure, it's no big deal," Tank said. "I've done it before, a few years ago in the Mighty Mac Swim—you know, that swim they do on Labor Day. The hard part was finding a wet suit that fit me. I must've searched a dozen dive boats before I found one I could squeeze into."

"What about search boats, Tank? There had to be at least a few in that area."

"Well, after burying me alive back in the forest, you, of all people, should know how long I can hold my breath."

"True. Where'd you come ashore when you got downstate?"

"McGulpin Rock, right at the top of the mitten. After that, I laid low until daybreak and then rode a bike to your place."

"A motorcycle?"

"No, a bicycle I found on someone's porch right there on the coast."

"You rode a hundred miles on a bicycle?"

"Sure. Have you ever heard of that annual bike ride from Lansing to Mackinaw City, the DALMAC? I used to—"

"Alright, Tank. We can talk about this later. Tell me about the surveillance on my house. Is it cops or a Surocco thing?"

"I can't tell for sure, Boss. Most of it's being done by whoever's in the black Impala parked out front right now, a couple houses down the street. I'm looking at 'em right now from your front window, but I can't make 'em out."

Harlan glanced at the horizon, where the sun had set a few minutes ago. It would be dark soon. He told Tank where he could find a pair of binoculars in the house. A couple minutes later Tank reported back.

"It's the guys from the forestland, minus the guy with the rifle."

"I'll be there in twenty minutes."

"Hold on, Boss. Maybe we should meet somewhere else, where it's safer."

"How should I come in?"

"Well, if that's your plan, do it the way I did, on foot from the east, through your neighbors' backyards. And then use the side door to your garage. By the way, Boss, I kind of busted up that door to get inside."

Harlan sighed. "Is there anything else I should know?"

"I guess. You might want to know about the food situation here."

"What about it?"

"Well, you know, I've been here a couple days, and basically there's none left, other than the dog food stored in the laundry room, which has actually started looking pretty good to me lately."

"I guess I should be grateful that the kid across the street took my dog in for a few days, or he'd probably be looking pretty good to you too."

"Sorry, Boss. I don't mean to be a bother while you're doing work that might clear me. I'd like to be more help."

"No worries, Tank. There is one thing you can do before I get there."

"Just name it."

"I want you to shave your damn head, like I told you to back in the forestland."

"But how did you know that—"

"How could I not know? I've seen the video for crying out loud, along with a hundred million other people. Now shave that damn mullet off, down to the skin, before I get there, you hear?"

"Okay Boss."

"And get yourself a mustache too."

"Well, I can't very well grow one before you get here."

"No, but you can glue one on with the spirit gum and false facial hair I have in the bathroom upstairs, in one of the drawers under the sink."

No lights were on in the house when Harlan came through the garage entrance into the kitchen. After his eyes adjusted to the dark, he wished he hadn't come home. The place was a disaster. Dirty dishes were everywhere, the wastebasket overflowed with smelly trash, and cupboards had been left wide open following Tank's plunder.

Harlan made his way to the front room, where he quickly discerned the outline of Tank's massive frame. It was perched on a stool by the front window. As Harlan got closer, Tank's facial features came into focus. They were made even scarier by the cosmetic changes. The big man didn't look up. He instead continued to peer out between the curtains while spooning the last of some uncooked bacon and beans straight from the can into his face.

"Nice of you to drop by, Boss."

"Nice of you to invite me," Harlan said, as he stepped over an empty box of Cheerios lying on the floor. "I love what you've done with the place."

Tank pointed out the Impala. Its engine was running.

"Looks like they're going to leave," Harlan said.

"No, I'm sure they're just warming up the car. They do that every once in a while after sunset."

"The same car stays out there overnight?"

"Yep," Tank said. "They must take turns sleeping. I'm not sure where they piss and shit. Only once in a while is there a different car out there to spell them, and usually not for very long."

Harlan left for the office to collect a few items and print off some documents he had put together while at the cabin. When he returned, he set the items on the coffee table.

Tank turned for a look. "That's your arsenal?" It was just two pistols and a stun gun.

Harlan nodded.

"What's the plan, Boss?"

"We need to find out the extent of Surocco's manhunt, whether it's just these two guys or something more, which I suspect it is, a lot more. I guess we'll have to make a move on these guys and try to find out what they know."

"Oh yeah, I like it," Tank said. "Can I have 'em for few minutes before you start asking questions?"

Harlan rolled his eyes. "Look, Tank, we have to approach this with—"

"Wait," Tank said, exploding to his feet. "I know what to do. In five minutes, you turn on the porch light and walk out to your mailbox and check your mail."

Tank grabbed the stun gun and ran for the kitchen door leading into the garage.

Harlan sprang from the couch and tried to catch up. "Hold on, Tank, you haven't told me what your..."

"plan is," Harlan said as the door closed behind Tank.

C42

9:12 p.m., Sunday, April 10.

Harlan thought about his options. He could do as Tank instructed, or he could just stay in the house until Tank got tired of waiting for him and returned. Then he recalled the harm that Tank had inflicted upon Phoenix the night Tank was stumbling drunk and *Phoenix* was the one with the element of surprise.

Five minutes later, Harlan flipped on the porch light and walked to his mailbox, which was located across the street from his house.

That's odd, he thought. He had been gone for days, yet there was nothing in the mailbox, not a single one of his daily papers or any of the usual junk mail.

On his return, Harlan stopped in the middle of the street when he heard a loud crash. He looked down the street and saw a garbage can coming to rest in front of the Impala. Tank Lochner followed it, clinging to the collars of two droopy individuals, dragging them off like a lion with its prey.

Moments later Harlan stopped again, this time to the voice of his next-door-neighbor, Mrs. Stella McDonald. She had just opened her front door and immediately spotted him.

"Did you hear that, Harlan? It sounded like a crash," the eighty-seven-year-old woman said before risking a sip from a steamy coffee mug uneasily secured in her trembling hand.

"Hi, Stella. I wouldn't worry about it. It's probably just Mr. Prosser's cat getting into someone's garbage."

Harlan knew that the woman despised cats, and especially Skeeter. Years ago he had wandered into her yard and dropped a live mouse right under her face while she was on her hands and knees pulling weeds.

"That good-for-nothin', flea-bitten Skeeter, always causin' trouble," Stella said. Harlan nodded and tried to say goodnight.

"Oh, Harlan, before you leave, let me get your mail and newspapers. Yesterday I noticed them overflowing from your mailbox and thought it best to bring them in—you know, so it wouldn't look like you were gone."

"Well, thank you, Stella, I really appreciate that. You can't be too careful these days, with all the hoodlums on the streets."

"You can say that again, Harlan. I'm sure you've heard all about that Traverse City Bagman who struck in the UP last week."

"Who hasn't?" Harlan said. "I just hope that scary monster never returns to Traverse City."

C43

9:22 p.m., Sunday, April 10.

Harlan stopped outside the side door to the garage. From inside he could hear the sounds of human suffering. He waited a few minutes and then entered.

"Is that you, Harlan? Call him off, please!" Vincent begged from beneath the bagman. Both hostages were pinned to the concrete floor between Tank's massive thighs as he administered open-handed slaps, back and forth, across their faces.

"Have you answered his questions?" Harlan asked.

"I told him everything I know, man. Please, make him stop!"

"Did he, Tank?"

"Yep."

"Okay, then, that's enough. You can stop now."

He didn't.

"Tank, did you hear me? What are you doing?"

"Just slappin' 'em around a little extra."

Harlan retrieved a roll of duct tape from a shelf and dropped it on the floor next to Tank. "Okay. When you're done with that, tie them up. I'll be back in a—"

He paused. Something occurred to him. Working his way around Tank, Harlan searched their hostages.

"I already disarmed 'em, Boss," Tank said.

Harlan shook his head. "That's not what I'm looking for." He eventually found their cell phones and the keys to the Impala and took the items with him when he left.

A few minutes later, Harlan returned to the garage with his pickup truck. By then, Tank was done disciplining their hostages and had them seated back-to-back, bound and gagged, on the floor in the middle of the garage.

"What'd they tell you?" Harlan asked.

"Kind of what we figured," Tank answered. "Surocco's after you, big time, with a manhunt that includes some pros from Philly. They're supposed to dump you in the bay, the way it happened to Leo. But they're not after me, at least not until I'm in the joint."

Harlan handed a cell phone to Tank. "It's mine. I'll call you on it later from one of their cells," he said, nodding toward their hostages.

"We're not splitting up again, are we?"

Harlan nodded.

Tank looked like a disappointed school kid. "Are you still upset with me for the thing I did in Iron River?"

"No. I just need your help with something I can't do right now."

"Yeah, what's the plan, Boss?"

"You'll hear all about it in a minute."

Harlan produced another cell phone, turned to Vincent, and asked, "What's the password?" Vincent mumbled something. "Come again," Harlan said after removing Vincent's gag.

Harlan put the gag back on Vincent's face, booted up the cell phone, and pulled up Angelo's name from the contact list. He then sat down next to Vincent and motioned for Tank to join him, on Vincent's other side.

"Look pretty for the camera, Vincent," Harlan said as he raised the phone to a selfie position and tapped "FaceTime."

Angelo took the call. "What's going on Vin—"

Several seconds of silence ensued while Angelo stared back at them. Harlan had the phone positioned so that Angelo would see clearly the face of his only surviving son, mouth gagged, between his and Tank's faces.

"What the hell is this, Holmes? Turn my son loose or I'll... I'll..."

"Or you'll what, hire some more guys from Philly to come get me?"

"Listen, you son of a bitch—"

"Oh c'mon, Angelo, how about shutting up and listening to me for a change, so maybe you can find out how to get Vincent back unharmed."

Angelo took a deep breath. "Alright, Holmes, what do you want?"

"I want you to let me do my job."

"What job?"

177

"Nailing the guy who killed Leo."

"You had a chance to do that last week, to nail that big bastard right there with you now. That's him, isn't it, the big guy right there in that asinine disguise?"

"Tank Lochner's never whacked anyone in his life," Harlan said. "But that'll change if anything unfortunate happens to me in the next twenty-four hours."

"I've never popped a guy's cherry either," Tank said, "but that'll also change if you hurt my boss." He then grabbed Vincent by the back of the neck, turned his head, and planted a big kiss on his gagged mouth.

Vincent writhed and let loose a muffled scream.

"Shut up, bitch, or I'll slap ya' around some more!" Tank shouted as he feigned a backhand to Vincent's face.

Vincent winced and screamed again.

"Well, Angelo," Harlan said, "will you stand down so I can finish my work, or should I turn the bagman loose?"

"Can you control that sadistic son of a bitch?"

"He's not so bad, Angelo, if you're nice to him and me."

Tank smiled broadly for the camera.

Angelo's angry expression turned sullen. "If he didn't kill Leo, who do you think did?"

"Tomorrow, Angelo," Harlan said, "we should know everything—the killer, the motive, the whole nine yards. I just need to put a few more things together, and I need to be able to move about freely to do it."

As Angelo shook his head, Harlan saw someone pass through the screen behind him. "Who's with you?" Harlan asked.

"Never mind who's with me, Holmes. If you want my cooperation, you're gonna have to answer my questions."

"Alright," Harlan said, "what do you want to know?"

"For starters, just what the hell you mean when you say that you just want to *do your job* and *finish your work*. What job are you talking about? And who's paying you to do it? You're obviously not working for me anymore, you fucking con man."

The question stirred something inside Harlan, some kind of recurring reaction that was happening lately whenever he caught himself thinking seriously about why he was still working this case.

The reactions were getting stronger, and stuffing them down harder.

Harlan looked away from the phone and swallowed hard, as if that might prevent his voice from trembling when he answered. It didn't.

"He... he died right in front of me, Angelo... on that damn computer screen of mine. I can't just let it go."

"What's going on with you?" Angelo asked, his face enlarging on the screen as he moved closer to his phone, apparently trying to get a better look at Harlan.

"It's nothing, Angelo," Harlan said, regaining his composure. "I just want to get the guy who killed Leo, that's all. I'm doin' it for me and... and him."

At this point, Angelo's face was so close to his phone that all Harlan could see on his screen was a distorted image of the man's nose and one eye. "C'mon, Holmes, tell me who you think killed Leo."

"Not yet," Harlan said, shaking his head.

"Well, just what do you have planned for tomorrow?"

"A sit-down, where we'll confront Leo's killer with the evidence, and if we're lucky, he'll come clean."

"Where's this gonna happen, Holmes?"

"Well, it's not gonna happen at all if you don't give me some space to put it together."

"Alright, if I back off, when and where is this sit-down gonna happen?"

"You'll get a call from me tomorrow afternoon, around four. I'll tell you then where it is. And sometime after my call, you'll get one from Tank Lochner telling you where to send someone for Vincent and Phoenix during the sit-down."

"Why won't *you* be the one telling me about their location?"

"Because I won't know where that is."

Angelo either jerked back his head or suddenly extended his hand holding the phone. His whole face was now on Harlan's screen.

"Wait a minute," Angelo said. "Are you telling me that Vincent and Phoenix are gonna be held hostage by that Neanderthal, and nobody, not even you, is gonna know where they are?"

"Yeah, baby," Tank interjected, "and we'll be havin' ourselves a real good time."

Harlan quickly turned the phone away. "That's enough" he whispered to Tank. Harlan knew that the deal had to be closed soon. Angelo might well have already dispatched some soldiers to the house on the chance that he and Tank had remained there after nabbing Vincent and Phoenix.

"Holmes, where'd you go?"

"I'm right here, Angelo," he answered, returning to the phone.

"Listen, Holmes, I don't trust that freak."

"Angelo, I give you my word, no harm will come to—"

"Your word? What kind of fool do you take me for? I've seen for myself the way you've jerked around the cops. And I've heard all about the way you jerked around my men. You actually think I'm going to trust you?"

Harlan's sight blurred as tears welled in his eyes. But his voice did not shake this time. It seethed. "I mean it, Angelo. I'm gonna nail the bastard who killed Leo, if you'll just stand down and let me do it."

The person who had passed behind Angelo earlier now stood behind him, holding a cell phone to his ear. Harlan couldn't make him out. He seemed to be waiting, probably for an instruction from Angelo that would be relayed to men on their way to Harlan's house at that moment.

"Is that Phoenix I see behind you?" Angelo asked.

"Yeah," Harlan answered.

"Let me talk to him."

Harlan walked around to Phoenix, removed the gag from his mouth, and held the phone in front of the two of them.

Angelo shook his head with a look of disgust. "Do you remember at the funeral home the other day," he said, "when you practically begged me for a chance to make things right?"

Phoenix nodded.

"Well, this is your chance. And I'm telling you, Phoenix, it's the last chance you'll ever get. You understand?"

Phoenix nodded again.

"Okay, stop looking at me, and look at the son of a bitch holding the phone, right there next to you. He says he's been jerking you around because the bagman didn't kill Leo, that somebody else did it, and he's gonna nail the guy if we give him some space to do it. And when he talks about Leo, he damn near cries, like he really means what he's saying. But I don't know what to make of him. He's burned you twice. I gotta believe you'd never let that happen again. So tell me—and dammit, Phoenix, you have to get it right this time—should I trust him?"

Phoenix stared at Harlan.

Harlan stared back, his vision still blurred by the tears that had welled in them.

"What was it you said?" Phoenix asked.

Harlan cocked his head. "When?" he asked.

"Back in the forestland," Phoenix said, "the first time I saw you cry, you said something—you shouted something—right when the first tear ran down your face."

A look of realization came across Phoenix's face. He turned back to the phone.

"He means what he's saying, Angelo."

C44

9:55 p.m., Sunday, April 10.

"So you know what to do, right?" Harlan asked.

"I got it, Boss. Call Angelo Surocco tomorrow afternoon, a quarter past four, and tell him where these two are. And then I'm supposed to just leave them there for his guys to pick up."

The two were in the garage, going over Tank's assignment while they finished securing Phoenix and Vincent in the backseat of the pickup truck.

"And you know what *not* to do, right?"

Tank sighed. "Yeah, I know, no jerking Surocco around, no assaulting police officers, basically, none of my usual stuff."

"Alright, then, I really have to go," Harlan said. "Are you okay to finish this up?"

Tank nodded. "I don't know what to say, Boss. You keep taking chances to do something that would clear me of what happened to Leo. I just wish there was more I could do for you."

"You know, Tank, I hate to say this, but about all you can do for me after this is act like we've never met. I'm already in deep shit, and if I'm ever linked to you, it'll get worse for me and no better for you."

Harlan shook the man's hand and said goodbye, expecting to talk with him by phone later that evening, but never see him again.

A few minutes later, Tank was ready to go. He slammed the pickup's tailgate shut.

Suddenly, a sleek mass of jet-black hair shot out from under the truck, right between Tank's feet. He stumbled backward, regained his balance, and then watched a black cat make a run for it. In its path stood a large metal trash can in front of the neighbor's garage.

The cat tried to hurdle the can but came up short and, instead, reorienting its body in midair like only a cat can, segued from the top of the can with a blast from its hind legs that launched it onward, like a diver exploding off a springboard.

Following the launch the cat let loose a scream, as if complaining at whoever had placed the obstacle there to begin with. The garbage can then spun twice and crashed.

Tank hurried to the driver's door, opened it and jumped in, and then—"Oh, man, the keys." He had left them in the bed of the truck.

As Tank returned with the keys, the front door of the neighbor's house flung open and a woman bellowed, "Skeeter, get out of my yard you no-good, mangy old—"

Tank looked up. The woman was staring right at him.

"Who the heck are you?" she shouted. "And what are you doing in that garage?"

Tank fumbled for an answer. "Uh... I'm Harlan's cousin, just here picking up a couple of... uh... things that he doesn't want in his garage anymore."

"Well, where's Harlan?"

"Out running a few errands."

The woman tilted her head and looked intensely at the big man. "You look familiar," she said. "Real familiar. I'm certain I've seen you somewhere before. My name's Stella MacDonald. What's yours?"

Just about any fake name would have worked well in this situation. But Tank still managed to choose poorly. He just couldn't get his train of thought to steer clear of the only bogus identity he had recently memorized.

"Learned Hand," he said, wishing immediately he could take the words back.

"Leonard who?"

"No ma'am, it's *Learned Hand*."

"What the hell kind of name is that?" Stella asked.

"Actually, ma'am, I'm named after a very distinguished historical figure, a man who served honorably on the United States—"

He stopped himself, realizing that the exchange was tracking one that had been replayed many times on television when the story of the Traverse

City Bagman was embedded in the cable news cycle.

"I just know I've heard that name somewhere before," Stella said.

"I doubt it, ma'am. It's not very common."

"Well, Learned, your parents must have been pretty hopeful. I'll bet they thought you'd grow up to be some kind of intellectual."

Tank nodded and tried to say goodnight.

"Hold on, Learned. It's really bothering me that I can't figure out where I've seen you before. Tell me, where are you from?"

Tank resisted the urge to say Cadillac, Michigan, which of course was where he had told the UP cop his Uncle Learned resided. But that train of thought led him to an even worse choice.

"I'm from the UP... uh... wouldn't ya know, eh."

"You don't say. Anywhere near Iron River, where the Traverse City Bagman struck last week?"

Oh crap, Tank thought. He could practically see the tumblers slowly turning in the woman's head.

"Uh... what's that, ma'am... you asking me something about the Motor City Madman?"

"No, for gosh sakes, the Traverse City Bagman. You know, the thug who attacked that cop in the UP last week."

At this point, it seemed impossible for Tank's decision making to get any worse. Yet it did. He thought better of trying to deny knowledge of such a newsworthy event, so he opted for the opposite course.

"Oh, that guy," Tank said. "Sure, I've heard of him. He's the monster who attacked my Uncle Benny."

Stella's eyes widened. "Wait a minute," she said. "Are you saying the cop who got thrashed by that bagman is your uncle?"

"Yeah."

"Well then why didn't your cousin Harlan say something about him when we talked about this just a little while ago?"

"Uh... cuz he's a cousin on the other side, once or twice removed, and, uh—"

"Oh never mind, Learned. The way my old brain works, I won't remember where I've seen you until some memory stuck in my head somewhere shakes loose and wakes me up in the middle of the night."

C45

10:02 p.m., Sunday, April 10.

Harlan had left his house a few minutes ago, driving the Impala left behind by his visitors. "C'mon, Nikki, pick up," he said into Vincent's cell phone. He had texted her earlier from the same phone and told her he'd be calling from it in a little while. "Maybe she didn't read the—"

"Mr. Holmes?"

"Yeah, Nikki. Sorry to call so late. I had some unwanted houseguests and it took forever to get rid of them. I was hoping you might let me drop by your place so we could talk about something that's kind of urgent."

"What's so urgent that it can't wait until tomorrow?" she asked.

"Can I tell you when I see you?"

Nikki escorted him through her small apartment and offered him a seat at a table in an area that served as both a living and dining room. There was a laptop on the table opened to what appeared to be a document. Before Harlan was close enough to make out any details, Nikki closed the laptop. "You're lucky I was up working on something," she said.

Harlan set a manila folder on the table before sitting down. The folder was stuffed with documents.

"This looks like it might take a while," Nikki said, glancing at the folder. "Would you like something to drink?"

"Sure. Maybe just a glass of—"

Just then a child wearing Spiderman pajamas appeared behind Nikki and grabbed her hand.

"I'm sorry, Nikki, I didn't even know that you had—"

"Give me a minute to put Luke back to bed," she said.

When she returned, Nikki set a glass of water in front of Harlan and sat across from him at the table. He tried to engage her in some small talk about her son. Her responses were short.

"Well, maybe I should just get to the point."

"Please do." Nikki said.

"Last week I found this hidden at the Surocco cottage," Harlan said as he reached into his shirt pocket and removed the USB flash drive. He set it on the table and said, "It contains some password information that got me into an online cloud storage system containing, among other things, some GTU law exams."

"Okay," Nikki said, "and you're telling me this because..."

"Because clearly one or both of the boys was cheating on exams at GTU Law," Harlan said.

"And this is what couldn't wait until tomorrow, Mr. Holmes?"

Harlan nodded.

"And this is something that Mr. Surocco has kept you on the payroll to investigate?"

"Well, I'm not exactly getting paid for what I'm doing these days."

"Okay, Mr. Holmes, then what, exactly, are you *not* getting paid to do *here* in my apartment at ten o'clock on a Sunday night?"

"If you'll just bear with me, Nikki, you'll see."

She placed her elbows on the table and leaned forward. "Alright, I'm listening," she said.

Harlan took a sip of water and then removed a document from his folder and placed it before her. It was a three-column spreadsheet. The first column listed the names of nine courses offered at GTU Law and the professors who taught them over the past three years. Harlan pointed at the column. "The exams for those nine courses were the ones I found stashed in that cloud."

Nikki's eyes scanned down the page and then returned to Harlan. "Where in the cottage did you find the flash drive?" she asked.

"It was in one of the upstairs bedrooms, locked in a wall safe that only Leo and I knew the combination to."

"So the exams for these courses were in Leo's possession?"

Harlan nodded as he reached into the folder again and withdrew nine documents. He set the stack in front of Nikki, next to the spreadsheet. She thumbed through the first eight quickly. The last in the stack was an exam in advanced criminal law that was scheduled for the following afternoon. Nikki spent a full minute looking at that one.

"Practically none of the profs release their exams," she said. "How did Leo get these?"

"I don't know how Leo got them, but I have a theory about how Joe Rylands got them in the first place."

"What makes you think that Joe ever had them? You just said that the password was on a flash drive that only Leo and you had access to."

"Joe obviously had access, Nikki. Just look at the second column of the spreadsheet, the column titled *Joe*. It lists his grades on the first eight of those exams."

Nikki looked at the spreadsheet. "So what if Joe got straight A's on those exams," she said as she looked up. "He's a good student. What makes you think he cheated?"

"Well," Harlan said, "those are the only A's he's ever received on exams at GTU Law."

"How do you know about—"

"In fact," Harlan added, "he's barely averaged a C+ on the rest of the exams he's taken over the years."

"Where did you get—"

"And he's scheduled to take the ninth exam listed there, for advanced criminal law, tomorrow."

Nikki looked back down at the spreadsheet and paused. "This last column here," she eventually said, "the one titled *Leo*—why does it list only three grades?"

"Because he didn't take the other five exams. Those were courses he either took from another prof or didn't take at all."

"And Leo's three grades," she said, "the A- and two B's, how do they compare with his other grades?"

"They're right in sync with his B+ average."

After another pause, Nikki asked, "Where'd you get Joe's grade information? His transcript is a private record—actually school property—available only to him and a few people at the school through a password-protected portal."

"That password was also on Leo's flash drive," Harlan said as he picked the device up from the table and returned it to his shirt pocket.

"How did Leo get Joe's password information?"

"I have no idea," Harlan said.

"But you claim to have a theory about how Joe got ahold of these exams in the first place. So you think Joe had them first, and then Leo got them from Joe somehow."

Harlan nodded.

"Okay, what's your theory?"

"Look again at the first two courses listed on the spreadsheet, Nikki."

Nikki sighed. "I don't need to," she said. "You're trying to draw my attention to the torts exam in Joe's first semester and his remedies exam in the second, aren't you, because those were given by Professor Caparo, my boss."

Harlan nodded.

"And you figure that the boss's secretary—who's been romantically involved with Joe since he started law school—would have had access to those two exams."

Harlan nodded.

Nikki smiled and added, "And who knows, she might even have access to a shared computer drive at the school where some of the other profs—the ones not scared of technology—post their exams for internal use."

"Well, I can't say that I knew specifically about a shared drive," Harlan said, "but something like that helps explain the other exams."

"I'd tell you that you're full of shit, Mr. Holmes, but you're not. What you are, though, is a mystery."

"What do you mean?"

"You've obviously worked some long hours, without pay, putting together this evidence of cheating. But what difference does it make to you?"

Harlan looked away.

Nikki leaned forward. "C'mon, Mr. Holmes, you didn't come here at ten o'clock on a Sunday night just to put this in my face. You're up to something."

"Just doing my job."

"Yeah, right," Nikki said, rolling her eyes. "And what the hell is your *nonpaying* job these days—proving that Joe and I are cheaters and that maybe Leo wasn't? Stop dickin' around, Mr. Holmes, and tell me why the hell you care about Leo's possible involvement with our exam cheating before he... he was—"

Oh shit, it's happening again, Harlan realized as another bout of emotion hit him on the heels of Nikki's remark. And by the look on her face, she saw it.

Harlan tried to look at her and say something, but he couldn't. Her question about his motives had derailed him, the same way he had been derailed earlier that evening when Angelo Surocco asked him why he was still working the case. His reaction this time was even more intense. He wasn't sure he could suppress the tears.

"Are you okay, Mr. Holmes? You look like you're about to get sick. Can I get you something, maybe some more water?"

The man needed to talk with someone about this, preferably someone who knew and cared about him, but he had nobody like that in his life these days. Inexplicably, he opted for her.

"There was a GPS device on Leo's truck the night it went into the bay. I put it there. And it was transmitting a signal to me at the time, on my computer at home."

"You watched it happen?"

Hearing somebody else say it out loud was excruciating. A tear broke through. Harlan wiped it off his face and looked away.

"Mr. Holmes, do you understand what's happening to you right now?"

Harlan said nothing as he stared into space.

"You're grieving over the loss of Leo."

He turned to look at her but said nothing.

"You don't get it, do you?" Nikki said. "Sometimes men can be such dumb asses."

Harlan was startled out of his silence by the woman's abrupt style of grief counseling. "Well, I guess I came to care about him, but I have no idea why. He was such a conniving little son of a bitch."

"Just like you, Mr. Holmes."

"Like me?"

"Sure, don't you see it? Until this whole thing happened with Leo, I thought you were some uptight ex-cop who played everything by the book. But then I saw the way you played those two cops outside Joe's hospital room last week so we could get in to see him. And later on Joe tells me that he heard something about a con you ran on Mr. Surocco's guys to keep the bagman alive, for God knows what reason. And now here you are, in my apartment on a Sunday night, obviously trying to play me. You've got me pegged as some kind of wild card in some scheme of yours, don't you?"

Harlan couldn't help but smile.

"Oh yeah, you're just like Leo," Nikki said. "You thrive on this kind of action, making big plays. But Leo will never make another one. Somebody took that from him when they threw him into the bay. And you're taking it personally for some reason. My guess is that it has something to do with how you got booted from the police force. Leo once said that you can get real moody about that. Yeah, you're out to prove something alright, but not who's been cheating on exams."

She paused, returned a smile, and added, "Now, why don't you tell me what you're really up to, Mr. Holmes, you conniving little son of a bitch."

Harlan laughed. She had totally snapped him out of his funk. "I'll make you a deal, Nikki. I'll tell you all about what I'm up to, if you'll do two things for me."

She leaned forward.

"First, I think you should stop calling me Mr. Holmes. Obviously, I'm only older than you in years."

"That's easy enough, Harlan. What's the other thing?"

"You have to tell me, first, about the play *you're* making on Joe tomorrow."

A long silence passed between them. Nikki glanced at her laptop, then at the stack of documents on the table, and then back at Harlan. He leaned forward and separated the final exam for advanced criminal law from the others.

"The metadata on this one—the exam Joe's taking tomorrow—is unusual," he said.

"The *meta* what?" Nikki said.

"It's a Word document, Nikki. Behind the text of its digital version there's stored all kinds of background information, metadata, about the document, like who created it, when they created it, who last revised it, all kinds of information like that."

"And what's so unusual about the metadata on that one?"

"It's not one of Professor Caparo's exams, yet the last person to revise it was you. That makes no sense, unless you also work for this other prof, the one who taught advanced criminal law."

Nikki didn't respond.

"And according to the metadata," Harlan said, "you spent over ninety minutes revising it, but the word and character counts remained absolutely unchanged. All I can think is that you moved things around for some reason, maybe the order of the questions... or maybe..."

"The order of the picks," Nikki said.

"What do you mean by *picks*?"

"The answer choices that students pick from for the multiple-choice questions, I changed the order of them on the version of the document I gave to Joe."

"Okay, maybe you could elaborate on that a little."

"Look, Harlan, the first time Joe asked me to help him cheat, I refused. But he told me a sad story about how he had some learning disability that slowed him down on exams, especially the multiple-choice questions. He told me all he needed was a little more time to work through them. It wasn't like he needed to really cheat, at least that's what he said. In fact, he told me that he didn't want any answer keys for those questions."

Nikki paused as Harlan glanced into space. "What is it?" she asked.

"Just thinking about the hours I spent in Leo's cloud looking for those answer keys. It struck me as useless to have the questions but not the answers."

"Well," Nikki continued, "Joe told me that he wanted to figure them out himself by working through the questions at home, at his own pace. And then when he sat for the exam, the first thing he'd do is fill in the multiple-choice answer sheet with his own memorized answer key—without having to take the time to read through all the questions. That would leave him with almost the entire exam period to work on the essay questions, which he said he wasn't even going to look at in advance."

"And this all began," Harlan said, "with what you described as a *sad* story Joe told you about a learning disability."

"Uh huh."

"Do you believe it—that he has some disability?"

"Not now, but at the beginning I did. That's why I stole the first exam for him. But I told him that I wouldn't do it again and that he needed to see a doctor and get his disability documented so the school would have to give him extra time on exams."

"Did Joe ever do that?" Harlan asked.

"No, I don't think he ever saw a doctor about it," she said, "at least not one who'd give him the diagnosis he needed."

"Why did you keep helping him?"

Nikki sighed. "Believe me, Harlan, I didn't want to. We argued about it at the end of practically every semester, when he'd start pestering me about whether I could get any of his exams from the shared drive. He was so stressed about the B average he needed to keep his scholarship. Like your research into his grade point average shows, he had to have A's on those stolen exams to make up for lower grades he was getting in other classes."

"So why did you tamper with tomorrow's exam?"

"Well, the argument we had this semester got ugly. I told Joe that there simply was no need to cheat on any final exams scheduled this week. It's his last semester. He's already received, and spent, his scholarship money. Even if he gets straight D's, he'll graduate."

"But he insisted," Harlan said.

Nikki nodded and looked as though she might take a turn crying, as she told Harlan about what had happened.

"You know, Joe, every time I do this, it puts me at risk too," Nikki said.

"At risk of what, losing your dead-end job?"

Nikki was stunned by Joe's anger and arrogance. She tried to explain, but it came off more like begging. "Please, Joe, I have a five-year-old son. I need my job."

"You're a frickin' secretary, Nikki. And you'll be quitting anyway, after I graduate and we move to Chicago."

"Oh, you think so."

"Easy, Nikki. Don't turn this into some kind of deal breaker. Just do this thing for me one last time, like you've done many times before without any problems."

"But why? There's no need."

"I shouldn't have to explain this. It should be enough that I'm telling you to do it."

"Are you serious?"

"Of course I am. Look, I have to think ahead about my career, and my GPA is something that will follow me everywhere I go."

"Oh, I see. It's all about *your* career and *your* GPA following *you* everywhere *you* go. What about what *I* want for *me* and my son, *Luke*."

"Enough, Nikki. Just do it, or maybe we *will* have ourselves a deal breaker."

"So you did it one last time," Harlan said as he glanced at the exam that sat between them.

"Oh yeah, I did it alright."

"What exactly did you do?"

Nikki opened the exam to the multiple-choice questions. "Take a look at some of these questions," she said.

Harlan began skimming through a few of them. Each question consisted of a short description of facts, usually a paragraph long, followed by a question about some legal issue raised by the facts. After the question came five answer choices, lettered A, B, C, D, and E, for students to choose from. The instructions told students to choose the best answer for each question— there were forty questions in all—and fill in their answers on a machine-readable scantron sheet.

After Harlan had turned a couple pages, Nikki stopped him. "Okay," she said, "you see those lettered answer choices for each question, right?"

"Sure, the items lettered A to E."

"I rearranged those on the document I gave Joe so that answer A on the real exam appears as answer B on the document I gave him, and answer B on the real exam appears as answer C on his document, and so on, until answer E on the real exam, which I made answer A on his document."

"I see," Harlan said. "Basically all you did was bump all the answers up a letter."

"Yep."

"And you did this for all forty questions."

"Sure did."

"And you say that Joe's practice is to figure out the answers and create his own answer key, and then he memorizes his answer key and reproduces it on the scantron sheet when he sits for the exam."

"That's right," Nikki said. "Joe's probably spent most of the weekend figuring out, correctly, at least ninety percent of the answers to the questions on the document I gave him, which means his answers to the *real exam* will be off by one letter every time. When A is the right answer, he'll be answering B, when B's the right answer, he'll be answering C, and so on."

"So the play you're making on Joe is to cause him to fail this exam and not graduate."

"That's not really my goal," Nikki said. "He could still manage to get a D on the exam if he crushes the essay questions."

"Well then, what's your aim?"

Nikki opened her laptop, refreshed the screen, and turned it toward Harlan. He read through the entire document. It was a nearly finished letter of resignation—and confession—addressed to Professor Caparo and Dean Fletcher.

The confession included a list of all the exams that Nikki had stolen for Joe over the years. The list matched the one on Harlan's spreadsheet. The letter also explained the pattern of wrong answers that Joe would provide for the multiple-choice questions on tomorrow's exam.

"I've been trying to decide how to deliver it," Nikki said, "by email, regular mail, or the way I probably should, by actually walking it into the school and apologizing in person."

"What about your plans to—" Harlan stopped himself, thinking better of asking about her plans to marry Joe. But he couldn't stop the impulse to look at her left hand. She wasn't wearing an engagement ring.

"Joe's not getting an explanation," she said.

Harlan glanced back at the letter on the laptop. "Who's Dean Fletcher?" he asked.

"She's the dean of students, the one who's supposed to keep all the twenty-something-year-old school kids in line."

"Oh yeah," Harlan said, "she's the one who Tommy MacPherson visited last week to ask about Craig Davies. Would she be the one to confront a student caught cheating on an exam?"

Nikki nodded.

"What's she like?" Harlan asked.

"Oh man, that's the hardest question you've asked all night," Nikki said, trying to stifle a laugh while glancing back at a hallway that led to her son's bedroom. "In a word, I guess I'd describe Dean Fletcher as *intense*. She's so passionate about professional ethics and the school's honor code, it's ridiculous. But the students sure do take her seriously. I mean, toward them, she's like an overbearing mother hen. She hovers over them, and if she catches one of them getting out of line, man, look out."

Harlan recalled something. "Tommy described her as braniac schoolmarm. What do you think—is she smart?"

"That's what makes her so damn scary to the students. Her brain's like a web browser on steroids."

"How about the kind of smart you are—you know, able to read people and think on her feet?"

Nikki gave Harlan an appreciative smile before offering her assessment of Fletcher's common sense. "Well, maybe not so much. She was the last person at the school to know about Leo's March Madness pool."

Harlan could relate to that.

"Say, why all the questions about Dean Fletcher?" Nikki said. "Isn't it your turn to tell me about the play *you're* trying to put together here, *Boss*?"

"Oh jeez, that reminds me," Harlan said. "I have to make a phone call soon."

"To who?"

"A co-conspirator of mine—Tank Lochner."

"What?" Nikki exclaimed, apparently forgetting all about her sleeping son down the hall. "You can't be serious!"

"Sure I am. He's a material witness to the homicide Joe committed."

Nikki's mouth fell open. Nothing came out.

"Let me tell you all about the play that Tank and I are putting together. And when I'm done, maybe you'll want to join our team."

C46

12:05 a.m., Monday, April 11.

Tank was exhausted. Before getting some rest, he took the added precaution of plying his bound captives with whiskey and sleeping pills. As they drifted off, the cell phone that Harlan had loaned him rang.

"What's happening, Boss?"

"Just heading home to get some rest. I'm beat."

"I hear that, but you might wanna find somewhere else to sleep tonight."

"Why?"

There was a long pause. "C'mon," Harlan said, "tell me what's going on."

Tank explained what had happened after the two split up earlier that evening. He tried his best to conclude on a positive note. "So I think you should play it safe and stay somewhere else tonight, in case that neighbor lady of yours figures out who I really am. But I'm telling you, by the time I left your house, I'm pretty sure I had her sold on my fake identity."

"Really," Harlan said. "Stella McDonald thinks she met my three-hundred-pound cousin, Learned Hand, also the nephew of Officer Benny Carduzi, alone at my house removing stuff from my garage in the middle of the night."

"Well, not when you say it like that. But you should have heard some of the Yooper talk that I dazzled her with, eh."

"Oh, yeah, I'm sure you nailed it, cousin Learned."

"I'm sorry, Boss. I know it seems like I keep screwing up every time you send me off on my own. But maybe she won't figure it out, and we can just..."

"Okay, Tank, let's try not to worry about this. How's everything else going?"

"Everything's cool."

"So you and those two guys are at least an hour's drive from Traverse City?" Harlan said.

"Yep."

"And you know what time you're calling Angelo Surocco tomorrow."

"Yeah, Boss, right after you call him at four to tell him about the five o'clock sit-down."

"And all you're going to do is—"

"Just tell him where he can find his two guys."

"And you're not going to—"

"I know, no stunts. I have to let these sons of bitches walk after what they did to me."

"Look, Tank, I know those guys put you through hell back in that forestland, but you really have to try to put that out of your mind right now."

"Got it, Boss. Just forget all about that place and what happened there."

After he hung up, Tank checked on Vincent and Phoenix. They continued to sleep soundly, nestled slightly beneath ground level in the shallow grave within which, just a few days ago, they had caused Tank to be buried alive. The dirt that had been piled on him remained piled beside the grave, and the shovel that had been used to bury him still stuck out of it.

C47

4:41 p.m., Monday, April 11.

"Officers Summers and Tice are here, Dean Fletcher."

The voice was transmitting from the phone in Dean Fletcher's office at GTU Law to another phone in a conference room down the hall and around a distant corner. Both phones were set on speaker mode, making everything said in each room audible in the other.

Dean Fletcher leaned toward the conference room phone. It was on the middle of a long table surrounded by chairs. Harlan Holmes and Nikki Ybarra sat opposite her at the table. The three were wrapping up a lengthy meeting.

"Thank you, Mrs. Palsgraf," Dean Fletcher said. "Please direct the officers to the conference room."

Harlan checked his laptop one last time. A recording device planted in Dean Fletcher's office was working well.

Riley entered the conference room ahead of Frank. "Alright Harlan," she said. "Why don't you tell Frank and me why we had to drop everything to be here right now."

"So you can arrest the person who killed Leo Surocco, after we get his statement," Harlan answered.

Riley glanced at Nikki Ybarra and then looked sternly at Harlan. "Joe Rylands?" she said.

Harlan nodded.

"What exactly do you have on him?"

"There's no time to tell you right now. The interrogation is about to begin."

"How do you expect me to conduct an interrogation without knowing what you have?"

"Actually, Riley, I have someone else in mind as the interrogator."

"Who?"

Before Harlan could answer, the voice spoke out again from the phone in the middle of the room. "Dean Fletcher, a Mr. Angelo Surocco is here."

Dean Fletcher leaned over the phone. "Thank you, Mrs. Palsgraf. Please direct him to the conference room."

Riley could barely contain herself. "Please, tell me he's not who you have in mind."

"Of course not," Harlan said.

"Who then? You?"

"No."

Riley scanned the room quickly and shrugged. "Well?"

"Dean Fletcher has graciously agreed to conduct the interrogation."

Frank erupted first. "What? The mother hen?" Then Riley began to complain as Frank continued, making it hard to discern what either was saying.

Angelo arrived while the officers talked over one another. He immediately strode around the table toward Harlan, but Dean Fletcher intervened. His scowl quickly faded as she introduced herself and offered condolences for the loss of his son.

Another announcement from the speaker phone then silenced the room.

"Dean Fletcher?"

"Yes."

"The exam proctors have detained Joseph Rylands, as you requested."

"Okay, Mrs. Palsgraf. Please see that he is escorted to my office immediately. And make sure that his escort brings along his multiple-choice answer form."

"Yes, ma'am."

Dean Fletcher then leaned in close to the conference room phone and tapped its mute button so that sounds in the conference room would no longer transmit to her office. Sounds in her office, however, would continue transmitting to the conference room. The room remained silent as she rose from the phone and left. On her way out, she looked only at Frank, her eyes narrowing disdainfully.

C48

5:01 p.m., Monday, April 11.

When Joe arrived, Dean Fletcher directed him to a metal chair. The old-fashioned, overstuffed furniture usually in her office had been removed earlier that day. She sat down opposite him. Between them was a coffee table. On it, she placed a multiple-choice answer form marked "Answer Key." Alongside that document she placed the answer form that Joe had completed for the exam he had just taken.

"Joseph, I'm afraid there's been an allegation that you cheated on the exam," she said as she slid the two documents across the table toward him.

"Who says?" Joe exclaimed, without looking at the documents.

"Just look for yourself. It's obvious."

Still averting his eyes from the documents, Joe objected again. "Look, I studied hard for this exam, and I definitely did not—"

"Be careful, Joseph. In all the years I've been doing this job, I've unfortunately seen many students in this kind of situation. And lying to cover it up often gets them into more trouble than the initial wrongdoing."

Joe sighed and began comparing the two documents. A perplexed look set in almost immediately and deepened as his eyes scanned downward and side to side. Soon his head swung in sync with his eyes, faster and faster, and then came to an abrupt stop.

A long pause followed. "I... I don't... understand," he eventually stammered. His face glowed red, like that of the proverbial child caught in the act. "How did my answers end up being wrong this way, by one letter every time?"

"The explanation is actually quite simple," Fletcher said. She took a small sip from a cup of freshly percolated coffee and then continued. "Ms. Ybarra altered the stolen exam before giving it to you."

"She altered what?"

"The exam that you coerced her to steal for you—she downloaded a digital copy of it and moved the answer choices around before giving it to you."

"So my answers would make this pattern?"

Fletcher nodded.

"And she told you she did that?"

"Yes, earlier today," Fletcher said.

His face, still red, expressed a mix of surprise and anger. "She set me up?"

"It seems she was done with your deceitful enterprise after stealing eight exams for you over the past few years."

"She told you there were eight more?"

Fletcher nodded.

"Look, Dean Fletcher, I swear, what happened today was just an isolated—"

Fletcher tried to interrupt. "Joseph—"

But Joe continued. "Look, you can't possibly take the word of that... that woman... that secretary... over my word, and I'm telling you—"

"Joseph, didn't I just warn you not to lie?" Fletcher said, as she reached back to her desk and retrieved a two-column spreadsheet. She leaned forward and replaced the multiple-choice answer forms with the spreadsheet, all the while staring over the top of her reading glasses at Joe.

Once again Joe's eyes scanned downward and side to side, his head eventually in sync. This time, however, his expression showed no surprise. The sheet's left column listed the eight courses for which he had obtained stolen exams, and the column next to it listed the straight A's he had received on those exams.

Of course, Dean Fletcher had access to Joe's transcript and knew full well that those were the only A's Joe had ever received on exams he took at GTU Law. And after her meeting with Harlan and Nikki earlier that day, she had full knowledge of a lot more. She knew that Joe had cheated to get every one of those A's in order to keep his scholarship; that he'd been doing it with the help of an insider who compromised the integrity of all exams on the GTU S-Drive; and that all along he'd been covering up his treachery by lying to her, Professor Caparo, and some other faculty about an anxiety issue that he claimed had caused his erratic exam performance.

Despite already knowing the whole truth, Dean Fletcher proceeded to elicit from Joe admission after admission, on every detail, in the style of a hard-boiled schoolmaster coming down hard on a wayward student.

She dragged him through the minutia of his modus operandi, again and again, for every stolen exam. She picked at the dark recesses of the insecurities that drove him to do it. And, at every opportunity, she scolded him for his treachery and the harms it inflicted on his victims—his fiancé, his classmates, his teachers, the school, and the reputation of the legal profession itself.

The eavesdroppers down the hall might question her approach, she thought. But she'd been in this kind of situation with students before, and she knew exactly what she was doing.

Twenty minutes into the interview, Joe's hands began to tremble when he recounted particularly incriminating events. At forty minutes, perspiration began to penetrate his outer shirt. At sixty, his eyes began to squint. Before the interview, Fletcher had positioned his chair so that it would face the setting sun through her office window.

"Would you like a drink of water, Joseph?"

"Yes, please."

She retrieved a cold bottle of spring water from a refrigerator in her office and set it on the table in front of him. Before sitting back down she paused to study him. His hand trembled slightly as he tipped the bottle back and poured it through a throat that gulped hard as if constricted.

It was time to *begin*.

Mustering all of the schoolmarm firmness she could, Fletcher stared at Joe over the top of her reading glasses, sat down, and leaned forward. "Do you know what really concerns me, Joseph, more than anything else you've described?"

Joe's expression went blank. Fletcher continued to stare into his eyes. At this point during a disciplinary meeting with a student, she usually launched into a long lecture about professional ethics and the duties undertaken by those privileged to practice law. But not today.

"What concerns me most is how widespread your cheating actually went," Fletcher said.

"What do you mean?" Joe asked. "I... I've told you everything. Wh-what widespread cheating?"

Fletcher clenched her teeth. "Bullshit, young man. Copies of all the exams you stole were found in digital files maintained by Leo Surocco."

Joe didn't respond. The hand in which he held the water bottle trembled.

"Answer me right now—just how widespread is your network of cheaters?"

Joe took a deep breath and said, "Honestly, Dean Fletcher, there is no network of—"

"I want names, young man—the name of every one of your co-conspirators—right now."

"But Dean Fletcher, I never gave any of those exams to—"

"Names, dammit!"

"But... but..."

"Joseph, do I have to warn you again about lying?"

"I swear, Dean Fletcher, Leo... Leo..."

"Leo what?"

"He stole them from me."

"Leo Surocco took these stolen exams from you without your knowledge?"

"Yes."

"Then how do you know?"

"He told me."

"Yeah, right," Fletcher scoffed. "Do you expect me to believe that one of the most clever individuals I've ever known stole these exams from you and then turned around and told you about it?"

"I swear, I'm not lying. Leo stole those exams from me and told me about it later."

"When?"

Joe's eyes darted around the room as he stammered. "It was... a... a long time ago." His gaze then settled into a distant corner of the room.

"That's not possible, Joseph, not according to the metadata."

"The *meta* what?" Joe asked.

She pushed past the question. "Metadata in Leo's files shows that he downloaded all of the exams, including the eight older ones, at the same time—only fifteen days ago."

Joe responded as though he were speaking to someone else in the distant corner, where his gaze remained. "I guess he might have told me about it a little more recently, maybe... maybe..."

"Maybe sometime shortly after Mr. Lochner had left the cottage the night you two fell down the stairs," Fletcher said, as if opining about some mundane detail.

"Mr. who?" Joe exclaimed, his eyes returning to Fletcher's.

"Mr. Lochner," she repeated calmly. "I believe he goes by the name Tank."

"The Neanderthal bagman?"

Fletcher nodded and then sipped her coffee. "Yes," she said, "and Mr. Lochner has said, unequivocally, that just before he left the two of you at the cottage that night, he specifically recalls hearing Leo say—"

"That bagman is full of shit! I'm telling you, Dean Fletcher—"

Fletcher slammed the coffee cup down on the table, sending the coffee that remained in it flying. "No, Joseph, I'm going to tell you!" she shouted as she leaned forward. "Leo Surocco never cheated on an exam in his life. He had only recently downloaded the stolen exams from your files, which I'm sure he told you that night. In fact, knowing Leo, a privilege I will always cherish, he would have put that hard evidence right in your face."

"Wait a minute, Dean Fletcher."

"No Joseph, I'm not done." She leaned forward further, putting her face only inches from his. "He was threatening you with that hard evidence, Joseph—hard evidence of your cheating—threatening to rat you out if you didn't shut up about his gambling activities. At one point, he even demanded that you step up and serve as his new front guy in those gambling activities— or he'd take you down—didn't he, Joseph?"

"Dean Fletcher, I'm telling you—"

"That little son of a bitch had you over a barrel. He was going to destroy everything you worked, lied, and cheated for: graduation from law school, a career as a lawyer, your whole life. And that's when you—"

"Dean Fletcher, I... I didn't—"

"Don't you lie to me, Joseph Rylands!"

"I... I—"

"Joseph!"

"It... It was—"

"Tell me, Joseph, *now!*"

"It was an accident! I swear it was an accident!" Joe burst into tears. "Oh

God, I... I didn't mean to hurt him."

Fletcher settled back into her chair and returned to calm. "Well then," she said, "why don't you elaborate on the facts, and we'll explore the existence *vel non* of *mens rea.*"

Everyone in the conference room had been riveted to the last few minutes of the conversation transmitting through the speaker phone before Fletcher took a short break to retrieve something from her desk. Their anticipation of what might come next was palpable.

Nikki filled the intermission. "What does this *mens rea* stuff mean?" she asked, looking at Harlan.

Everyone at the table turned toward Harlan. He took a deep breath. An attempt to really answer the question could get complicated. What Dean Fletcher had obtained so far was Joe's admission to the act, or *actus reus*, of a criminal homicide—the killing of a human being. But even killing someone is not a crime if done by "accident," as Joe was claiming. A culpable state of mind—or *mens rea*—must accompany the homicide for it to be criminal.

Harlan opted for a simpler answer: "It means that Joe Rylands is swimming with a shark."

Everyone except Riley then returned their attention to the speaker phone. Riley turned hers to a piece of paper, on which she jotted down a note that she slid across the table to Harlan. It read, "What did that bagman tell you while you aided and abetted his flight from justice?"

Harlan paused over the note. He then glanced not at Riley but at two uniformed cops who had joined her shortly after the interrogation began. They had positioned themselves by the conference room door.

C49

6:17 p.m., Monday, April 11.

Dean Fletcher returned from her desk. She set an ashtray on the table between them and smacked the top side of a pack of Marlboro Reds into the palm of her hand several times.

While packing down the tobacco, she looked at a nearby picture of her condo in South Carolina, where she planned to retire in a few years. She found herself thinking about making it sooner. *I'm getting to damn old for this shit.*

Her attention returned to Joe after she peeled the seal off the pack. "You smoke?" she asked as she removed two cigarettes from the pack.

"Isn't indoor smoking illegal?" he said.

Ignoring the question, she lit one for herself and slid the other toward him, along with the lighter. Joe shrugged and lit his as well.

Back in the conference room bewildered looks spread across the faces of everyone, except Frank. "I love this woman," he said, beaming with approval.

Through the speaker phone they heard her go back to work.

"Okay, Joseph, start with the first thing you remember after falling down the stairs that night."

3:33 a.m., Tuesday, April 5.

"Joe, are you okay?"

Leo's head seemed to bob and weave as Joe opened his eyes and tried to respond.

"I... I think so... but my head..."

Leo's face finally came into focus and, over his left shoulder, that of the guy who'd attacked him on the loft.

Joe gasped as he stumbled to his feet, trying to flee. "Look out, Leo, that son of bitch is right behind you!"

Leo placed a hand on Joe's shoulder and guided him to a chair in the great room. "Easy does it, Joe. Everything's okay."

Joe tipped his head back and gaped at the enormous beast standing just a few feet away, staring at him curiously. Still panicked, Joe grabbed hold of both arms of the chair and pushed himself into its backrest, struggling vainly to create more distance between himself and the beast. "Hurry, Leo, call the cops! Dial 911! Do something!"

"I'm telling you, Joe, everything's cool. Isn't that right, Tank?"

Tank nodded his head, but continued to study Joe intensely.

Joe's grip on the arms of the chair began to loosen. "Really, Leo, you know this guy?"

"Sure, he collects for my bookie."

"He does what... for who?"

"He's a bagman, Joe. His boss booked a bet I made on Bucknell, and he's here to collect. But I don't have the money—not yet, that is."

"And that's why he was beating the shit out of you?"

"Well, yeah, he's a bagman. That's what he does. But everything's cool now. Like I was saying to him just a minute ago, I'm going to visit my dad in Chicago today to get the money, and then I'll wire it to my new partner for payment to him."

"With double the vig," Tank added.

"Absolutely," Leo said.

"You're going to drive to Chicago to ask your dad for money?" Joe asked.

"Uh huh."

"For the March Madness pool winners too?"

"Uh huh."

"So when you called him—"

"That didn't work out. I have to see him in person."

"And you're going to wire the money to—"

"My new partner," Leo said.

"What happened to Craig?"

Leo shrugged. "Apparently he left town after a business meeting with Tank earlier tonight."

Joe glanced at the bagman, who nodded his head matter-of-factly in agreement with everything Leo was saying, as if it were all just standard procedure.

"So who's your new partner?" Joe finally asked.

"Well, like I told Tank, that will be you, Joe. You'll be dealing directly with Tank, going forward."

Joe lurched forward in his chair over the objection of his bruised ribs. "No way, Leo! I'm not getting involved with this... this monster, or any of your gambling debts."

"Oh, come now, Joe, you haven't even heard the terms of the deal I'm proposing."

"What deal?"

"Hey, Leo, I'm not so sure about this guy," Tank interjected.

"Don't worry, Tank. His head still hurts. He'll be fine once I straighten him out."

"What deal?" Joe asked.

"The deal by which you shut up and do what I say, Joe, and I let you graduate from law school."

The answer silenced Joe.

"This doesn't feel right," Tank said. "I think I'd rather work with College Boy."

"Are you serious?" Leo asked.

"Sure. He's still okay with me," Tank said. "We just had a little misunderstanding."

Joe's mind drifted while Leo and Tank continued talking. About all he overheard was Leo confirming Tank's preference to work with College Boy.

What the hell does he have on me? Joe wondered. He asked Leo that as soon as Tank left the cottage. But Leo ignored the question. He was rapidly tapping his thumbs on the screen of a smartphone.

"What are you doing?" Joe asked.

"Just writing an email."

A large clock in the great room gave a quarter-hour chime as Joe was about to ask another question. He looked at the clock instead. It was 3:45 a.m. Joe started thinking about logistics.

Leo's drive to Chicago would be over three hundred miles, and much of it would include congested morning traffic, picking up outside Gary, Indiana, and continuing through Chicago's metro area. He'd then have to meet up with his father, talk him into covering his gambling debts, and wire the money to College Boy in time for him to pay the March Madness winners at nine o'clock, or at least within an acceptably late time frame.

"You're not gonna make it," Joe said.

"I might."

Joe shook his head and sighed.

"You worry too damn much, Joe. This isn't even your problem anymore. Didn't you hear Tank and me just a minute ago? College Boy's back on line as my front guy."

"I still have a problem, Leo, because I know that you ripped off the March Madness money."

"Big deal, so you know. Why's that a problem?"

Joe didn't respond.

"It's not like *you* ripped off anyone's money, Joe. You're just a bystander."

"But not an innocent bystander," Joe said, "and you know why."

"Why don't you tell me, Joe. What makes you so guilty?"

Joe didn't respond.

"You are one serious piece of work," Leo said, shaking his head. "It's that asinine honor code that Dean Fletcher's always talking about, isn't it? Do you actually accept her bullshit? Do you really believe that you have an ethical duty to rat me out?"

"It doesn't matter what I believe. It's what she believes," Joe said. "She's gonna boot your ass out of school for embezzling that money. Why should I go down with you?"

"I haven't even been caught yet, asshole—assuming that Caparo can keep his mouth shut about what you've already told him."

"What are you talking about, Leo?"

"Oh c'mon, man, you think I don't know that you squealed to Caparo about me secretly sponsoring the March Madness pool?"

"That was a confidential meeting, Leo. How did you learn about it?"

"You just told me."

"No I didn't. You already knew, didn't you?"

Leo returned to tapping the screen of the smartphone before putting the phone away and jumping to his feet.

"I have to finish packing and get on the road," Leo said as he headed for the stairs. "If you want answers to your questions, check your Yahoo email account."

Both boys headed up the stairs to their respective bedrooms. When Joe got to his, he refreshed the screen on his laptop and signed into his Yahoo mailbox, which was the account he used for all personal email.

There was no recent email from Leo, at least not from any source that Leo normally used. But there was an email that purported to be from Joe himself, originating from his Gmail account provided by the law school—sent less than two minutes ago. This was the email account that Joe used for all school-related business. *I haven't used Gmail for days*, Joe thought. *Did Leo...*

Joe read the "Subject" line. It said, "Forward: Follow-up to our meeting." Next came the email's text, which said, "Check out the email that Caparo sent you, forwarded below, and the attachments I've added—you treacherous son of a bitch. Cheers, Leo."

Joe scrolled to the forwarded email from Professor Caparo. The professor had sent it to Joe some time ago, after their confidential section 9B meeting at which Joe had explained Leo's secret role as the real organizer of the March Madness pool and the risk of embezzlement he posed due to his gambling addiction.

The professor's follow-up email began: "Joe, this is just a friendly reminder of my advice that you report to Dean Fletcher the irregularities related to the March Madness pool that we discussed last week."

Scrolling further, Joe came to the attachments Leo had added. There were nine. His heart pounded as he opened and scrolled through several of them. They were the exams he had stolen and stored securely, he thought, in a password-protected, cloud-based storage system.

"Where'd you get these exams?" Joe shouted as he ran toward Leo's room.

"From the cloud that you stored them in after you stole them," Leo calmly said when Joe reached his doorway. Leo looked up from a bag he was packing, shot Joe a disgusted look, and then returned to packing the bag.

"But those files are password protected. And so is my Gmail account."

"You have habits that I've seen while living with you over the years," Leo said, keeping his eyes on his work. "One of them is occasionally getting up while you're online and letting out a big sigh, like you're frustrated with something, and then getting a daily planner from your backpack before returning to your online activity."

Joe thought about a few pages in the back of his daily planner, where he kept track of his password information, by hand, for all of his secure online sites, including his email accounts and cloud-based files. Ironically, he frequently changed his password information as a security measure, which led directly to his habit of having to revisit the daily planner whenever he forgot new passwords.

"So you looked at my daily planner," Joe said.

"And I snapped pictures of those pages in the back—you know, so I wouldn't have to keep going back to them when I wanted to check up on you."

"But what made you decide to spy on me in the first place?"

"Because you're a *Wolve*, Joe."

Joe immediately understood the misnomer. A proud graduate of the University of Michigan, he was a big fan of the school's sports teams, his beloved Michigan *Wolverines*. But not everyone in Michigan feels the same way about the Wolverines. In fact, some love to hate them, and the misnomer, *Wolve*, when spoken with disgust the way Leo had spoken it, is a way of expressing that contempt.

"What does me being a Wolverine have to do with you prying into my online stuff?"

Leo zipped shut his bag and looked up. "Do you remember asking me for advice about the bracket you submitted for ESPN's March Madness Challenge?"

Joe nodded.

"Man, you were totally stoked about your Wolves drawing a second seed in their region."

"Sure," Joe said. "I had them running the table. So what?"

"That's right, yet you weren't willing to put a mere ten bucks down on those Wolves for a play in *my* March Madness pool. Do you remember me asking you what you had against my pool?"

Joe reflected for a moment and eventually nodded. "Yeah, I told you that I didn't like the structure. It struck me as boring to just pick an ultimate winner. I like picking through all of the rounds."

"That's not all you told me, Joe."

"Yes, it was."

"No, it's not, my man. You don't just have habits that I've noticed over the years—you have *tells*."

Joe was confused. Leo offered a hint. "Do you have any idea how many hands of poker I've already managed to play in the short time since I've been old enough to get into the casinos?"

Joe nodded, recalling an occasion in the past when Leo boasted about reading changes in a guy's behavior—tells—whom he caught bluffing at a poker table. "Okay, what's your point, Leo?"

"That I knew you were lying about your reason for staying out of my pool. And since then, you've given more tells of serious misgivings almost every time the subject of the pool comes up. And it's come up a lot, especially around College Boy, because other than March Madness, there's not a damn thing going on in this wasteland of northern Michigan this time of year."

"So you started snooping around because you suspected me of... of..."

"Being a low-life snitch, or at least a risk of becoming one," Leo said, "especially because of the way you've bought into GTU's lame-ass honor code."

"And when you found out I... I met with Caparo, you snooped around some more to see if you could find something to hold over me, to shut me up, like you said before?"

"You know what they say, Joe. Sometimes the best defense is offense."

"Who else knows about this?" Joe asked.

"You mean, about your cheating?"

Joe nodded.

"Besides you, me, and Nikki?"

"How do you know about Nikki's involvement?"

"I can't believe you're asking me that, Joe. First you rat me out to Caparo, and now you insult my intelligence."

"Okay, besides you, Nikki, and me—who knows?"

"I imagine Harlan Holmes knows, or will eventually, because he's so into my shit, and I'm so into yours."

Joe shook his head. "For all the complaining you do about that devious son of a bitch, you're no different than he is."

"I'll take that as a compliment, Joe. I've actually come to admire Mr.

Holmes' deviousness. Now, as much as I'd love to spend the evening rubbing your nose in *your* character flaws, I need to get on the road—and you need to get your sorry ass out of my way."

Leo swung a backpack over his shoulder, grabbed another bag and a cell phone, and started for the door.

Joe stepped forward, blocking the way. "Not until you tell me where I can find your digital copies of those exams."

"Yeah, right, Joe. Just get the hell out of my way, you snake."

Leo tried to push past Joe. At the moment of bodily contact, a rush of adrenalin and anger seized Joe. He grabbed hold of Leo's jacket and slammed him into a wall next to his bed. The phone and both bags fell to the floor with the thud of Leo's head smacking against the wall. Leo's eyes rolled back, and he stumbled toward the doorway.

Joe charged forward, again got hold of the jacket, and drove a knee into Leo's groin, causing him to stumble further.

Oblivious to the pain radiating from his bruised ribs, Joe continued forward. "Where the hell are you keeping those exams, Leo!"

When there was no response from his reeling friend, Joe reacted with a frenzied push.

Leo stumbled backward toward the loft's rail. And then he flipped over it. His descent ended on the great room's hardwood floor, head first, twenty-five feet beneath the rail.

C50

6:50 p.m., Monday, April 11.

There was a break in the interrogation, and Angelo and Riley were busy sending text messages. Harlan was also busy on his phone, arguing with someone on the other end from whom he was ordering a pizza.

"But all I have is a credit card," Harlan said. "Why can't I pay with that?"

Riley finished her text and stepped toward Harlan. She stopped beside him and folded her arms. Harlan covered the phone. "Hey, Riley, you got a few bucks?" he asked.

"What for?"

"The pizza guy will only take cash, and I'm a little short."

She rolled her eyes.

"Actually, it might help if everyone who wants pizza kicked in a few bucks," Harlan said, raising his voice to address everyone in the room. "I'm sorry to ask like this, but my client hasn't paid me for a while."

Angelo rolled his eyes and stepped toward Harlan. "The pizza's on me," he said as he peeled two bills off a wad of cash.

"Thanks," Harlan said.

As soon as the phone call ended, Riley grabbed Harlan's arm. "C'mon," she said, "out in the hallway where we can talk. You've been avoiding me long enough."

Angelo grabbed Harlan's other arm. "Hold on, Detective," he said. "I'm the client. I come first."

"You really think I owe you money?" Angelo asked after he and Harlan stepped into the hall.

"Well, I have been putting in a lot of unpaid hours lately," Harlan said.

"But I guess I could understand why you might not want to pay me, you know, seeing as how I freed the bagman and... uh... kidnapped Vincent and all."

"When *was* the last time I paid you?"

Harlan thought for a moment. "Last Wednesday when we met at the coffee shop, before we visited Craig Davies."

"Oh, yeah, that's right," Angelo said. "What I gave you then probably didn't cover much more than your expenses."

Harlan nodded.

"And you're sure I haven't paid you since."

"Uh huh."

"You're absolutely positive," Angelo said, as though he thought Harlan was overlooking something.

"Well, yeah, Angelo. It was Wednesday night, just after you last paid me, when I scammed Phoenix and Vincent and freed the bagman. The very next day you ordered a hit on me. At that point, I'm pretty sure you took me off the payroll."

"How do I know you're not scamming me right now? Lately you've shown quite a talent for that sort of thing."

Harlan shrugged. "I guess I could tell you I'm not, but that'd probably just make you more suspicious of whatever the hell it is you suspect."

Angelo froze. "That's uncanny," he said, staring at Harlan. "That... that's exactly the kind of thing *he* used to say when I... I can't get over how much you just reminded me of... *him*."

Harlan started to feel the onset of one of his uncontrollable grieving episodes. He turned away, but Angelo stepped around him and looked into his eyes. "Are you about to cry?" he asked, stepping closer. "I'll be damned— you are."

Harlan suppressed the tears, but as he answered a crack in his voice confirmed the emotion he had already shown. "People keep saying how much we're alike... both a couple of hustlers... and I guess it gets to me sometimes." He swallowed hard and continued. "Look, Angelo, just forget about the money." He then started for the conference room door.

"Wait," Angelo said. "I really don't care if I'm being hustled right now. You got the guy who killed my son. I owe you for that."

Angelo withdrew an envelope from inside his jacket. It was still sealed, which meant it contained all the cash initially stuffed inside, ten grand if his past practice continued. Harlan shook his head as Angelo extended the envelope toward him. "Just take it," Angelo said. Harlan did.

Phoenix approached as Harlan took the envelope and the two men shook hands. "Please, Angelo, don't tell me you called me up here so I could see you playing nice with this guy."

"I just need a smoke," Angelo said.

"But why the hell would you give him cash after the ballsy move his bagman made?"

Harlan sighed. "What'd he do this time?"

"Like you don't know," Phoenix said, rolling his eyes.

"I don't think he does," Angelo said.

"Careful, Boss, this sleuth can run a con like nobody I've ever seen, except maybe Le—"

"So what if he does," Angelo said. "He got Leo's killer. Everything's square as far as I'm concerned."

"Are you shittin' me, Angelo? We're just gonna let him and that bagman walk?"

Angelo turned to Harlan. "What are you going to do about them?" he said, nodding in the direction of the two cops from the conference room. They had followed Harlan and Angelo and were now positioned down the hall, watching.

Harlan shrugged.

C51

7:01 p.m., Monday, April 11.

Dean Fletcher waited in her office, hoping that Joe wouldn't return from a bathroom break. In all her years at GTU, a student had never been the victim of a criminal homicide, let alone one committed by a classmate. And even this case, she thought, might have been prevented if she had just been more diligent.

Hindsight tortured her. *How did I miss so much? Joseph's erratic exam performance. A huge March Madness pool. I'm supposed to be the dean of students—the mother hen around here.*

Her thoughts were interrupted by a tap on the door. It was Joe, returning from the bathroom. Fletcher sighed deeply. *Why did he come back?*

"You believe me, don't you, Dean Fletcher?" he said as he returned to his chair.

No way. He wants me to console him? All she could offer was a perfunctory nod.

"I mean about it being an accident. I wasn't trying to push him over that rail. And after he fell, I didn't mean to drown him. I thought he was dead."

She managed to reengage. "What exactly did he look like after he fell?"

"This may sound strange, but he looked at peace. There was no blood. And he was perfectly still, just lying there on his back."

"And that's what made you think he was dead, how peacefully still he was?"

"Not just that, Dean Fletcher. I actually got close and tried to talk to him. I shook him too. But there was no response. His pulse and breathing must have been incredibly weak. I checked for both and didn't find anything.

217

I swear, I thought he was dead."

"And then what happened?"

4:08 a.m., Tuesday, April 5.

What would have happened if that bagman had done this? Joe thought as he stood beside Leo's body. Seconds later, he went to work.

His injured head and ribs complained as Joe dragged Leo's limp body outside to the pickup truck. He took Leo's keys from his pocket before loading him into the bed of the truck. Then he slammed the tailgate, double-checked the fasteners for the bed cover, and returned to the cottage.

On his way to the stairs, Joe noticed it for the first time—blood, lots of it, especially on the rug in front of the staircase. It looked almost fluorescent against the white fibers. Then he remembered. One of the many things about the bagman that made him look so scary was the blood on his face, a fresh streak running down one side of his face and a dry smear on the other. *He must have gotten banged up during the fall,* Joe thought.

Joe double-checked for blood where Leo had fallen. There was none. He then stepped into the bathroom and checked himself. There was a smudge on one of his sleeves, but no injury to him that could have caused it. *That's the bagman's blood on me and out there,* Joe thought.

He caught himself smiling during a pause before the bathroom mirror. It was like looking at someone else wearing his pajamas. The smile melted away.

Joe returned to the rug. *That's too obvious for the bagman to overlook,* he thought. Besides, there were samples on the stairs that blended into the dark wood. Some of those could be more plausibly overlooked, and they would still suffice for DNA analysis. He snatched up the rug and stuffed it into a large plastic bag.

The clean-up job proceeded with a combination of wet and dry towels applied to all but the bottom two steps of the staircase. Joe was especially meticulous about cleaning spots on the great room floor where a few stray smudges of blood had been tracked by Tank and the boys after the fall down the stairs. He couldn't risk leaving a bloody print of his own showing that he was up and about after his fall. When he finished, he stuffed the towels into the plastic bag that contained the soiled rug.

Then Joe went upstairs. He stopped on the loft and scanned the carpet for blood that might have been tracked on it. There was none.

But there was something protruding from the carpet's shag fibers on the far side of the loft, beneath the window. Joe stepped toward it. *Oh yeah, Leo's Rolex watch,* he recalled. *The bagman didn't want it. He must've thrown it aside before he attacked Leo.*

Joe left the watch in place and stepped into Leo's bedroom. *None of Tank's assault happened in here,* he thought, *so it shouldn't look like any did.*

Joe picked up the packed bags that Leo had dropped during their scuffle and placed them on the end of Leo's bed. He then scanned the room while standing beside the bed, but he didn't look under it.

In his own bedroom, Joe opened his backpack and, from his daily planner, removed the pages containing his password information. Those pages would end up in the plastic bag downstairs that contained the dirty rug and towels.

Then he refreshed his laptop and permanently deleted the email that Leo had sent earlier—from both his Yahoo "inbox" and his Gmail "sent items."

My glasses, he thought, recalling that he had slipped them on earlier when reading the email. *I wouldn't have stopped to put these on before going after the bagman.* He returned them to his nightstand, and things around him got blurry.

After returning to the lower level, Joe grabbed the plastic bag of items he had collected and headed for the front door, the same door that the bagman presumably had used to come and go from the cottage. Joe wiped the doorknob with a sleeve as he thought the bagman would if covering up. And then, as he proceeded down the driveway, he saw some of the bagman's tracks. *Oh man, look at the size of those footprints. What should I do with them?*

Joe then realized why he could see them in the middle of the night, even without his glasses. *All of the outside lights are on.*

He returned to the cottage, shut off the lights, and left the bagman's trail intact.

C52

7:29 p.m., Monday, April 11.

The sight of Joe devouring pizza and gulping down cherry cola appalled Dean Fletcher. He dug into the box for his third slice, totally immersed in the carnage. *Doesn't he even wonder where it came from?* Fletcher thought.

Taking advantage of the distraction, she walked her soda over to her desk and discreetly spiked it with a couple ounces of something she kept in a lower drawer. *Maybe this will make him tolerable.*

"Joseph, do you mind talking while you eat?" she said when she returned.

Joe murmured something through a mouthful of food. She took it as a yes.

"Do you recall what time it was when you left the cottage?"

Joe pulled his mouth up from the straw to his soda and swallowed hard. "Actually, I think I remember hearing... excuse me," he said through a muffled belch. "The clock in the great room, I think I heard its half-hour chime just before I left. That would have had me on the road at about 4:30."

Fletcher recalled what Harlan had said about the truck's movement. According to the GPS program, it left the cottage at 4:32.

"And did you drive directly to—"

"The GTB Marina, yeah," Joe said. He then stuffed the remainder of the third slice into his mouth and began digging into the box for another.

Fletcher looked up directions from the cottage to the marina while Joe worked on converting his mouthful into a swallowable mass.

"According to MapQuest, the distance you drove was a little less than two and a half miles," she said, looking up from her laptop, "and it's usually just a five-minute trip along M-22."

"It took me at least twice that time."

Fletcher paused, recalling that the GPS recorded his arrival twelve minutes later, at 4:44. "What took you so long?" she asked.

"I'm practically blind without my glasses. I had to take it slow."

"And what happened after you arrived at the marina?"

4:43 a.m., Tuesday, April 5.

As the pickup truck crept along the top of the marina wall, Joe couldn't help but recall better times at this spot, fishing and drinking beers with Leo and Craig. The best spot for fishing, Leo always said, was at the end of the marina wall. Joe quickly learned, however, that the claim was just an excuse for Leo to drive the truck into the bay on top of the wall.

He was one crazy son of a bitch, Joe thought. There was virtually no margin for error—just a few inches to each side of the pickup—on the wall's slick water-level surface. Leo had made a point of driving it fast while casually chatting with his petrified friends.

On this occasion, Joe was taking it especially slow, with his door open, constantly watching the wall's left edge and keeping the left front tire a few inches from it. But eventually he found that the crowned surface tended to hold the truck's front wheels in place, making steering almost unnecessary.

Joe stopped the truck and climbed out of its sliding rear window onto the covered bed. He stood up and surveyed the area ahead, which was illuminated by the headlights. It was hard to see without his glasses, but he was able to make out the remainder of the wall. Toward the end, it ramped up several feet above the water's surface.

If only there was a way I could push it in, Joe thought. *But it'll just hang up as soon as a wheel slips off the wall... unless... it has momentum.*

Joe scrambled off the back of the truck and hurried on foot back to the shore. He waded into the frigid water and searched along the wall. It didn't take long to find what he was looking for.

His soaking wet pajamas clung to him as he hoisted himself and a fifty-pound boulder onto the truck's covered bed and then worked the boulder across the bed and through the rear window.

Once in the cab, Joe released the latch for the fold-down back seat, which provided interior access to the bed, but he did not fold the seat down. After working his way up front, Joe rolled the boulder onto the driver-side floor and leaned it against the brake pedal. He then opened the door and paused, not so much to catch his breath or to rest his bruised ribs as to figure out the position he needed to be in for this to work.

There's no room to stand out there, Joe thought as he looked out the door at the three inches of space between the truck and the edge of the wall. *But maybe I don't have to stand out there to do this. I just have to be able to reach my hand to the brake and gas pedals.*

Joe opened the driver-side door as wide as it would go and stretched himself on his right side across the driver's seat. His legs dangled out of the door, left leg on top of right. The gear shifter, which stuck out of the floor between the front bucket seats, was directly in his face.

He paused again to visualize the rest of what he needed to do. The engine, still running, was all he could hear. *All I have to do is drop it in "Drive," then reach down there for the boulder and roll it over to the gas pedal, and then get the hell out of here.* He glanced out the door and beyond his feet. *Right out that door and into the water, where I'll let myself get cold, real cold, before running down to the BP station for help.*

He worked the gear shift from "Park" into "Drive." The weight of the boulder on the brake held the truck still.

Then he rolled the boulder onto the gas pedal. The truck accelerated. He had to get out fast. But almost as quickly as he jerked himself up, something tightened around his neck and jerked him back down.

He tried again, and again he was jerked back down by something around his neck. It wasn't until his third failed attempt that realization hit him— followed by the dashboard. His head slammed into it after the truck hit the water, and as it did his neck broke through the thing that had tied him to the shifter.

His titanium chain necklace, an engagement gift from Nikki, had looped over the floor shifter when he laid himself across the seat, and it had been catching on the knob at the top of the shifter every time he tried to rise up.

"Then I was out cold for the second time that night," Joe said. "And the next thing I remember is the freezing cold water waking me up, and me somehow being trapped in the bed of the truck, with Leo. I have no idea how I got in there."

"Well, you unlatched the fold-down seat, right?" Fletcher asked.

"Yeah, I did that so that I could later *claim* that I escaped through it—but I didn't plan on actually doing that."

"I suppose the seat could have folded down when the truck hit the water," Fletcher suggested. "And once you were free of the necklace, your body could have tumbled to the back of the truck."

"But it's such a tight fit to squeeze through that opening," Joe said. "It doesn't seem like I could have just tumbled through it while unconscious."

Fletcher paused. Suddenly her eyes widened. "What is it?" Joe asked.

She recalled something Harlan had said about Leo's body being found draped over the fold-down seat, with his feet tangled in some fishing and swimming gear in the bed of the truck. *Maybe Leo came to first and was trying to climb through the opening, over Joe's body,* she thought, *but because Leo's feet were tangled up behind him, instead of pulling himself out, he pulled Joe in.*

"What is it?" Joe repeated.

"Probably nothing," Fletcher answered before tipping back her drink and heading to her desk for another—this one neat.

C53

7:52 p.m., Monday, April 11.

Dean Fletcher poured several ounces of whiskey into a tumbler at her desk. She was done being discreet.

"Is that liquor?" Joe asked.

"Ole George Rye Whiskey," she said.

"From the Grand Traverse Distillery?"

"Yep, double barreled Ole George."

"Can I have some too?"

Fletcher shook her head. She felt more than done with him—and her job of thirty years. "What you can do, Joseph, is leave my office." She tipped back the tumbler, gulped down the drink, and immediately poured another.

"Holy shit, Dean Fletcher, you're pounding straight whiskey in your office, right in front of a student!"

"You're not a student anymore, and I don't give a shit. Now get the hell out of here."

In the conference room, all eyes but Frank's converged on Harlan, as if he could explain Fletcher's behavior. He just shrugged.

"Yeah, you go, girl," Frank said, looking at the speaker phone on the table.

"Hey," Phoenix said, "I thought she was supposed to be some kind of schoolmarm, not some—"

"Quiet," Riley said.

"Hold on a second, Dean Fletcher," Joe said. "We haven't answered the question yet."

"What question?"

"You know, the question about *mens rea* you said we were going to explore."

"Seriously, Joseph, you're not done talking about this?"

"Well, I might be, because I don't think I committed any serious crimes. Is your legal analysis the same?"

She choked on a sip of whiskey.

"What's the matter, Dean Fletcher?"

"Are you out of your mind?" she bellowed through a hard cough. "I realize that you've cheated your way through three years of law school, but haven't you learned anything?"

"So you don't agree?"

"Let me put it this way," she said, rolling her eyes. "If the events you described were presented as a fact pattern for an essay examination given at this law school, the students would need at least three hours to write about all of your felonies."

"Like what?"

"You really want to know what I think?"

Joe nodded.

She took a deep breath and shrugged. "Well, most obviously, you intentionally used unwarranted force against Leo when you attacked him on the loft."

"That's just misdemeanor assault," Joe said.

"Goodness no, Joseph, it's at least involuntary manslaughter because it caused Leo's death."

"No it didn't," he responded defensively. "The cause of death was drowning, and when I did that, it couldn't have been a criminal homicide—because I had every reason to believe he was already dead."

She paused to consider Joe's state of mind when he pitched Leo into the bay. If he really thought that Leo was already dead, criminal negligence might be the limit of his culpability—a route to involuntary manslaughter, but perhaps no more. So she continued down the path of an alternative

225

theory that might get to *voluntary* manslaughter, or possibly even *murder*, if he'd help.

"Oh please, Joseph, a drowning death may be what the coroner says, but I would expect a graduate of this law school to know that there can be more than one cause of death for purposes of criminal responsibility."

Joe's expression went blank.

"Do you really need this spelled out?"

He nodded.

"Well, okay," Fletcher said, and then she launched into a technical discussion of legal causation, speaking as if she were reading from a legal encyclopedia, the effects of the whiskey notwithstanding.

A confused look on Joe's face deepened as Fletcher droned on about some concept dubbed "concurrent causation"—a label she used to describe "two or more events that combine to produce an indivisible harm." In this case, the assault and the bay dump were the concurrent causal events; they combined to produce the indivisible harm, Leo's death.

"It doesn't matter that the assault happened well beforehand," she said. "If you hadn't done that, you never would have dumped him in the bay."

Fletcher paused and watched Joe struggle to wrap his brain around her analysis. She was linking his assault of Leo back at the cottage with his drowning of Leo nearly an hour later and over two miles away. Eventually he came up with a predictable rebuttal. "But obviously," Joe said, "pitching Leo into the bay was the more *proximate cause* of the drowning." He asserted.

"Oh c'mon," Fletcher scoffed, "it's not like you left Leo for dead somewhere and then an hour later an airplane just happened to fall out of the sky and finish him. No, Joseph, for purposes of proximate causation, there was sufficient connection between your assault of Leo at the cottage and your subsequent effort to cover it up by pitching him in the bay."

Joe continued to struggle. Finally he guessed: "What you're saying is that the assault at the cottage also caused the drowning, so whatever intent I had during the assault, it applies to the homicide too?"

"Yes," she said, "if I was prosecuting this case, that's where I might peg your *mens rea* for the homicide—whatever your mental state was with reference to the initial assault back at the cottage."

"And that's how you get to involuntary manslaughter?"

"I said *at least* involuntary manslaughter. When you shoved Leo, you at least intended to cause him *some* unwarranted bodily contact. But if I was prosecuting the case, I'm sure I could prove *more* culpability."

"How?"

"My goodness, Joseph, it's too bad for you that ignorance of the law isn't a defense."

"Please, Dean Fletcher, could you just get to the point?"

"Very well," she said, the same way she would to a student who came to class unprepared. "Think for a moment about your own version of the assault. You said that, at some point during the struggle, you drove a knee into Leo's groin, right?"

"Yeah."

"And, according to you, that knee to the groin completely subdued Leo, right?"

"Well, yeah, it pretty much put him on his heels."

"And then, after you subdued him, you pushed him over the rail of the loft, which was right behind him, correct?"

"But... but—"

"But nothing, Joseph—that's what happened, right? You completely subdued him with a knee to his groin, and then, while he helplessly suffered from that blow, you pushed him over that rail, which you knew was right behind him, correct?"

"Well... yeah... I suppose I did, but—"

"Joseph, it really doesn't matter how much you insist that, subjectively, your state of mind was innocent. If the jury thinks that your conduct manifested an *intent to cause serious bodily injury or death* when you knowingly pushed Leo at that nearby rail after subduing him—as you just admitted—they're going to see this as *voluntary* manslaughter or perhaps even *murder*."

"But... but—"

"Then, of course, there's the larceny you committed."

"Larceny? What are you talking about?"

"The larceny of Mr. Surocco's pickup truck."

"But I didn't steal the truck. I just pitched it into the bay."

"Oh please, Joseph, try to think like a lawyer here. One doesn't have to actually steal property—as in converting it to one's own use—to be guilty of larceny. That's certainly *sufficient*. But it's not strictly *necessary*. Indeed, why don't you reflect back on your studies of criminal law and tell me, precisely, the crime's necessary elements." She looked at him, fully expecting an answer. "Come now, Joseph, a lawyer cannot properly advise a client about a legal concept, like larceny, unless he knows its essence."

"Please, Dean Fletcher, don't treat this like one of your Socratic teaching moments."

"So disappointing," she said, genuinely upset by his failure to recall the basic elements of this simple common law crime. Simple to her, anyway. All she had to do was open, in her head, one of the many legal hornbooks lodged in her photographic memory and read it aloud.

"If you consult just about any authority on the subject," Fletcher said, "it'll tell you that a larceny happens when someone takes the personal property of another *with intent to permanently deprive that person of the property*. So intent to steal is not strictly required. For example, I can commit a larceny by taking something of yours *with intent to destroy it*, and thus permanently deprive you of it. In fact, some courts have held that a larceny occurs when someone simply takes another's property *with an intent to do something with it that would create a substantial risk of destruction*—you know, like pitching Mr. Surocco's pickup truck into a bay, where submersion in the water might total it."

"But what if the truck could be fixed and returned to Mr. Surocco?" Joe asked.

"So what? What matters is what you intended when you took it—not what happened to it later. A shoplifter is guilty of larceny the moment she grasps and moves the item she intends to steal—even if she immediately changes her mind and sets it back down on the shelf—because it's that first moment of movement, with the requisite intent, when the *actus reas* and *mens rea* concur and the crime is complete."

"But... but..."

"Now, for a crime like malicious destruction of property," Fletcher continued, "harm must actually come to the property. So if Mr. Surocco's truck *was* in fact destroyed or significantly damaged, that's another crime we could add to the list."

"List? What list?" Joe nervously asked.

"The list I'm just getting started."

"There's more?"

"Oh heavens, yes, Joseph. Just think about all the crimes you committed between the time you shoved Leo off the loft and when you pitched him into the bay. You destroyed evidence, you attempted to frame poor Mr. Lochner of murder, you..."

Back in the conference room, Frank had become so enthused by Fletcher's methodology that he jumped to his feet and began shadow boxing to demonstrate figuratively the absolute beat down she was putting on Joe intellectually.

"For crying out loud, Frank, sit down," Riley said.

"Wait a minute, Dean Fletcher," Joe pleaded. "What about not guilty by reason of insanity? I was out of my mind when I pushed Leo and then did all that other stuff."

"I'd say you're out of your mind right now to even suggest that."

"You don't think insanity is a viable defense?"

Fletcher wandered back to her desk and poured herself another drink. "Not a chance, Joseph. What you described just minutes ago was anger and adrenalin triggering your violence, which at the very least was heat-of-passion manslaughter. Nothing you said even remotely suggests an emotional illness, let alone one that overcame your will or rendered you unable to tell right from wrong. Face it, young man, after the jury hears what you've told me here today, you're toast."

Joe's eyes darted around the room, and his face turned red. "What do you mean about the jury hearing what I've said here today? I'd never repeat anything I said here—only to you."

"You won't have to," she said.

Fletcher knocked back her drink and then leaned directly over the phone on her desk. "Mr. Holmes, I'm done with him."

C54

8:25 p.m., Monday, April 11.

"We'll talk later," Riley said to Harlan before she and Frank left for Fletcher's office. The other two officers in the conference room remained behind.

Harlan paused before leaving. He had no exit strategy and couldn't come up with one. Eventually he left the room and slowly made his way toward the elevator. He glanced back. The officers were following him. Close behind them followed Nikki, and some distance behind her Phoenix, who spoke on his cell phone as he walked.

When Harlan reached the elevator, he pressed the down button and looked at the floor. *Just like Joe Rylands, I'm toast*, he thought.

Soon after pressing the button, he heard the sound of elevator doors closing on the floor directly beneath him, level three. Then the doors opened in front of him and he stepped in. He pressed the first-floor button as the officers and Nikki stepped in behind him. She held the doors for Phoenix, who paused to finish his phone conversation and then stepped in close to Harlan.

The elevator was barely underway when it stopped and its doors opened—on the third floor—and in walked eight large guys wearing dark suits, followed by Vincent, Tommy, and Angelo. "Make some room, dammit," Angelo said.

"Youse guys hoyd da man!" one of the big guys shouted. *The guys from Philly?* Harlan wondered as they squeezed him, Nikki, Phoenix, and the two cops to the back.

Phoenix tilted his head toward Harlan. "I expect you to return these," he whispered while pushing something into Harlan's hand. The elevator was too crowded for Harlan to raise the object above his waist to see it. But clearly it felt like a pair of glasses. "Why are you—" Harlan began. He stopped, however, as did the elevator—this time on the second floor—when he felt the sudden grasp of many strong hands taking hold of him, followed immediately by a sensation of weightlessness as his feet lifted several inches off the floor.

Harlan was then whisked, airborne, through the crowded elevator toward the front. Along the way, he felt something get pulled over his head and something else get crammed under one of his arms. When Harlan arrived at the front of the elevator, Angelo shoved him off and shouted, "Get lost, sleuthhound!"

As the elevator doors closed behind him, Harlan removed the thing on his head. It was a Detroit Tigers baseball cap. The thing under his arm was a matching Tigers jacket.

After he shoved Harlan off the elevator, Angelo pressed the close button.

"Let us the hell out of here!" one of the cops in the back shouted as the doors closed.

"Oh, you wanted off?" Angelo said. "Okay then, let me see. Where's that... uh... oh, there it is," he said, as he pressed the emergency button.

A shrill alarm immediately sounded and the elevator stopped abruptly between the first and second floors. "Sorry about that," Angelo said. "I must have hit the wrong button. What do I do now?"

"Just pull the damn button back out!" an officer shouted. "But now I can't see any of the buttons," Angelo said, "not with the way everyone's crowding me."

Laughter poured out of the elevator behind him as Angelo emerged first, onto the ground level, followed by the slow-moving migration of his men, who continued to delay the two cops stuck in the back.

"Hey, watch it with the police brutality, man!" someone inside the elevator shouted, apparently in response to the officers' efforts to push through the mass of tightly packed bodies.

As Angelo strolled into the lobby, he spotted Riley Summers, waiting. "Hi Detective," he said.

"What the hell's going on in there?" Riley asked as she looked passed

Angelo and toward the elevator.

"I dunno," Angelo said. "I can't see in there any better than you can."

It was just minutes before sunset when Harlan emerged from a stairwell door on the ground level and stepped into the long shadow of the school's southeast corner, sporting his new Detroit Tigers gear and a pair of mirrored sunglasses. On the school's north side was the main parking lot. That's where he had parked the Impala. But now the parking lot was full of cops, so he opted to depart on foot.

He was just a few steps into his escape when the iPhone in his pocket vibrated. He pulled it out of his pocket and looked at it. It was a text message from "Harlan Holmes."

Oh yeah, I still have Vincent's phone, and mine is still with…

"Hey Boss, pick your head up," the message instructed. Harlan did, and there, in the Bay Shore Inn parking lot next door, he saw Tank Lochner crouched down beside a vehicle that resembled Harlan's old pickup truck.

Harlan walked quickly, but not urgently, toward Tank, trying to figure out how the big man could possibly be waiting for him in an ideal spot for a getaway when Harlan himself didn't know until he emerged from the building where he was.

Another familiar face appeared as he approached. It was Dozer's. The dog popped his head out of one of the truck's back windows to greet him.

Riley rushed out of the front doors of the school and into the parking lot on the school's north side. She scanned her surroundings, skimming past a guy wearing Tigers baseball gear who was walking toward the Bay Shore Inn.

Her head snapped back, however, when she heard the bark of a dog coming from that direction. She squinted. The man was approaching the head of a German shepherd sticking out of a pickup truck. *Is that Harlan and that dog of his?* she wondered. Just then an enormous bald-headed man rose up beside the vehicle and extended a hand toward the approaching Tiger fan. *And Tank Lochner?*

She watched the two men shake hands.

"Hey, Riley," Frank said, approaching from behind. "We might have a lead on the bagman."

Frank told her about a call that had come into the station only thirty minutes ago reporting the theft of a dog. "One of our guys already checked it out and learned that the complaining witness is a neighbor of Harlan Holmes, and the stolen dog is actually his dog, Dozer. The neighbor says he was boarding the dog while Harlan was gone on business."

"Did he see the thief?"

"Yeah, clear as day, right through his kitchen window. He saw this big bald-headed guy just casually walk into his backyard, pick the dog up like a bag of groceries, and walk off with him back to some tricked-out pickup truck parked right in front of the house. The thief was so damn big that the poor guy was too scared to do anything but call the cops."

Riley looked back in the direction of the Bay Shore Inn. The pickup certainly fit the description. It had chunky all-terrain tires mounted on satin-black alloy wheels, a massive grill guard, and a chrome sports bar with auxiliary lights. She continued watching, silently, as it pulled out of the Bay Shore Inn parking lot and turned left onto Front Street.

"I was thinking," Frank said, "that maybe we should ..."

Riley ignored him. Just a few yards away, she saw Phoenix Wade holding the door of an Escalade for Angelo Surocco. She hurried over to him. "Hold on, Mr. Surocco, please."

"What's up, Detective?"

"I need to know what happened when your crew caught up with Tank Lochner."

"Whoa, Detective," Tommy interjected. He stepped in front of her. "Did I hear you read my client his rights?"

"No."

"So you're not arresting him for anything."

"No, I just want to talk with him about something."

"In that case, we'll be on our way."

"It's okay, I don't mind," Angelo said as he waved Tommy off. He then lit a cigarette and gave Riley a look that actually seemed friendly.

Riley smiled at him uneasily and continued. "Look, Mr. Surocco, I heard all about your meeting with Craig Davies at that efficiency cabin in Waters, including how it ended with you paying him to lie low while you chased down the bagman."

"And who'd you hear that from?" Angelo asked without blinking.

"Joe Rylands."

"How about College Boy? What did he say?"

"Well, he said exactly the same—"

"Bullshit, Detective. I'm willing to try to help you with what I think concerns you right now. But please, knock off the interrogation tactics and be straight with me. What did College Boy really say?"

"He told me that hell would freeze over before he'd say anything about what happened in that cabin."

"Even after you threatened him with obstruction?"

Riley nodded.

"Yeah baby!" Phoenix shouted. "Welcome aboard, College Boy!"

"So right now," Angelo said, "all you've got is the word of a low-life murderer about something he claims I intended to do, but that he never witnessed me doing—am right, Detective?"

"Yes."

"Well then, how about we speak hypothetically," Angelo said, again offering a friendly smile.

Riley paused to think about what he was suggesting. "Okay, Mr. Surocco, maybe you can tell me what you think *might happen if, hypothetically speaking,* your men were to learn the whereabouts of a man believed to have killed your son."

"You mean, hypothetically speaking, someone who my guys had every reason to believe beat my son nearly to death and then pitched him into a bay to drown in ice-cold water, trapped inside a pickup truck?"

"Yes."

"Well, if they actually got their hands on him, I would hope they'd put that son of a bitch through the same kind of torture. Not that I would ever direct them to do that sort of thing, mind you. But it's comforting to at least imagine them taking it upon themselves to kidnap the bastard and drag his ass out to the middle of nowhere and—"

Angelo paused and looked directly into Riley's eyes. "Oh, why even fantasize about something like that," he said, "when you and I both know that Harlan Holmes would never allow it."

"But how could Harlan stop them?"

"Well, gee, Detective, you know that con man as well as anyone. He'd pull one of his stunts, and my guys would probably fall for it because they underestimated him." Glancing at Phoenix, Angelo added, "Of course, this is all just pure speculation about something that never happened."

"Of course," Riley said, as she, too, glanced at the chauffeur, who shrugged his thick shoulders and smiled at her from a face that had been badly battered since she last saw him.

"Okay, so you remembered me mentioning where Dozer was staying," Harlan said, after completing his first round of questions. "Now, why don't you tell me about my truck. Where'd you get the idea to install all the gaudy upgrades?"

Tank glanced over from the driver's seat. The two were traveling east through Traverse City, on Front Street. "Pretty sweet, huh, Boss, the new wheels, the sports bar and lights—"

"Sure, Tank, just the kind of add-ons I've been meaning to get since I bought it ten years ago—used."

"You think the exterior stuff is cool," Tank said, obviously pleased with himself, "just listen to this." Tank dropped the shifter into neutral and floored the gas pedal. "You hear that, Boss? You got yourself a brand new 454 big-block V-8 under that hood now. This thing hauls ass, man."

"When did you do all this?"

"This afternoon at a chop shop owned by a buddy of mine near Williamsburg."

"Where'd you get the money for it?"

"Well, one of Angelo Surocco's guys gave it to me early this morning out in that forest area where you and I first met."

Harlan sighed deeply. "I think you should stop calling me Boss."

"Why?"

"Because you never do a damn thing I tell you to do."

"I'm sorry, Boss, but—"

"Just tell me what happened, Tank."

4:02 a.m., Monday, April 11.

"Holmes?" a voice answered on the fifth ring. "Why the hell are you calling at—"

"You're Angelo Surocco, right?" Tank asked.

"Of course I am, you... you..."

"What's the matter?" Tank said. "You just realizing that this isn't a dream? Or are you having trouble figuring out who you're talking to?"

"Lochner?"

"That's right—the sadistic son of a bitch who's got your son."

"What the hell do you want? Did you do something to Vin—"

"I want what I'm owed," Tank said.

"What are you talking about?"

"The forty grand that Leo bet on Bucknell and said you'd pay—I want it."

"Are you out of your fucking mind?" Angelo said. "Or are you threatening to kill my other son if I don't give you money?"

"I'm not threatening anything, Surocco. I'm just offering an early release of Vincent and his friend if you pay what Leo owed, fair and square, and said you'd pay."

"Listen, dumb shit," Angelo said, "I've already gotten to Jimmy the Leg, and he's cancelled that marker."

"Well, Jimmy's not my boss anymore, and as far as I'm concerned, the money's still owed."

"Does your new boss know about the move you're making right now?"

"No."

"I can't imagine he does. What's to stop me from moving on him if I was to pay for this early release you're offering?"

"Because you have sense enough to know that if you move on Harlan Holmes before today's sit-down, you might never learn what actually happened to Leo."

"And just what the hell am I gonna learn," Angelo scoffed, "that after you terrorized Leo in the middle of the night, somebody else just happened to come along and murder him?"

Tank sighed deeply. "Look, I get where you're coming from," he said, "what it must look like to you, knowing that I showed up that night and kicked those boys' asses right before they ended up in the bay. I don't blame you for thinking I did it and sending your guys after me. If I was you, I would have made the same mistake. That's why I only want what Leo owed and promised you'd pay, nothing more."

"And what if I don't pay?"

"I'll do exactly what Harlan told me to do—call you sometime after four in the afternoon to tell you where to pick up Vincent and his friend. And they'll be fine."

"So you're gonna release them later on anyway, even if I don't pay?"

"Yeah, because I keep my word."

"I don't know," Angelo said, "forty large is a lot to pay for twelve hours. Let me talk to Vincent."

"No. You can talk to him when you get him back—how soon is up to you. But I'll tell you this much, he could use the early release."

"Why? What have you done to him?"

"It's not so much what I've done. It's more about what you've done, or what he thinks you're gonna do."

"What the hell are you talking about, Lochner?"

"Practically all night long the kid's been talking with his friend about how hard you're gonna come down on them when this is over. I think he's more scared of you than me. It might go a long way with him if you do this."

Tank heard a deep sigh through the phone. "You know," Tank said, "Harlan told me about Leo calling you that night for the money and you hanging up on him. Obviously, I don't know you that well, but my guess is that you would have given Leo the money eventually. You probably figured you were just making him sweat a little. I don't think you should do that with Vincent."

Tank continued driving east out of Traverse City while recounting how he handled the physical exchange of his prisoners for the cash delivered by Angelo's men.

"I guess there's just one other thing," Harlan said when the story concluded. "How did you know exactly where to find me when I came out of that school?"

Tank nodded at a cell phone sitting on the center console between them. It was the phone Harlan had loaned him. "Check the last incoming text message," Tank said.

The message had been sent by Angelo about an hour before Harlan's escape. It detailed the disguise he'd be wearing and his most likely escape route.

Harlan sighed deeply as he looked up from the phone.

What's on your mind, Boss?"

"I just would have never figured Angelo Surocco to have my back this way."

Tank smiled. "It kind of reminds me of what you did for me, Boss, back in that forest area, right after you smashed my face down in the mud of that shallow grave."

C55

7:30 p.m., Sunday, April 17.

Harlan turned on the radio and cut into a recording of the feature interview on NPR's Weekend Edition.

"Look, Rachel, I'm only suggesting leniency for these men. Sure, one of them assaulted a police officer and the other knowingly assisted his flight from justice. But I have reason to believe that there were extenuating circumstances."

Hey, wait a minute, Harlan thought. *That's—*

"But wasn't it just a week ago, Detective Summers, on this very program, when you described the fugitive as a threat to public safety?"

"Yes, I did."

"And you still acknowledge the seriousness of the charges against these men—one of them indeed a former state trooper—don't you?"

Are they actually talking about—

"Of course they face serious charges, Rachel. But these two men, Tank Lochner and Harlan Holmes, were themselves apparently threatened with grave danger if they didn't act as they did."

"Holy shit, they are!" Harlan shouted. He glanced at his passenger, Tank, whose eyes widened as he leaned toward the radio. The two men and Dozer were heading westbound on U.S. Highway 2, a remote two-lane route along the country's northern border, to a destination yet to be determined.

"What grave danger did they face, Detective?"

"I can't comment on the details, Rachel. The matter is still under investigation. Let me just put it this way. I think these men had good reason to believe that their lives depended on both of them being at large and in a position to prove Mr. Lochner's innocence in connection with the drowning death of Leo Surocco."

"He may have been innocent of that, Detective, but you can't just sweep under the rug that bagman's vicious assault of a police officer."

"Well, I think that at least some consideration should be given to the fact that—"

"And as for this private eye, Harlan Holmes, who we now know was acting in concert with the bagman at the time, what are you suggesting, Detective—that he simply be allowed to walk?"

"Look, Rachel, I'm just saying—"

"I'm sorry, Detective. But frankly, I'm having trouble accepting your sudden change of heart in this matter, and not just because my father has served honorably as a police officer for my entire life."

"Oh, I didn't realize that your—"

"It's because I have a reliable source inside Michigan's Department of State Police who says that you may have gone rogue as to this matter."

"Oh, that's just ridic—"

"According to my source, Detective, you knowingly let Harlan Holmes and that bagman slip through a police lockdown at GTU Law and escape Traverse City."

"I don't know where you're getting your information, Rachel, but—"

"My source says that there were security cameras running next door to the school in the Bayshore Inn parking lot. One caught these men leaving in a tricked-out pickup truck, and another caught you in the distance, apparently watching."

An extended period of silence followed the accusation. During the dead air, Harlan looked at Tank, who returned a bewildered look.

"Well, Detective, isn't there something you'd like to say?"

"Actually, there is, but not in response to the allegations of some nameless source. I recall that Harlan Holmes is a fan of this show, and I want to say something to him and Tank Lochner, if they happen to be listening right now.

"Hold on, Detective. I'm not about to let you—"

"Look, guys," Riley said, "I wanna help you, but you've gotta stop running."

A hot flush and a bout of dizziness hit Harlan on the heels of Riley's words. The truck swerved.

And then he woke up to a world still spinning.

"What the hell?" Harlan said between heavy breaths.

"You had some kind of attack, Boss, and passed out. Are you okay?"

The spinning slowed, and Harlan began taking in his surroundings. The truck was parked on the shoulder of the road, engine off, facing a wheat field that extended ahead to the city limits of Cut Bank, Montana. "How did we get here?" he asked.

"I grabbed the wheel and shut down the engine," Tank said.

Harlan placed his hands back on the wheel and stared ahead at the wheat field. He concentrated on slowing his breathing. *What's wrong with me?* he wondered.

"I've seen this kind of thing before," Tank said, "when collecting gambling debts. Some guys get overwhelmed by panic, you know, when I start leanin' on 'em. Is there something I can do to help?"

Harlan remained silent, staring ahead, brooding.

"It bothers you that the detective is trying to help, doesn't it, Boss."

"There's nothing I hate more than someone back on the force feeling sorry for me, especially her."

Tank shook his head. "I don't think that's where she's coming from," he said.

"After all the shit I pulled on her," Harlan said, "why else would she be trying to help me now?"

"Well, she's trying to help me, too, and we've never even met. I think she's just trying to do the right thing."

Harlan didn't want to argue with Tank. He wanted to be angry at her, the rookie detective whom he had trained to do his job before he was let go, who'd been doing his job for the past two years, and who just moments ago was doing it, in his face, right over the radio of the truck he was driving to nowhere.

241

Tank sighed. "You've gotta stop blaming her, man."

Harlan's grip on the steering wheel tightened. His knuckles went white as he turned to stare at Tank. "You got something you wanna say to me, *man?*"

"Well, actually, yes, but I don't think you're in the right frame of mind to hear it."

"That's just as well, Tank, because I don't need to hear the obvious."

"And what's that?"

"That I just need to get over the shit from my past and move on. I've been telling myself that for two years."

"And how's that been working for you, Boss?"

Harlan resumed his silent stare over the steering wheel.

"Look, Boss, I'd never tell you to just forget all about that shit and pretend that life is all good. Believe me, I've been right where you're at now, mired down in setbacks, going back to my old man ditchin' my mom and me when I was a kid, and then these guys she started hookin' up with and the things that some of those sons of a bitches did to me. Hell, things like that stay with you for all time."

Harlan's grip on the steering wheel loosened. He turned to look at Tank, but now the big man was staring at the field ahead. "Doesn't sound like a very good childhood," Harlan said.

Tank leaned into his seat and let his head drop back. "It sucked," he said. "I can still catch myself, to this day, blaming my mom and the men in her life for the shit that happens to me and wanting to kick all their asses for it."

"Sounds like they'd have it coming."

"Maybe so, but when my mind goes down that path, it punishes me, not them."

At that moment, Harlan felt something he hadn't experienced in a long while—the feeling that he wasn't alone. He had fallen into a deep hole, and in the past when others tried to help him, it always felt like they were standing above him, outside the hole, talking down at him about his predicament. Tank's approach was different. He opted to jump into the hole beside Harlan, and climb out with him.

Harlan continued to look at Tank, who seemed to be deep in thought. Tank's stare dropped from the horizon, down in the direction of his left arm. Harlan leaned over to see what Tank was looking at. It was a small tattoo on the inside of his left forearm. Before Harlan could make out the image, Tank looked up at him.

"You remember me telling you about how I swam across the Straits of Mackinac to escape the cops in the UP?" Tank asked.

"Yeah," Harlan said.

"And do you remember me telling you how easy it was because I had done it before?"

"Uh huh."

"Well, I lied. The truth is, I hadn't made a swim like that for over ten years, and I damn near drowned. My muscles cramped up on me like never before. Every part of me—my shoulders, arms, legs, everything—was failing. By the time I realized I was in serious trouble, I was at a point of no return, where the shore going back was as far away as the shore going forward."

"What'd you do?" Harlan asked.

Tank smiled. "I flipped the script."

"You did what?"

"I stopped fighting the water with my front crawl and flipped over, onto my back. I'm not very good at the back stroke, but I was good enough to at least breathe. And it let me to use some different muscles for a while and rest the ones that were full of lactic acid. I actually felt myself relax on top of the water and even took in the sight of a big night sky full of stars."

Tank stopped talking. The pause allowed Harlan to fully engage with the image.

"Okay," Harlan said, "you got me going on this. But what exactly is your point?"

"The moment wasn't just about the water beneath me, Boss. It was about everything above it, too, and the way the two came together to make a balanced whole."

Harlan let his hands slip off the steering wheel. In the rearview mirror he saw Dozer sitting at attention. He reached back and scratched the dog's head for what seemed a long while. Then he returned his hand to the ignition but didn't turn the key.

"Well," Harlan said, looking straight ahead.

Tank leaned toward him, but Harlan didn't turn his head. "Well, what?" Tank asked.

Harlan continued looking straight ahead, waiting for Tank to figure it out. Eventually he did.

"What's the plan, Boss?"

"Let's go home."

ABOUT THE AUTHOR

John Marks is an attorney in Michigan. He previously practiced law in California and has taught classes at law schools in California and Michigan. John and his wife, Dena, have traveled extensively but enjoy most the time they spend close to home with their children and grandchildren.

BLACK ROSE wriiting™

CPSIA information can be obtained
at www.ICGtesting.com
Printed in the USA
LVOW11s1810200917
549414LV00002B/458/P